Wiccan Romances

Amelia's Story

Nicola Hebron

To my parents, who have supported me throughout this
experience and all previous endeavors

Chapter 1

9th November 2017

"Amelia Elizabeth Taylor, I won't tell you again, you need to pay attention!" Yelled Amelia's father.

Amelia, known as Lia, was sat cross-legged, trying to listen attentively to the magic lesson being taught by her father; however the converted garage had lots of more interesting objects to focus on. The double garage was separated into a small kitchen area and an expansive living space, which had two walls covered in floor to ceiling bookcases, overflowing with books and other magical tools. The various beams and columns of the garage had a collection of dream-catchers, decorative moons, compasses and acorn pendants strategically positioned throughout. There were also a few gimmicky items like a witch's hat and a broom used to decorate in one small part of the garage. On one of the bookcases was a framed photo of the four siblings on their birthday, in which Lia was sat on Ben's lap posing in the hat, while Sam and Charlie laughed. The magic lessons had started two months ago on Amelia and her brothers', Ben, Charlie and Sam's 17th birthday, when they had discovered their paternal lineage was a long line of witches.

Amelia glanced over at her brothers, all of whom were sat comfortably on chairs throughout the room, which were centred around the circular table where her father was currently stood glaring at her.

"Sorry Dad."

"OK, so as I was saying, you all need to master controlling your powers, learn your triggers and finally you need to work as a team."

Amelia glanced over at Ben, the independent, charming and quiet leader of the four of them, who shrugged. As a set of quadruplets, the four of them were closer than typical siblings but that didn't mean that their closeness led to constructive team work as they had a lot of disagreements and differences. For example: the night before Sam and Ben had been arguing about whose turn it was to walk the dogs with Lia and as a result several plates and mugs had been broken.

"OK Dad, how do you want us to proceed?" Sam, the charismatic and driven quadruplet, who often acted as the voice of the siblings, asked.

"For now, I simply want you to work on controlling your powers. Each one of you has control of an element alongside your active powers of telekinesis and telepathy. Once you have mastered these then we can move onto the more difficult aspects of your craft."

"I don't understand how this all works Dad." Charlie, overly cautious and stubborn, piped up.

Charlie was having the most difficulty trying to adjust to the powers they had acquired; his natural belief was based in science and logic, so invisible magic abilities were beyond his comprehension. Amelia, the youngest of the quadruplets and the only girl, was quite open to the idea of magic existing but due to her more daydreamy nature she was having a lot of trouble mastering her powers. Ben and Sam had accepted the powers and were coming into their own with the control, they still had blips but overall, they were doing the best of the four of them.

"Charlie, I understand that you are having difficulty grasping this but you need to at least try and learn how to use your powers." David, their father, groaned. They had been having variations on this conversation for the last couple of months since the quadruplets had turned 17 and Charlie was still not interested in attempting to learn his craft.

"There is no basis for magic!"

"Charlie that's enough! We can talk about this later but for now I need everyone…. Amelia what are you staring at now?"

Ben quickly kicked his sister's ankle, as she had once again begun to focus on the huge bookcases that covered the walls.

"Oops, sorry Dad. I'm just fascinated by all these different topics, can I read any of the books?" She asked for the hundredth time since starting magic lessons. She hadn't been allowed in the garage until her seventeenth birthday and therefore was intrigued by the books she had recently discovered.

"Later, come on now guys! I only ask for two hours a week to try and teach you how to use your powers. Today's lesson is again focused on your telekinesis as this is one of your active powers. Now, I have been watching you guys and I've got some ideas of your triggers, this is what activates your powers. Ben your initial trigger is anger, Sam yours is your excitement, Amelia yours seems to be when you get nervous or flustered and Charlie yours is frustration."

"How does that help us?" Sam asked.

"Well by knowing what your trigger is, we can begin to work on control and then we can work on using your powers without triggers."

"How are we meant to control our natural reactions?" Lia asked.

"It's not about controlling your reactions, it's just ensuring that you don't accidentally use your powers inappropriately." David explained. "Right, let's get started with today's lesson."

Lia adjusted her position in the chair so she was sitting with one leg crossed over the other and pulled out a notebook, which she balanced on one knee, to make some notes on what her dad was telling them. After an hour of listening to an explanation on how telekinesis worked and the best way to control their emotions, they were allowed to practise their powers.

In the centre of the table was a plain coffee mug and each of them had to try and move it towards them and then back to the centre again.

"I'm going to knock this one out of the park." Sam announced, as he got up to stand by the table.

Sam squinted his eyes at the mug and sure enough it began

to move towards him.

"Yes!" he shouted, which caused the mug to pick up speed and crash onto the floor.

"Sam! What have we just talked about? When you get it overly enthusiastic about something, it causes you to lose control of your powers. Alright Ben, your turn."

Ben stood up and again squinted at the mug, somehow Ben managed to get the mug to do exactly what was needed.

"Excellent." David said, nodding to Ben.

"Amelia? Would you like to have a go next?" he asked his daughter, who was no longer paying any attention to the class and was doodling in the notebook she had been using.

"I can try."

Lia got to her feet and walked slowly to the table. She squinted her eyes like her brothers had however the mug did not move.

"Why don't you try using your hands? When your mum startled you the other day, she said that you waved your hands then all the books and paper on your desk went flying."

"Why would my powers be different to Ben and Sam though?"

"Because you're different." Smirked Sam, trying to wind his sister up.

"As I was explaining earlier, telekinesis can be accessed in two ways, either by your eyes or by your hands, yours might be controlled through your hands."

Lia sighed but lifted her hands up, she focused on the mug and gestured that it should come towards her. Sure enough, the mug did begin to move in her direction. Unfortunately, at that moment Charlie sneezed, causing Lia to jump and send the mug flying into the wall.

"Oh no!" Charlie exclaimed, as Sam and Ben dissolved into laughter at their siblings' misfortune.

"Well, this proves my point about your powers being linked to things that make you jump Amelia. Have a seat and we will try again." David stated, going to collect another mug and pick up the shards from the one that had just been broken.

Charlie slumped in his seat and looked down at the ground but Lia still patted him on the shoulder as she walked the long way back to her seat.

"Don't worry Charlie, it's not your fault." She said, as she passed him.

"It's not that I am worried about." Charlie snarled into his lap, his sister's natural empathy picking up on his low mood. "Dad! I am not taking part, this whole thing is a sham and I will not be a part of it!"

"This is a magic lesson Charles and you all have to learn to control your powers."

"NO!" Charlie snapped, before shoving himself out of the chair and stomping out of the room.

"OK, Ben you are dismissed, Sam and Amelia could you have another couple of goes at trying to move a mug. I will be back shortly."

Lia stood up after her father left the room but rather than heading over to the table, she wandered over to the bookcases that had been capturing her attention over the last few weeks. The shelves were filled with books that were written through the centuries and covered a wide variety of topics and subjects, including spells, potions and magical creatures. Lia wandered along the shelves, staring at the books, wondering how she could not have known that they were in here until a few weeks ago.

"Hey Lia, we are supposed to be practising this whole telekinesis thing, you don't want to get caught looking at the books. Dad will kill you." Ben advised, as he left the room.

Sighing wistfully, Lia turned back to the table where Sam had placed two new mugs and was trying hard to concentrate on getting his to move. Following her brother's lead, Lia took her place at the opposite side of the table and raised her arms. The mug began to move as she gestured for it so she smiled and kept her arm moving until slowly the mug made the journey, coming to rest in front of her. In an effort to get the mug to move a bit faster on its return journey, she flung her hand out, however she accidentally caught the edge of the tablecloth and pulled everything off the table.

"Lia!" Sam yelled, frustrated that his efforts had been disrupted.

"Sorry!"

"Forget it."

"What is happening in here?" David asked, as he re-entered the garage.

"I was trying to get the mug to move a bit faster but my hand got stuck in the table cloth and well..." Lia trailed off, gesturing to the mess at her feet.

"You know what, let's just call this lesson over." Some progress had been made at least, David decided.

Sam quickly left the room whilst Lia stayed to put the table back to rights. Once everything had been replaced she packed up her stuff and headed into the main house. As soon as she walked into the house, Betty and Veronica, the two family Golden Retrievers ran into the hall and began jumping up at her.

"Hi girls, is it time for a walk?" She asked, grabbing her walking boots and coat from the cupboard. She clipped both leads in place. "Mum! I'm taking the dogs out, I'll be back in time for dinner!"

Lia headed out down the driveway, letting the dogs run around ahead of her while she tried to untangle her headphones from her coat pocket. At the end of the drive, she paused to put her headphones in her ears.

"Lia, wait up!" Ben called, as he jogged down the drive, trying to zip up his jacket.

"Oh, hey, what's up?"

"You know you aren't supposed to walk the dogs by yourself in the dark."

"I use the same route every day, I see the same people. How much danger can I be in?" Lia asked, passing Ben one of the dogs' leads.

"I'm just repeating what the parents have already told

you."
Sighing, Lia took her headphones out of her ears. They walked in silence for a few minutes, along the path which led to the local woods, letting the dogs walk ahead of them, sniffing the trees around. Lia loved the woods, particularly in Autumn when all of the leaves were changing colour. At the entrance, Lia paused as she heard some rustling in the bushes, Ben moved so he was positioned slightly in front of her. The bushes continued to rustle as a large Husky jumped out of the bushes and leapt up at Lia.
"Hi!" Lia cooed, shifting so she could pet the dog without being knocked over.
"Buster! Come here!"
"He's over here, Aidan!" Ben called out.
"Ben didn't expect you out here!" Aidan called out, as he followed his dog out of the bushes.
"Lia was walking the dogs, thought I would give her a hand." Ben explained, as he shook his friend's hand.
"Hi." Lia mumbled, as she continued to pet Buster.
Lia stumbled backwards as Buster leant his full weight against her legs, causing Aidan to grab his dog's collar, pulling him away from her. Smiling, Lia shifted so that she could focus on the dogs and look at Aidan without being obvious. He looked at ease, wearing a pair of faded jeans, black shirt and unzipped grey hoody. She had known Aidan for years and had a crush on him for nearly as long. Consequently, whenever he was around, which was a lot of the time as he was Ben's closest friend, she turned into either a babbling idiot or a mute. Lia glanced down at the dogs when Aidan looked over at her and busied herself taking off Betty's lead.
"You alright Lia?" Aidan asked, watching her closely.
"I er, ye.."Lia mumbled.
Ben smirked but put his hand on his sister's shoulder as a sign of support. Her crush was well known to everyone, except maybe Aidan who seemed ignorant of the fact that Lia wasn't herself when he was around.

"You guys beginning or ending your walk?" Aidan asked, petting Betty who had wandered up to him.

"Just starting, you?" Ben responded, letting Veronica off her lead so she could join Betty who was now examining the bushes.

"Same, let's get going then." Aidan stated, moving forward, whistling to Buster who had once again vanished into the bushes.

The dogs ran ahead enjoying the freedom of being off the lead. The curvy path was the perfect place to walk dogs, as it followed the perimeter of the woods and the dogs were allowed off their leads. Ben and Aidan went on ahead as Lia dawdled through the woods, trying to get rid of the red blush that had come from her being around Aidan. Lia knew the woods like the back of her hand, she had been playing in them with her brothers since they had moved to this house when the quadruplets were five. As she had gotten older, she would come into the woods to daydream or fantasise about Aidan, to worry about the school work that she had to do or to simply have a couple of minutes peace when her brothers had all their friends round. She loved sitting underneath the tall trees and reading during the summer holidays.

After they had been walking for a few minutes, Lia got caught up in a daydream about Aidan and didn't notice that he and Ben had disappeared round one of the path's curves and out of sight. Lia was pulled out of her harmless fantasy when another couple of dogs came running out of the trees up to Lia. Kneeling Lia stopped to pet the dogs, she saw them everyday and always made a fuss of the cute Cocker Spaniels.

"Lia, where are you?" Ben called.

"Just behind you." Lia called back, standing back up, brushing the grass and leaves off her knees.

"Which bit of stay in sight don't you understand?" Ben yelled, when Lia came round the corner to where the boys stood waiting for her.

"The rule is I have to have you, Sam or Charlie come with

me if I'm walking the dogs when it is dark, I don't remember being told anything about having to stay with you when you go steaming ahead!" Lia grumbled.

Aidan cleared his throat, making Lia jump as she had briefly forgotten he was there. Ben shrugged and turned away from his sister, before stomping ahead to where the dogs were hovering. Aidan stood awkwardly between the two siblings debating which one to go with. In the end, he stuck with Lia as he knew better than to try and talk to Ben when he was annoyed. In silence they all continued their walk around the path. Once they had come full circle, they clipped the leads back on the dogs. Lia grabbed the leads and headed off with both dogs, leaving Ben and Aidan.

"Mum, I'm back. Ben is at the bottom of the drive with Aidan, he will be up in a few minutes." Lia called, as she hung up her coat and the leads in the cupboard. She dropped her walking boots in the shoe rack on the floor of the cupboard.

Standing at the bottom of the Taylors' drive, Aidan and Ben stood, mirroring each other's stance of slightly leant back with their hands shoved in the pockets of their jeans, as they discussed the plans for the weekend.

"Do you know what's up with Lia?" Aidan asked out of the blue.

"What do you mean?" Ben queried.

"Well, she seemed really happy on the walk until you two had words and I've seen her at school and she just seems a little different." Aidan explained.

"I don't think there's anything going on with her; she hasn't said anything to me anyway." Ben mumbled thoughtfully.

"So, no new guys or anything in her life? Aidan asked, dropping eye contact with Ben.

"I don't talk to her about things like that, she's my sister." Ben groaned.

"Forget it." Aidan said. "I was going to offer to walk the dogs with Lia if you wanted but needed to check I wouldn't be stepping on some guy's toes by hanging out with her."

"What?" Ben exclaimed.

"I can walk the dogs with Lia, I have to walk Buster and if all your parents are worried about is her being alone in the woods, she wouldn't be if I was with her." Aidan explained.

"Why?" Ben asked.

"I've heard her arguing with Sam a few times and I was there today when you had words with her." Aidan clarified.

"Right, but what does that have to do with you offering to walk the dogs with Lia?" Ben questioned.

"Trying to prevent World War Three in your house. If you, Charlie and Sam don't have to argue about dog walking then it gives everyone a bit of peace." Aidan commented nonchalantly.

"I'll check with Lia and let you know." Ben decided, after a few seconds.

With that, both boys nodded at each other and went their separate ways. Ben headed up the driveway to the house, while Aidan headed off down the street. Back inside, Lia grabbed her school bag from the bottom of the stairs where she had dropped it coming in from school and walked up the two flights of stairs to her bedroom, hoping to get another glance at Aidan before he headed home. She and her parents had bedrooms on the second floor whilst the three boys had the first floor to themselves.

Once in her room, Lia took her History textbook out of her bag and dumped it next to her laptop so she could continue working on the essay she was currently writing. Lia claimed that her room had an order to prevent her mum, dad and Charlie from complaining but in reality, as it had been for years, it was quite simply a mess. Her desk was covered in pads, papers and books in no particular order; her laptop was balanced haphazardly on the chair where she had dumped it the night before, having spent half the night on Youtube.

"Amelia? How do you work in here?" Charlie asked,

appearing in the open doorway to her bedroom.

"The same way I have always done. I simply move the unnecessary onto the pile on the floor or work sat on my bed." Lia explained, plopping down on to her unmade bed.

Charlie sighed and shook his head as he glanced around the disorganised mess his sister called a room, there were dirty clothes spilling over the top of the laundry basket, a leaning pile of clean clothes about to topple over on top of one of Lia's chest of drawers, books scattered on the floor and any number of other surfaces.

"Dinner's ready." He announced, with one last head shake before heading out of the room.

Lia grabbed one of her slippers from where she had kicked it off that morning and glanced around her room for the second one. When she couldn't find it straight away, she kicked at the cushions and stuffed animals that had fallen off the bed in the night. Still not able to find the slipper, she checked under the bed and sure enough there it was. Pulling both slippers on, Lia quickly left the room so she could get down to the kitchen.

As usual, Lia was the last one into the kitchen. Grinning as pasta bake was her favourite, she grabbed the plate that had been left for her, accepting that it probably had the smallest portion as her brothers would have stolen a few forkfuls. Taking her place next to Ben and opposite Sam, she helped herself to some bits of garlic bread. For the next few minutes the meal was eaten in silence.

"How was Aidan, Lia?" Sam asked, pulling a face at his sister "Did you actually manage to form a whole sentence?"

"Sam." Warned Diane, their mum.

"What? She needs to get over this crush, it's ridiculous." Sam complained.

"It's fine, Mum." Lia said, lowering her gaze to her plate.

"He offered to walk the dogs with you, if you want." Ben commented. "He seemed to think that it would be better for you than walking with one of us."

"That's nice of him." Diane observed.

"Why would he offer that?" David enquired.

"Ben and I might have had words, while out with dogs."

"No, you wandered off by yourself, which is the one thing you know you are not supposed to do, so I reminded you." Ben retorted.

"I have been walking the dogs all year. I don't need someone to come with me."

"We've already discussed this Amelia. As it is dark outside and you are walking through the woods, it is in your best interests to have one of your brothers walk with you." David interjected.

"Fine!"

"So, one of us still has to go with her?" Charlie asked.

"Yes."

"Moving on." Diane started. "How was everyone's day?"

"Mine went really well, I had a chat with my Chemistry teacher and I now have some additional study materials to help with my coursework." Charlie announced. "Also, I am ahead of the rest of my class in Maths and Physics, so have been given a couple of separate assignments to ensure that I get the A grade I need."

"Geek." Ben muttered under his breath.

"Ben." David warned.

"What? He always brags about how far ahead of the rest of the class he is. He's always getting extra work and his main friends are his teachers." Ben argued.

"Ben!"

"Whatever."

"Well, how was your day Benjamin?" Charlie smirked.

"Know something, Charles?" Ben snarled.

"Oh crap!" Sam laughed.

Lia stared at Ben and Charlie who engaged in a silent battle of wills over who would talk next. Lia knew instinctively due to her brothers' behaviour that Ben must have failed a test or got into a fight protecting someone that had gotten him in trouble at College and that Charlie, being nosy and a teacher's pet had found out about it. Deciding that she did not want to get involved in whatever

Ben had done, knowing that it would likely result in him being punished, Lia turned her attention back to her dinner and quickly ate the last few mouthfuls before one of her brothers, having finished their dinner, tried to help themselves.

"Children! Behave!" David yelled, when Charlie started to say something and Ben kicked him under the table. "I think that dinner is over for tonight. Lia, it's your turn to clear the table and deal with the dishwasher."

Lia waited until her brothers had left the table before she began stacking the dishes to carry through to the kitchen, her mum gave her a hand by carrying in a few of the glasses through on her way out of the dining room.

"How is your Law coursework coming along, Sweetheart?" Diane asked, watching her daughter load the empty plates into the dishwasher.

"It's going OK, I've got a couple of hundred words done but still have quite a bit of research to carry out, I'm thinking about heading into town to hit up the library at the weekend."

"Sounds like a plan, do you have much other homework that you need to get done?"

"Erm, I have a mini History essay which I am about halfway through and I'll hopefully finish it off tonight and a few mini assignments with some Psychology data due next Tuesday."

"OK, I will let you get to it then."

Diane left the kitchen to head into her office, leaving Lia to finish off her chores. Once the dishwasher was loaded she switched it on and left the room. She checked in the main living room and saw Sam and Ben engrossed in watching sport on the television. In the smaller living room, Charlie had a documentary on pause and was getting set up to do some research on one of his school projects. Deciding that she didn't want to watch TV with her brothers, Lia went up to her room where she switched Netflix on her laptop and settled herself on her bed with her History textbook so she could read the necessary chapters.

Chapter Two

10th November 2017

"Ugh." Lia groaned, as her alarm went off for the fifth time in fifteen minutes.

"Good morning, it's time to get up if you want a lift to school." Diane all but sang, as she breezed into Lia's room.

Lia rolled onto her side to glare at her mum as she placed a cup of tea on Lia's desk at the other side of the room. "Thank God it's Friday" she thought, as she kicked off the duvet and shoved her feet into her slippers. She wandered out into the hallway and down to the kitchen to pop some bread into the toaster. As she was always running slightly late, she never had time to have anything but toast as she wasn't a fan of cold cereal. Leaning against the counter, she glared at Sam and Charlie who were wide awake, eating breakfast at the table.

"Ben still in bed?" David asked, entering the kitchen.

Sam grunted his agreement as Lia's toast popped up. Grabbing the toast, Lia quickly sat down at the table to spread jam onto it. Once she was finished, she grabbed her plate and left the kitchen to go up and get ready. She was always running late so never had time in the mornings to eat with her brothers.

"Tap on your brother's door!" David called after her.

"Ben! Dad says to get up!" Lia yelled, knocking on his door.

Lia and Ben were not morning people, it always took them much longer to get up than Sam and Charlie, who rose early no matter what day it was. Knowing that Ben still wouldn't be awake, Lia popped his bedroom door open and opened the heavy hall curtains letting a bit of light into his dark room. She debated actually going into Ben's room but realising she was running late she settled for a second set of loud knocking until he groaned. Leaving Ben to wake up on his own, Lia continued up to her bedroom, eating her toast en route. Once in her room, Lia slumped onto her desk chair to finish off her toast and drink a few mouthfuls of tea. Finished with her breakfast, she pulled out her diary to see what lessons she had that day. She had a double lesson of English Literature first thing followed by History, then a free period and finally a second lesson of History. Lia also took Psychology and Law but thankfully she did not have either of those that day.

Sighing, Lia sipped her tea whilst debating what she needed for the day and what to wear. Realising she had History twice and that meant spending two hours in the same room as Aidan, she decided on her better jeans and one of her flattering jumpers; a dark blue, slightly low cut, cable knit Jack Wills jumper. Registering that she was still going to school, she coupled the jumper with a bright pink strappy vest which had lace across the top, which would give a level of decency but still draw the attention that she hoped for. She knew that it didn't matter, as Aidan would only ever see her as Ben's sister but she couldn't seem to stop trying to get his attention.

"Pathetic." She muttered, as she pulled her clothes out of her wardrobe and dumped her clothes on the bed.

The benefit of sharing the second floor of the house with her parents, was that Lia technically had a bathroom to herself. There was an ensuite in her parents' room and a bathroom downstairs, which the boys were supposed to share. However, the bathroom door was closed so she tried the door.

"I need to shower!" She yelled, to whoever was in her bathroom.

"I'll be out in a minute!" Ben called. "Charlie is in our bathroom and he has been in there for ages, I think he's doing one of his experiments."

Lia leant against the wall next to the door waiting for her brother to finish whatever he needed to do in the bathroom. When Ben wasn't out quickly, Lia headed back into her room and grabbed another mouthful of tea whilst sorting out her desk so the stuff she needed was all in one pile. Once everything was semi-organised, Lia picked up her small school bag and placed her pad, pencil case and glasses in it, then dumped her textbooks into the rucksack that she kept all her books in.

"Bathroom's all yours." Ben stated, popping his head around the door.

"Thanks."

Lia wriggled past her brother and into the bathroom. She quickly turned on the shower and fiddled with the temperature gauge. Turning the spray on full blast, Lia stepped under the piping hot water and began to sing along to her morning playlist, playing on her phone. Almost mindlessly, Lia began to wash her hair and then when her hair was clean, she lathered herself up with her peach scented shower gel. Once she had finished in the shower, she turned the water off and clambered out, wrapping herself up in the purple fluffy bath sheet, before using a smaller matching towel to create a turban for her hair. Cleaning her teeth, Lia examined her face, deciding if she needed to add any concealer to her daily make-up regime of eye liner, mascara and lip gloss. Deciding against it, Lia left the bathroom and headed back into her bedroom where she selected her morning playlist off her Ipad and danced around as she got ready for school.

"Amelia, I'm leaving now." Diane called, as she walked down the stairs, forty minutes later.

"I'll be two minutes I'm just trying to find my left boot."

"If you actually tidied your room occasionally you wouldn't have this problem every morning." Charlie quipped, from the bottom of the stairs.

"Shut up!" Lia said, shoving her brother out the way so she could catch up with her mum.

"You are just in time, I was just about to leave." Diane observed, opening the front door as Lia grabbed her coat out of the cupboard.

Lia slid into the front seat of her mum's Audi, as Charlie ran out of the house. Lia glanced up at him confused. The three boys had all elected to go to the local college for their studies which meant their dad drove them in, whereas Lia had opted to stay at the school she had been at the last four years. She had made this decision because her two best friends were continuing to study there and also slightly because Aidan had stayed although she would never admit that to anyone. Her only reservation about staying at school was that a couple of the girls who had been bullying her throughout her time at the school had also opted to stay but as they took different subjects, Lia decided that they wouldn't really be able to bother her.

"Mum? Do you have time to take me to college before you drop Lia at school? Charlie asked, pulling open the back door of the car.

Diane checked her watch, sighed and nodded.

"You should have mentioned it last night really Charlie." Diane commented, as she pulled out of the driveway.

"Sorry, I just realised I needed a couple of books from the library and I could do with an extra hour or two preparing my Physics presentation."

The next few minutes of the journey continued in silence. Lia pulled her phone from her pocket so she could check whether anyone had messaged her that morning. Having responded to the couple of messages she had received, she shoved her phone back in her bag's pocket. Her mum pulled the car up to pick up Aidan, as their families had been sharing lifts to and from school for the last couple of years. Since they had started in Sixth Form, one of Sam's friends Carl had joined them, he would walk the couple of streets to Aidan's, to make Diane's pick-ups easier on the way to school.

"Morning." Diane said, as Aidan slid into the car next to Charlie.

"Morning Diane, Lia, Charlie good to see you." Aidan replied.

Lia waved and then immediately pulled her phone back out. The last two months without her brothers as buffers, had made the drives to school much more awkward so she was grateful for Carl's presence the last few weeks.

"Did Ben talk to you about walking the dogs together last night Lia?" Aidan asked, tapping her on the shoulder.

"He did, but you don't have to do that." Lia mumbled.

"It's no problem, I have to walk Buster and it saves one of your brothers having to go with you."

"I think that's a wonderful idea Aidan." Diane piped up. "Why don't you try it tonight Lia?"

"OK." Lia mumbled, blushing bright red.

"Out you get Charlie." Diane remarked, as she pulled up outside the college.

"Thanks Mum."

Once Charlie was out of the car, Diane pulled out of the car park and continued the remaining ten minute drive to the school.

"Thanks Diane." Aidan called, as he got out of the car.

"Yeah, thanks." Echoed Carl, following Aidan.

"I know you are nervous about walking the dogs with Aidan but I have to admit I agree with what Sam said last night about you needing to get over your crush. It has been going on for a number of years and I feel it is time you learnt to spend some time with Aidan. You never know he might start liking you back." Diane commented, as she turned to face her daughter who had yet to move from her seat.

"Mum, I'm fine. I don't need any help besides I barely even like him anymore." Lia muttered, staring at her boots.

"Whatever you say. It's still nice of him to offer to walk the dogs with you and it will stop a lot of arguments between you and your brothers."

"OK, there's Heather and Siobhan." Lia said, clambering out of the car.

Lia walked quickly over to her friends. Heather who was a tall atheletic looking blonde and Siobhan the slightly smaller girl with fiery red hair, reflective of her Irish ancestry. When Lia joined up with them it was like the beginning of a bad joke 'a blonde, brunette and red head walk into a bar...' Lia had been friends with Heather since Reception and their bond had remained strong all the way through school despite the fact that they were polar opposites. Heather was outgoing, sporty and made friends very easily and she had plans to become a Physiotherapist after university, Lia on the other hand was more reserved, a complete clutz and quite quiet around new people, she wanted to be a publisher or editor after university as she loved books. Siobhan had joined the two of them at the age of ten and she had immediately fit into the group. She was pragmatic like Heather although far more logically minded but she also had Lia's reserved but kind nature.

"Morning." Lia said, coming to a stop in front of her friends.

"Have you done anything with the data that we have been given for Psychology?" Siobhan asked, as they walked into the school.

"Not yet, I was planning to go to the library on Saturday to get some work done on the data and finish off my Law Essay, as it is always quiet and my house won't be as all the guys will be round to watch the football. I also might pick up a couple of History books as Mr Brooks has mentioned an essay a couple of times." Lia explained.

"Isn't it great though, to be with all those fit boys every weekend?" Heather asked laughing.

"Sure, as long as you aren't me in front of Aidan." Lia sighed. "My mum has arranged for me to walk the dogs with him tonight, because that's not going to be a complete disaster."

Her friends shook their heads and laughed as they walked up to their lockers. Lia pulled her keys out of the front pocket of her handbag and opened her locker, she shoved her backpack into her locker, then pulled out her copy of Wuthering Heights for her English lesson.

After her two hour English class, Lia stopped by the school café to get a cup of tea and to have a five minute sit down. English was the only A Level that she took where she wasn't with anyone she knew really well, so it tended to be the class that she focused best in, as there was less to distract her but she always came out feeling a little bit drained.

"Hey Lia!" Aidan called, plopping down next to her at the table she was sitting on.

"Hi." Lia managed, going tomato red, another unfortunate consequence of being near Aidan.

"Have you got any of your textbooks for Mr Brooks' History lesson?" Aidan asked.

Lia nodded, picking up her tea and taking a small sip as a method of hiding her nervousness.

"Would you mind if I shared with you? I left mine at home."

"No problem."

"Thanks, you're a life saver." Aidan smiled, as he got back up from the table and headed over to Carl and several of their friends, who were on the other side of the café.

"What did Aidan want?" Heather asked, coming up behind startling her, causing Lia to send her drink flying across the floor. "Sorry didn't mean to scare you."

Staring at her hands, shocked by what they had just done, Lia shook her head slightly, trying to deny that she had just telepathically sent her drink flying across the school café.

"Don't worry about it." Lia said, managing a small smile as her friend sat down next to her.

"So, anyway what was Aidan over here for?"

"Oh, he just wanted to share History textbooks."

"You know, I think you aren't the only one with a crush."

"I think you are losing it, Aidan sees me as Ben and Sam's sister and that's all."

"Hear me out." Heather laughed. "He always comes over when he sees you are alone, he often shares textbooks with you and he knows you and your brothers have been arguing about the dogs, so he has come up with a solution to stop you from fighting and that allows him to spend time with you."

"You are delusional." Lia retorted, shaking her head at her friend.

"Who's delusional?" Siobhan asked, joining them at the café table.

"Heather. She seems to think that Aidan likes me back." Lia stated sighing.

"I can see why she thinks that, he obviously cares about you." Siobhan observed.

"He cares because he has known me a long time and he is my brother's best mate, it would be weird if he didn't speak to me."

"You know, I wish you both luck, you both seem reluctant to believe the other one likes you." Heather stated.

"Let's move on." Siobhan quipped, she was always the peace maker between Heather and Lia.

"Do either of you two have a free period after lunch?" Lia asked.

"I have Biology." Heather replied.

"I have Geography, sorry." Siobhan said apologetically.

"Oh well, worth a try." Lia smiled.

The first bell went, so the girls got up from their table and headed for their lockers. Lia paused at the drinks machine and got a bottle of water for her next lesson. Catching up with her friends, she quickly swapped her copy of Wuthering Heights for her History textbook. The three of them all took History so it was the one class where they actually all sat together. As Lia locked up her locker, she noticed Aidan and Luke, Heather's boyfriend, hovering by the exit.

"Hi." Lia said, as she walked over.

"Did you do the reading for class today?" Luke asked, as they headed over to their classroom.

"Nope." Aidan commented, as Siobhan and Lia both nodded.

"I read part of it." Heather commented, linking hands with Luke.

Once inside the classroom, the five of them took their seats on one side of the u-shaped row of desks, Luke, Heather, Siobhan, Lia and then Aidan. Once they were all seated, Lia placed her book between her and Aidan so they could both see it, then pulled out her pad and pens so she could take any notes needed. Mr Brooks took his place in front of the whiteboard and waited less than patiently for everyone to settle in.

"Right OK, I hope that everyone has had a chance to do the required reading as we are going to be doing a recap session today on the origins of the War of the Roses, so you can all write your 5000-word essay next week." Mr Brooks announced.

Aidan dropped his head a bit so as not to make eye contact with Mr Brooks. Lia sensing his discomfort, shifted the notes she had been making the night before so he could read off them if necessary.

"Right! First question! Luke, who was the War of the Roses between?" Mr Brooks asked, beginning his round robin questions.

"The House of Lancashire and the House of Yorkshire."

The questions passed around the class relatively successfully, there were only a couple of answers that were either incomplete or incorrect. Mr Brooks then went on to detail the various points that would need addressing in their essays that were due in two weeks.

"You will need to back up all points that you make in your essay with quotes and reasoning. You cannot just use your textbooks for this essay you must use other research, and no Wikipedia is not an acceptable research tool." Mr Brooks announced, as the bell for lunch rang. "Our second lesson today will be a self study session to give you a bit of a head start with your essays."

"Lia, do you have a free period after lunch?" Aidan asked, as they all left the classroom.

"Yeah I do."

"OK, I'm gonna find out what Carl has this afternoon and if he's free, see if any of our parents can pick us up early." Aidan commented.

"I don't mind working in the library, it's much quieter and I can usually get more work done." Lia stated, thinking if they couldn't get a lift home early, there was a chance, that she could spend a bit more time with Aidan as well as getting a head start on her essay.

"I don't really see the point in hanging out here if we don't have to, I'll see if I can sort out a lift home early and let you know." Aidan said, partly ignoring Lia's comment.

Lia checked the line in the café and decided that she could wait a little while before going to get any food. She followed Siobhan into the library as Heather wandered off to get some food with Luke.

"What work do you want to start on?" Lia asked, as she sat down at the computer next to Siobhan and logged in.

"I have a Geography assignment that I need to finish so I've got to get my head down." Siobhan explained, as she pulled out her headphones.

Shaking her head, Lia followed her friend's example and fished her headphones out of her bag. Once she had settled on the new Niall Horan album to listen to while she worked, she pulled her memory stick out of her bag and plugged it in to the computer. For the next fifteen minutes, she sat typing up all of her notes from her English class.

"Hey, I'm going to grab a sandwich in the café, can you watch my bag for the next five minutes?" Lia asked, once she had finished typing up all of her English notes.

Siobhan nodded but didn't look up from what she was doing at the computer. Trusting her friend, Lia pulled her purse out her handbag but left the rest of her stuff by the computer she was using to prevent anyone else from deciding to work there. She walked quickly to the café and was pleasantly surprised to see that there was virtually no queue to get food. Pausing in front of the sandwiches, Lia scanned the options in front of her to see what she fancied. Toying between getting a simple cheese one and tuna and cucumber she picked both up and examined them. Deciding that she did not particularly fancy having fish breath all afternoon and not being sure if she had any mints in her handbag, Lia picked the safe option of the cheese sandwich. She then picked up a bottle of apple juice and debated between getting a cookie or an apple. In the end, she chose both because it was easier than trying to eat healthily and then eating a load of chocolate when she got home.

Spotting Heather, Luke and Carl sitting with a few other of their friends she walked over with her food. Lia settled down on the bench next to Heather, aware that the girls who had been bullying her and Siobhan throughout their time at school often sat in this group at lunchtime. Smiling at Luke when he nodded at Lia by way of greeting, she unwrapped the sandwich that she had just bought and spotting Aidan at the other end of the table, and not wanting to seem like a pig, she bit into it carefully. Lia sat eating her sandwich, half listening to Luke and Heather debate their plans for the weekend and half day-dreaming. After a couple of minutes, she heard the sound of sniggers coming from left of her. From underneath her eyelashes Lia looked over to her left and saw that Marie, Ben's ex-girlfriend and her friend Sophie had now joined the group. Trying to ignore the two girls' constant whispers and pointed looks, Lia stared intently at the bottle of apple juice in front of her.

"She's pathetic, clinging to Matt, Carl, Luke and Aidan." Sophie whispered loudly to Marie.

"Yeah, it's like she doesn't realise that they only put up with her because of Sam and Ben." Marie agreed.

Lia had been hearing variations of the same thing for years but it had gotten worse since Sam and Ben had left school to go to college. Lia jumped slightly when Heather squeezed her knee, letting her know that she could also hear everything that Marie and Sophie were saying and that Lia had her support. Trying to ignore the girls, Lia opened her apple juice and took a couple of sips.

"I don't know how Heather puts up with being her friend." Marie stage-whispered to Sophie.

Realising that they weren't going to stop making their comments and that they were beginning to get under her skin with their nasty remarks, Lia screwed the top back on her drink and rapidly gathered up the remains of her food, before bolting from the table. Spinning quickly, Lia bumped straight into Matt, who was just coming over to join the group.

"God. Look where you're going Lia." Called Marie laughing.

"Such a clutz." Echoed Sophie.

"Sorry." Lia mumbled to Matt, before she dashed out of the café back to the library.

Lia quickly logged herself back into the computer she was using and then let her hair fall in front of her face to hide the tears of embarrassment, which were starting to fall. Lia felt Heather put her hand on her back and spotted Siobhan now watching her. Sniffling, Lia brushed her hair back from her face and sat up so she could face her friends.

"You OK?" Heather asked, pulling up a chair from a nearby table so she could sit between her friends.

"I'm fine, just embarrassed, I was trying to get away from them before they could make any jokes at my expense but now I've made it so much worse." Lia mumbled, turning her attention to her knees.

"Just ignore them!" Heather sighed. "It doesn't matter what they think of you."

"I wish they would just go away." Siobhan declared. "They have made mine and Lia's lives hell and the only reason they don't do the same to you anymore is because you are with Luke."

"I'll talk to Luke, see if he can say anything to get them to lay off you." Heather proposed.

"Don't! That's what has made me such a target for them recently." Lia protested.

When both girls looked at her confused, Lia explained that Ben and Marie had been dating and that she had gotten fed up with all of the comments that Marie and Sophie were making about her, so she had told Ben about the comments and Ben, being highly protective of her, had subsequently broken things off with Marie.

"So basically, Marie blames me for breaking her and Ben up." Lia finished.

"Ben was going to end it with her anyway." Aidan stated, as he came up behind Lia.

"What?" All three girls asked.

"Yeah, he really didn't like her bossing him around and she was often quite critical of him so he wanted to end it. When you told Ben what she had been saying about you, he just ended it sooner than he planned." Aidan explained. "We all know how much of a cow she can be and Sophie is just as bad. I wouldn't let them upset you."

"Thanks Aidan." Siobhan said, shifting back to her work.

"Yeah, thanks Aidan." Heather echoed, as she turned her chair back around so that she could sit with Luke and they could talk.

Lia sat in her chair watching Aidan as he gave her an assessing look.

"Are you OK?" he asked, crouching down in front of her.

"I'm fine, I'm just embarrassed that's all, you don't need to worry." Lia managed, not making eye contact.

Aidan squeezed her hand as he stood up and then took a look around the library. Clearly deciding that he was going to stay with Lia, he sat down at the table with Heather and Luke. Once Aidan had pulled out a pad so he could do some of his doodles/art, Lia turned her attention back to the computer. She pulled up her electronic copy of Wuthering Heights and began highlighting some of the passages that had been mentioned in her English lesson earlier then annotated those paragraphs with all the information necessary plus making some of her own observations about the phrasing and the use of adjectives.

The bell to signal the end of lunch came just as Lia was finishing up with her notes. Siobhan, Heather and Luke packed up and headed off to their classes, leaving Lia with Aidan.

"Amelia, the computers are needed this session, would you mind logging off?" Mrs Shephard, the school librarian asked.

"Of course not." Lia responded and began saving her work onto her memory stick and then logged off. "Am I OK to work in here?"

Mrs Shephard nodded, so Lia shifted all of her work onto the table where Aidan sat. Aidan glanced up and smiled at Lia as she got herself set up. She pulled out her History textbook and began to reread the first four chapters in readiness for planning her essay. Whilst she was reading, she used tabs to mark the pages that she felt would come in handy when she actually started writing the essay. After working in silence for about thirty minutes, Aidan tapped Lia's hand to get her attention.

Unfortunately, that startled Lia, causing her to wave her hands, sending all of the papers and books on the table flying.

"Didn't mean to startle you." Aidan commented, mildly amused by Lia's reaction.

"It's OK." Lia muttered, once again staring at her hands.

Lia scrambled off her chair and began to quickly to gather up the books, pads and pens that she had accidentally thrown off the table. When she went to pick up Aidan's pad, Aidan put his foot down on top of it preventing her from picking it up. Lia glanced up.

"I've got this one." Aidan said, crouching down to pick up his pad. "Anyway I was going to say that I need a drink, do you want to move our stuff into the café for a bit?"

Lia paused for a couple of seconds, debating between spending more time with Aidan and her need to plan out her essay. Her crush on Aidan quickly won out over the sensible option so she nodded and shoved her stuff haphazardly into her bag. Following Aidan out of the library, Lia continued fiddling in her bag, trying to come up with something to say. As they entered the café, Lia glanced around and spotted Matthew, Alex and Joe, the remaining school group of Aidan, Ben and Sam's friends.

"Do you want a cup of tea?" Aidan asked.

"Yeah, just let me find my purse."

"Don't worry about it, this one on me."

"Um, thanks."

Lia stayed in the main café area, watching Aidan through

her lashes, while he got their drinks. Returning from the till, he passed the cup of tea to Lia and then he walked over to join his friends. Lia followed very slowly, debating whether she wanted to join them or whether she would rather go back to the library. As she hovered near the table, Aidan took her drink from her hands before pulling her gently down into the seat next to him.

The guys all talked around Lia, chatting about football and F1, things that Lia knew very little about but having three brothers she was completely used to this sort of conversation. Sipping on her tea, Lia let the conversation flow around her allowing herself to daydream about her magical powers and what she could do with them.

When the bell went, signalling the end of fourth period, Lia drained the last of her tea and then stood up to head back to the library, as she loved to read and the group of lads weren't paying attention to her. Once she had returned, she placed her bag on the table closest to the History section and began to look through the books on the War of the Roses. She pulled a couple of books out of the shelves and flicked through the contents page to see how much of the origins of the war and the other topics she needed for her essay were covered. Putting two back back in their place, she pulled another couple out of the shelves and repeated her routine of checking the contents of all the books. Once she had picked the best five, she walked over to Mrs Shephard to check the books out.

"Mr Brooks' origins essay?" Mrs Shepard asked, as she scanned them.

"Yep, got any tips?"

"Plan it out properly."

Smiling, Lia picked the books up off the counter and walked to her locker to put them all in her rucksack. Checking her watch, she realised there wasn't much of the day left; she pulled her rucksack onto her shoulders, then headed towards the school's entrance so she could wait in the late Autumn sunshine for her lift.

"You ready to head home, Lia?" Carl asked after a few

minutes, joining Lia who was leaning against the wall just outside the school.

"Mmmmhmm." Lia agreed, as Aidan joined them.

"I can't wait to get home." Carl stated.

"There's my dad." Aidan said suddenly, spotting his dad's beaten up, blue Corsa pulling up near where the three of them were standing.

Lia bent down and grabbed her rucksack off the floor and balanced it on one of her shoulders as she scrambled across the backseat of the car, allowing Carl access to the remaining seat. Placing the rucksack on the floor by her feet, Lia pulled her phone out of the front pocket of her smaller bag.

"You out tonight, Aidan?" Mark, Aidan's dad, asked.

"Yeah, I'm going to walk the dogs with Lia, then me and Ben have talked about heading into town later." Aidan commented with a smile, catching Lia's eye in the rearview mirror.

Lia caught Aidan's eye and half smiled when he winked at her, before she dropped her gaze back to her phone and began typing in the group chat she had with Heather and Siobhan.

Lia: Do you think I could fake a headache to get out of this dog walk? Lol x

Heather: NO!! x

Siobhan: What is so bad about going on this dog walk? X

Lia: Most friends would have said that faking a headache is fine lol x

Lia: Me and Aidan have never really spent anytime alone together, some friends or at least one brother is always around x

Lia: What if it's horrific? What if we have nothing to say to each other? What if I accidentally reveal my crush on him and he laughs? X

Heather: And I'm the dramatic one? Lol x

Siobhan: Best just to get it over with rather than stress about what could potentially go wrong x

Heather: Yep and then tell us all about it x

On that comment Lia smiled and slid her phone back into the pocket of her bag.

"You going to be at yours over the weekend Lia?" Carl asked suddenly, turning to face Lia.

"Erm, I'll potentially be about on Sunday but I'm not planning to be around during the day on Saturday. Why?" Lia queried.

"Yeah, why?" Aidan echoed, with a touch more annoyance in his voice than he had planned.

"Just wondered, me, Jake, Jack, Phil and Liam were planning to come over but I always feel a bit like we take over your house and disturb any plans you might have wanted to make." Carl explained, a bit defensively looking between Lia and Aidan.

"You're not bothered by that, are you Lia?" Aidan asked, turning in his seat so that he could look at Lia.

"No, it's fine, I'm used to it by now." Lia stated, after a moments thought.

"Are you sure?" Carl checked.

"Yeah, it's not a problem." Lia assured them, when they both kept staring at her.

The rest of the trip back to their houses, like the majority of their car journies continued in relative silence apart from the occasional sounds of phones vibrating as messages came in. After about ten minutes, the car pulled up against the curb near Carl's house. Aidan quickly got out of his seat and pulled the seat forward so that Carl could get out. As Aidan climbed back in the car, Carl waved before turning and walking up his drive towards his house. Once the passenger door was closed the car pulled away from the curb and continued the couple of minutes drive to Lia's house.

"I'll see you later." Aidan said, once Lia had climbed out of the car.

"See you later." Lia echoed, watching wistfully until the car was out of sight.

Once the car had driven away, Lia turned and wandered slowly up to her house, near the garage she saw that her dad's silver people carrier was already parked in its usual spot. Lia glanced at her watch and noted that it was early for her dad and brothers to be home. Slightly puzzled, Lia unlocked the front door and was immediately greeted by the sound of her dad and Ben arguing.

"Hello!" Lia called, as she shut the door and bent down to pet the overexcited dogs, who were surrounding her, whining and jumping in excitement.

"Not now, Lia." David yelled back.

Lia winced at the angry tone of her dad's voice and immediately stopped petting the dogs and headed upstairs. At the top of the first set of stairs, Lia stopped, crouched down and scooted so she could listen to what was going on but was out of sight should her dad or Ben come to the bottom of the stairs.

"Your behaviour is completely unacceptable." David shouted. "What the hell were you thinking?"

"It was a spur of the moment decision." Ben yelled back.

"It doesn't matter whether you planned it or not, it's still completely unacceptable." David continued to shout.

"I stand by my actions." Ben exclaimed.

"You need to apologise." David yelled.

"Never going to happen." Ben shouted back, before storming out of the house and slamming the door behind him.

Lia jumped when the door slammed but quickly got to her feet to ensure that she didn't get caught eavesdropping. Tip-toeing up to her room, Lia quietly shut the door behind her and strategically pulled up her Psychology data to make it look like she had been studying the whole time should her dad come in. After hearing the car start, as her dad left to pick Sam and Charlie up from college, Lia immediately relaxed and stopped pretending to study then began to actually work on the topic in front of her. Before she got too engrossed in the work in front of her, Lia set an alarm on her phone to remind her that she needed to get changed to walk the dogs.

After just over two hours of studying Lia's alarm went off,

rousing her from her detailed analysis of her Psychology data. Pushing away from her desk, Lia stretched and walked over to her wardrobe and swapped the jeans she had been wearing for her slightly older jeans she used when walking the dogs. She then pulled a thick hoody over the top of her jumper.

"It's only a dog walk." Lia told her reflection, when she caught sight of herself in the mirror.

"You walking the dogs with Aidan today?" Sam asked, strolling into Lia's room.

"Haven't you ever heard of knocking?" Lia retorted, turning to glare at her brother.

Sam simply winked and laughed when Lia threw a cushion at his head. When Sam caught the cushion Lia stuck her tongue out at him, making Sam laugh more. After a few seconds of face pulling Lia gave in.

"Yes." Lia said, once the laughter had died down.

"Great, I'll tell Jake he's cool to come over now. Ben's MIA so I would have had to walk with you if you were too chicken to walk the dogs with Aidan." Sam teased, as he headed out of Lia's bedroom.

Lia shook her head at her brother's departing back and huffed out a breath, she made a mental note to text Ben to check on him when she got back. Lia then went back to getting ready for the dog walk by grabbing her phone and shoving it in the back pocket of her jeans. With one final critical glance at her appearance, Lia headed downstairs where she attempted to pull on her walking boots whilst the dogs danced around her, jumping at her in their excitement to go on their walk. Lia was just clipping their leads on when she heard the knock on the door.

"Hi." Aidan said, when Lia opened the door.

"Hi." Lia echoed, before turning back to the house to yell that she was off and shutting the door.

The dogs all strained on their leads, forcing Lia to walk a little faster than she would normally as she and Aidan headed down the path towards the woods. They both kept glancing at each other and then staring at the floor when the other one caught them.

"Well, this is awkward." Aidan observed, when they paused at the entrance to the woods and took the leads off.

"Huh?" Lia managed.

"I just can't believe we have nothing to talk about." Aidan explained. "We've never had a problem before."

"We are usually in a group." Lia commented.

"True." Aidan said thoughtfully.

The next five minutes of the walk continued in awkward silence, punctuated by one of them starting a sentence but trailing off before they finished it. Focusing on not making a fool of herself in front of Aidan, Lia failed to notice the Cocker Spaniels run up to her and made a high pitched startled noise when one of them jumped at her.

"Lia?" Aidan queried, glancing round at her.

"I'm fine." Lia said, bending down to pet the dogs as her typical bright red blush spread over her cheeks.

"Don't you see those two dogs every day?" Aidan asked teasingly when Lia started to walk again.

"Well….. erm…" Lia replied.

Aidan grinned at Lia, she immediately smiled back and just like that the rest of walk was filled with companiable teasing and discussing past memories. At the end of the circuit they stopped and put the leads back on the dogs, Lia felt a small pang of sadness that the walk and her time with Aidan was over and fell silent to think.

"Same time tomorrow?" Aidan asked when they reached the Taylors' drive.

Feeling relieved that this wasn't a one time thing, Lia smiled as she nodded her agreement.

"Great, see you tomorrow."

"Bye."

Chapter Three

16th November 2017

"Right, so we have discussed the fact that all of you will be able to control one element: Amelia you can control water, Charlie you can control earth, Ben you can control air and Sam you can control fire. The ability to call on these elements will come in handy when you come up against your enemies." David explained.

"Hold on a sec, Dad." Sam interrupted. "You never said anything about having enemies."

"If you would just let me finish explaining, I will get to the part about them." David replied. "So, as you are aware you have an ancestor called Isaac and he is the last member of our family to have control of all four elements as an individual. Now, legend has it that over 800 years ago Isaac became aware of a plot to take over the village that our ancestors had been controlling for the last three centuries by a village that had been their rival for as far as records go back. The chatter that had been overheard gravely concerned Isaac because it mentioned an enemy sorcerer who had come from the big town in the south. Going about his business in the village, Isaac heard more talk regarding the sorcerer and his penchant for killing any witch who appeared in his path and taking their powers for his own gain. Based on this talk, Isaac decided that he would defend his village if and when it came under attack from their opponents. However, realising that there was a risk that he could lose control of the elements to the other sorcerer due to the use of dark magic, Isaac wrote a spell, which if he chanted would prevent the elements from being in one body again. The spell meant that the first born of each generation would inherit control of one element until the day that four were born at once. After months of small attacks between the two villages, killing of cattle and the burning of unoccupied buildings, the final straw came when two farmers from Isaac's village were decapitated. With the spell in his pocket, Isaac rode out with the other villagers to battle for their village. Unlike Isaac, the fiendish sorcerer hid behind his villagers, waiting for his chance to attack Isaac. Charging into the battlefield, armed with a sword, bow and arrow, Isaac fought valiantly to protect his village. Using both his powers and his weapons, Isaac was able to deplete the number of human rival warriors, enabling his village to win the battle. Unfortunately, Isaac was mortally wounded when he was shot by a number of arrows by some advancing opposition fighters, including two to the stomach and one to the chest. Surrounded by rival villagers to prevent him from escaping, Isaac chanted the spell, initiating the power splitting. The enemy sorcerer arrived moments after the spell was cast and vowed that his family would use whatever means necessary to obtain control of the elements and as a result our families have been feuding ever since."

"So, you are saying that a family of evil witches are now going to try and kill us because of a centuries old feud." Charlie asked shocked.

"What I am saying is that there are other witches, including the family from our past, out there who will want to steal your powers and use it for their own gain but there are also some good witches around as well." David explained, sitting down heavily on the edge of the table.

"Now I know you have gone completely mad." Charlie announced, springing from his chair. "You are sitting here telling your children that they have inherited some mystical powers which come from their paternal lineage and that we now have to use them to fight some centuries old feud. I mean come on, how ridiculous does that sound? Seriously! Have you been hit on the head recently?"

Charlie swung his arms out to vent his frustration, however because he was so wound up by the situation, he caused all of the books and ornaments to come crashing out of the bookcases. The whole room fell silent after the last of the books finished falling from the shelves and Charlie sank back into his seat.

"Does anyone have any questions?" David asked, after a few minutes of shocked silence.

"How would we know if someone else has powers?" Lia asked.

"Good question Amelia, there is no way to specifically tell if someone else has powers. It is not something that is regularly talked about because as Charlie has pointed out it does sound quite weird. However if someone was a witch there are a couple of methods they could use to let you know: the first would be through telepathy as all witches have this power, alternatively if it was appropriate they could tell you that they are a witch."

"Does every Wiccan family have control of the elements or are there other powers that can be used?" Lia continued fascinated, not giving her brothers a chance to ask any questions.

"Whilst the basic powers are all the same, such as telepathy, spell casting and potions, there are also a variety of different powers out there that other Wiccan families possess." David explained.

"What types of powers?" Sam piped up.

"Divination, empathy, healing…" David started.

"We could do with one of us having healing powers just for Lia's accidents." Sam joked, interrupting his dad.

"Funny." Lia muttered, sticking her tongue out at her brothers, when they smirked at Sam's comment.

"Other possible powers include: illusions, astral protection, invisibility, shape-shifting, teleportation, conjuring. This is by no means an exhaustive list, there are always other powers out there." David continued.

"What is likely to happen if we come up against this evil family?" Ben asked.

"Well, obviously they will want to steal your powers, so most likely they will launch the offensive by attacking you using their powers. This is the most appropriate time to use your powers in order to defend yourselves. However if they win they will capture you to steal your powers." David explained.

"How can they steal our powers?" Lia exclaimed.

"There are two methods, the old school method is to kill your enemy and to embrace the powers as they are expelled from the body. However, in the last 100 years someone has come up with a spell which can transfer powers from one witch to another." David admitted.

"Right, so to conclude this particularly enthralling magic lesson, we have to master our powers as quickly as we can just in case, we end up in some centuries old war with people who we may not be able to identify." Sam summed up, standing up. "I think I speak for all four of us when I say that we need a bit of time to process this information and that we would like to end the session now."

David looked at his other three children, all of whom nodded their agreement at Sam's suggestion. In a sign of silent agreement David waved his hand to dismiss them. Lia watched as her brothers left the garage and then got out of her chair to help her dad put all the books and ornaments away.

"Dad?" Lia asked, once most of the books had been put away.

"Yes?"

"Are there any books on the origins of our powers?"

David looked at the bookshelves for a couple of seconds, ran his fingers across a couple shelves, before pulling out three books that were bound together.

"These have been written by our ancestors over the centuries and cover the origins of how our powers came to be split." David said, passing the books to Lia. "These books are not to leave the house but you can read them if you want."

Lia took the books from her dad and gave him a quick hug. "Thanks Dad, you're the best." Lia stated, as she darted out of the garage.

Coming through into the kitchen, Lia put the books down on the counter so she could grab a glass of water and pet the dogs as they wandered over to her. Glancing at her watch, she realised that she only had a couple of minutes before Aidan came over to help her walk the dogs.

"Ben!" she called, as she took the stair two at a time.

"Yeah." Ben called from his bedroom.

Turning back, as she was partway up the stairs to her room, Lia jogged to Ben's room. "When Aidan gets here can you stall him for a couple of minutes."

"Why?"

"I'm still in my nice jeans, I need to find my trainers and get a warmer jumper."

"Whatever." Ben said, but he got up from his desk and walked downstairs.

"Thank you." Lia called, as she ran back up the second set of stairs to her bedroom.

Once in her bedroom, Lia quickly stripped off her jeans and hung them over the back of her desk chair. She then pulled open one of her drawers and rifled through until she found a warm woolly jumper which she pulled over the top of her pink checked shirt.

Aidan hesitated before he knocked on the Taylors' front door. He wanted to speak to Ben before he went on his daily walk with Lia. Over the last week the feelings for Lia, that he had been ignoring for the last year, had been getting stronger and he could no longer ignore them. Coming to the conclusion that he wanted to act on them, he was here a couple of minutes early so he could talk to Ben about what he intended to do. They had been friends for as long as he could remember and he wanted to ensure that asking Lia on a date wouldn't cause any friction between them.

"Stay." he ordered Buster, as he knocked on the door.

"Lia's running late." Ben announced, by way of a greeting when he opened the door.

"Got a minute then?" Aidan asked.

"Sure." Ben shrugged.

"Wanted to talk to you about something."

"Sounds serious."
"How would you feel if I asked your sister out?"
"Lia?"
"You have another sister?"
"You been thinking about this long?"
"On and off for the last year, more on for the last couple of months."
"I knew it! Sam owes me a tenner!"
"What?"
"Me and Sam have had a bet going for the last couple of months about this."
"OK, but that doesn't exactly address my point."
The boys fell silent for a minute while Ben thought about what Aidan had said. Shoving his hands in his pocket, Aidan turned away from his friend unsure what to do next.
"You serious about this?" Ben questioned, after a few more seconds.
Aidan turned back round, so that he could look his friend in the eye, as he nodded.
"Well, I can't speak for my sister but if Lia says yes then I will support it."
"Thanks."
"Just don't make her cry." Ben warned finally, before smirking in amusement at what he had just said and heading back into the house.

"Lia! The dogs need walking and Aidan's waiting outside!" Diane called, coming up the stairs to Lia's room after Lia had been in her room for a few minutes.
"I'm coming." Lia mumbled, as she hunted for her dog walking jeans and trainers under her desk.
Yanking her jeans on, Lia picked up both trainers and ran down the stairs. At the bottom of the stairs, Lia battled with her laces as she pulled on her shoes, grabbing her coat she quickly bottoned it up before taking a pair of gloves out of the pocket and putting them on. Once she was ready, she fetched the dogs' leads out of the cupboard.
"Betty! Veronica! Walk!" Lia called to the dogs.

"Hey!" Aidan said, from just beyond the front door.

"Hi, sorry I'm running a little late." Lia apologised.

"Lia I have known you for years, I am well prepared to wait a couple of minutes." Aidan chuckled, putting the lead on Veronica as Lia did the same with Betty.

Once the dogs had their leads on, Lia moved through the open front door, Buster had been waiting patiently outside until he saw Lia and jumped up, knocking Lia back into Aidan. Aidan caught Lia before she fell to the floor and once, she was safely on her feet, Aidan pulled Buster away from her.

"Sorry Lia, I swear he doesn't do that with anyone but you." Aidan said, standing between Lia and his overexcited dog.

"It's fine. Betty and Veronica do the exact same thing every morning, every afternoon and any other time I leave them for more than an hour." Lia babbled, reaching round Aidan to pet the now whining Buster.

Aidan headed out of the house with Buster and Veronica, Lia followed him with Betty. For a couple of minutes the two of them walked in silence. Once they reached the woods, they let the dogs off the lead so that they could run around. Lia stumbled over a stick that was in the middle of the path causing Aidan to grab onto her to steady her.

"That's twice you've stopped me from falling today, most boys like girls falling at their feet." Lia quipped, once Aidan let go of her arm.

Aidan smiled but didn't respond, Lia gave him a puzzled look but when he looked away Lia moved slightly away from him. Lia walked along the edge of the path slowly kicking at the leaves that were piled up along the edge of the path. Hearing some rustling slightly ahead of them, Lia moved so that she was stood slightly closer to but also a little behind Aidan.

Lia let out a sigh of relief when she realised that it was just the Cocker Spaniels. Aidan paused as Lia passed him so she could crouch down and pet the dogs as she did every evening. Once the dogs had run back to their owner, Lia stood up and wiped at the mud on the knees of her jeans.

"You've been quiet today." Lia commented, as they started walking again.

"Sorry." Aidan replied.

"Is everything OK?" Lia asked, grabbing at Aidan's hand pulling him to a stop.

Lia let go as Aidan tugged his hand away. Lia stood with her hands at her sides watching Aidan as he walked a few steps and stopped. Sensing something wasn't quite right, Lia walked over to the dogs all of whom had paused to watch the humans. Betty walked over to Lia's side and leant against her legs, Lia rested her hand on Betty's head soothing both of them.

"Aidan? Are you OK?" Lia asked, once he had eventually turned back to face her.

"Yeah I'm fine."

"Why are you acting so strange?"

"What do you mean?"

"You've barely spoken to me in the last ten minutes. Normally you ask me about History or you tell me stuff that you and my brothers are doing at the weekend." Lia explained.

Aidan walked over to Lia so he was standing directly in front of her.

"So I spoke to Ben earlier and I was just thinking about that."

"You two talk all the time, what is so different about today?"

"I was talking to him about you."

"Me?" Lia squeaked.

"Yes, you." Aidan confirmed. "I was asking Ben whether it would be a problem if I asked you on a date."

"A date?" Lia repeated.

"Yeah, I've been wanting to ask you out for a little while but I didn't want to make things awkward with Ben and Sam. However, I realised that going on these walks with you that I want to be with you, you know go on a date and see where it goes."

"What did Ben say?" Lia asked.

"He said he was OK as long as I didn't make you cry, then he smirked." Aidan said, with a smile and shrug. "So what do you say?"

Lia stood, staring at Aidan for a few seconds.

"You want to go on a date with me?" Lia asked.

"Yes."

"Yes."

Aidan smiled, then nodding he caught Lia's hand and began to walk forward, continuing the walk. Lia fell into step with Aidan and kept glancing down at their hands in disbelief that this was actually happening. The dogs ran ahead but kept them in sight.

After a couple of minutes, there was a strong gust of wind which blew some leaves off the trees and caused a few branches to snap. Aidan and Lia quickly rounded the corner where the wind dropped off, and they bumped straight into Dean Foulds. Dean was two years above them in school and had been suspended a number of times for fighting whilst at school. Before leaving school, he had been particularly keen on picking fights with Ben, Sam and Aidan whilst harassing Charlie and some of his friends.

"It's good to see you again Aidan." Dean snarled.

"Dean." Aidan said, steering Lia so she was behind him.

"Well isn't this cute, just a couple of lovebirds out on an evening stroll." Dean continued to snarl, moving closer to them.

Dean shoved Aidan back, when he took a few steps forward, staggering he managed to stay on his feet and take another step forwards. Aidan balled his hands into fists but kept them by his side, until Dean shoved him back again and advanced forward to take a swing. Aidan managed to evade Dean's fists and followed up by punching him in the stomach. Dean staggered backwards but managed to hit Aidan in the face, causing him to crumple to floor and Dean advanced on Lia.

Grinning, Dean stopped two metres from Lia. He opened

his palm and produced a glowing purple ball of electricity, which he launched at Lia. Lia dropped to her knees, ducking the ball barely. Dean regrouped and produced an electricity ball in each hand. Lia gasped but managed to spot a low hanging tree branch just above Dean's head. Using all of her strength, Lia waved her hands at the branch, somehow managing to pull the branch from the tree and hit Dean in the stomach. Dean's energy balls disappeared as he landed on his knees, winded.

Aidan groaned as he began to come to. Dean glanced round before pulling himself to his feet, glaring at Lia and then ran off back into the woods.

"Lia? Are you OK?" Aidan asked, crawling over to where Lia was kneeling.

"I'm fi… Oh my God you're bleeding!" Lia cried.

"It's fine, let's go." Aidan said, pulling Lia to her feet and whistling for the dogs.

Moving as quickly as they could, Lia and Aidan finished their walk in shocked silence. At the edge of the woods they put the leads back on the dogs. Lia clutched Betty and Veronica's leads and tried to stop the tears that were forming.

"You need to come in and get cleaned up." Lia announced from the bottom of the driveway, letting the dogs walk up the drive on their own, while Lia tugged Aidan's hand to get him to walk up the drive with her.

Lia pulled open the back door and let the dogs into the utility room, she then turned and took Buster off his lead so he could also come in.

"Mum! Mum!" Lia called, as she followed the dogs into the kitchen. "Aidan is bleeding!"

Diane rushed out of her office into the kitchen, quickly followed by Ben, Sam and David.

"What happened?" Sam asked, looking at the singed sleeve of Lia's coat.

Lia glanced at her sleeve and silently shook her head at her brother, signalling that she would talk about it later. Sam nodded, then gestured silently to Ben and his dad to look

at Lia. When they saw the singed sleeve of Lia's coat.
David took the coat off Lia and hung it strategically so the
sleeve was hidden
"Do you guys remember Foulds from school?" Aidan
asked, taking the ice pack Ben handed to him whilst Diane
examined his nose.
Ben and Sam nodded.
"Well, he ambushed me and Lia whilst we were walking
the dogs, we turned the corner at the top of woods and
there he was just standing there. He shoved at me a couple
of times then he started throwing punches. One caught me
at a dodgy angle and knocked me flat on my arse then I
don't know what happened." Aidan explained. "I think he
must have gone after Lia next though because when I
came to she was sprawled on the floor."
"He just knocked me over, then due to the wind, a tree
branch fell and hit him so he left."
Ben looked furious, as Diane walked over to check on Lia.
Diane ran her hands over her daughter's hair and down her
arms. Lia winced as her mum touched her left elbow, and
glanced up at her dad.
"Diane, why don't you take Amelia upstairs as she's
covered in mud?" David suggested.
Diane nodded her agreement and placed her hand on Lia's
back, guiding her out of the kitchen.
Aidan sank down onto one of the kitchen chairs and rested
his chin on his hands.
"Sorry guys." he said, once he had heard Lia and Diane
start up the stairs.
"What are you apologising for?" David asked, pulling up
the seat opposite him.
"I should have stopped him from getting near her."
"It's not like you hid behind her and let him attack her
first. He knocked you out. There isn't anything else you
could have done." Ben said. "No-one here blames you."

Upstairs in her bathroom, Lia yanked off her muddy, leaf-
covered clothes and dropped them in the sink so that mud

did not get all over the upstairs of the house. The downstairs was a lost cause due to the dogs. She then looked at the wound on her arm which was now stinging as well as bleeding. She grabbed some tissues and held them to her arm in an effort to stop the bleeding.

"Let's have a look at your arm." Diane said, walking into the bathroom.

Lia released her arm so her mum could have a look at the gash, which was just above Lia's elbow. The surrounding skin was also sore and red where the electricity ball had grazed her.

"I think that could need stitches." Diane commented. "But I will clean up the gash for now and if it's still bleeding after dinner then I will take you to the hospital."

Lia pulled a face at the thought of going to hospital for stitches but after a few moments silence she nodded her reluctant agreement to her mum's suggestion.

"OK, why don't you grab a quick shower to clean yourself off and see if that doesn't make you feel a bit better." Diane suggested, pulling the bathroom door shut behind her.

Lia turned the spray on full blast at the hottest temperature she could bear. She quickly stripped off the rest of her clothes and dropped them in the sink as well. Lia winced as she stepped under the spray but then stood underneath it, letting the water wash away all the dirt and debris that was covering her. Once the worst of the dirt was rinsed off, Lia crouched down and started to cry. After sitting sobbing for a few minutes, she stood up and washed herself quickly, being careful not to touch the wound on her arm.

Feeling slightly more human, Lia all but crawled out of the shower and wrapped herself up in her towel. Lia left the bathroom and retreated to her bedroom; she pulled on her thickest dressing gown and sat down on the edge of her bed. Betty wandered into her bedroom and rested her head on Lia's knee, Lia rested her hand on her dog's head and began to cry again.

"Lia? You decent?" Ben asked, from the other side of her bedroom door.

"Yep." Lia hiccupped.

"Dad sent me up with a cup of tea, he figured you needed it." Ben said, coming into her room. Gesturing at Betty. "She's not supposed to be in here."

Ben quickly set the cup of tea down on Lia's bedside table when he saw that she was crying and sat next to her on the bed, he put his arm around her and let her cry. Betty whined in sympathy and rested her head on Lia's lap. Lia rested her head on Ben's shoulder and petted Betty's soft head until her tears began to stem and she had stopped sniffling.

"He formed these weird energy balls with his hand." Lia cried, lifting her head from her brother's shoulder.

"We can talk about it later." Ben said, trying to sooth his sister. "Aidan is staying for dinner."

"Oh."

"Did anything happen before the attack?" Ben asked, smiling and hugging his sister.

"Go away Ben, I need to get dressed." Lia said, pulling away from her brother but she did manage a small smile.

Ben left his sister to get ready and walked back downstairs. He stuck his head round Charlie's door.

"Hey, Lia and Aidan were in a fight on their dog walk." Ben said, when his brother glanced round at him.

"Are they OK?" Charlie asked.

"Aidan has a bloody nose and a black eye, Lia has a massive gash on her arm and is quite shaken but they are pretty much fine."

"I'll head up and check on her." Charlie said, getting up from his chair.

"I've just got her to stop crying."

"Lia's crying?" Aidan and Sam asked, as they both entered Charlie's room.

"She was a minute ago, I think she's just in shock." Ben said.

Aidan ran his hands over his face while Sam patted him on

the shoulder. Charlie swivelled his chair all the way round and gestured to his bed so the others could sit down. The boys sat in silence for a little bit, coming up with a plan until they heard Lia's bedroom door open above them. Betty ran down the stairs followed by Lia.

"We are in Charlie's room." Ben called, before Lia could head down the second set of stairs.

Lia wiped the last few tears away from her face before she headed into Charlie's room. She hesitated at the doorway, unsure how best to proceed.

"How's the arm? Mum said it might need stitches." Sam asked.

Lia grimaced but didn't respond.

"Dinner's ready!" David called.

They all walked downstairs and grabbed a plate from the kitchen, then sat down at the table and began eating. The meal was consumed in complete silence apart from the occasional sound of cutlery hitting plates. Realising that Lia was struggling to use her left arm, David cut up the chicken that was on her plate but didn't say anything.

After the meal, Charlie and Sam began clearing the table, to give everyone a bit of breathing room.

"I'll drive you home, Aidan." David said, as they left the table.

"Thanks David, would you mind if I just had a word with Lia before we go?" Aidan asked.

David nodded as Lia paused in the kitchen doorway. Warily Lia walked with Aidan into the smaller living room; her brothers headed into the larger living room. She switched on the lights and then perched herself on the edge of one of the chairs.

"I understand if you would rather change your mind about going on that date." Aidan said, sitting in the chair opposite Lia, staring at the floor.

"I'm just a little shaken, but a date sounds fun."

Aidan glanced up from the floor so he could look at Lia's face. When he saw that she was smiling at him, he smiled back.

"So you two are finally going on a date?" Ben asked from the doorway, Sam and Charlie were hovering just behind him.
"Do you guys not believe in privacy?" Aidan asked.
"Not really." Ben admitted with a smile.
Shaking his head, Aidan smiled and got up from his chair, Lia followed his example and stood up as well.
"Lia?" Diane called.
"I'll see you at school tomorrow Aidan." Lia said, as she left the room.
"See ya."
Lia left the room and went into her mum's office.
"Let's have a look at your arm." Diane said, as Lia entered the room.
Lia shut the door behind her and slid her arm out of her jumper. She winced as the jumper caught on the gash.
"It's still bleeding." Diane said. "I'm sorry Sweetie but we are going to have to go to the hospital."
Lia walked backwards until she walked into the back of the door. She pulled the door open and edged towards the stairs but Ben was blocking the way up.
"Need to go to the hospital, Lia?" Ben asked, watching as his mum eyed up his sister.
"Mum says my arm is still bleeding and she wants me to get stitches but really it's fine." Lia said, trying to edge round him.
Ben managed to block Lia's escape.
"I'll go with you." he said, wrapping his arm around Lia steering her to the front door.
Diane picked up her car keys then passed Lia her boots and a different coat, Ben grabbed a hoody from the cupboard and pulled Lia out of the door.
The hospital waiting room was relatively empty when they arrived, Diane went up to check them in while Ben and Lia sat down on the plastic chairs.

They were finally seen shortly after 11 o'clock and Lia had to have 11 stitches in her left arm. Ben and Lia went to the pharmacy to pick up Lia's painkillers and antibiotics to prevent any infection, whilst Diane went to get the car. They met up at the exit and Diane drove them all home, Lia drifted off to sleep thanks to the traumatic events of the day and the painkillers. Once they got home, Ben lifted Lia out of the car and carried her into the house.

"Painkillers put her to sleep." he explained, as David held the door open.

"She's got a deep cut just above her elbow and second degree burns over fifty percent of her arm so she made need some time off school." Diane commented, as she shut the door. "She needs to keep it dry and watch for any signs of infection."

"I'll take her up to bed." David said, slowly taking Lia off Ben.

Ben followed David upstairs, while Diane went to get Lia a glass of water. David lay his daughter down on her bed and pulled her shoes off before tucking her into bed. David took the water off his wife and placed it on Lia's nightstand.

"Dad." Ben said, once they were all back downstairs. "Lia said something really strange when I gave her that cup of tea earlier."

"Hmm?" David responded, sinking onto the sofa.

"She said that Dean made energy balls with his hands and threw them at her."

David shot out of his seat and began to run up the stairs. Confused, the boys looked at their mum, who shook her head. Diane got up and walked into the kitchen, to put the kettle on so that she could make a cup of tea. She then organised glasses of fruit juice and coke for the boys.

"Amelia, Amelia, Sweetie, can you wake up." David asked, giving his daughter a gentle shake.

Lia let out a small moan and attempted to swat at David.

"I'm sorry Sweetie, but I do need you to wake up for just a little while."

Amelia opened her eyes and blinked at her dad.

"I just need you to tell me what happened when you saw

Dean Foulds earlier." David explained, when Lia looked confused. "Let's go downstairs so you can tell everyone together."

David handed Lia her slippers and gave her a hand getting out of bed. David picked up the glass of water and passed it to Lia who took a sip before trying to stand up. David led the way back downstairs to the living room with Lia following him slowly. Betty and Veronica appeared at the bottom of the stairs and whined gently until Lia stopped to pet them. Diane walked past holding a tray of drinks and beckoned Lia into the living room. Ben slid onto the floor giving Lia a spare seat on the sofa.

"OK Lia, I need you to tell me exactly what happened when you bumped into Dean earlier today." David said, crouching down in front of Lia.

"Well the beginning bit went exactly like Aidan said, although there was this massive gust of wind just before we turned the corner." Lia said, shifting so she could lean back a bit.

"What happened after Dean knocked Aidan out?" David demanded standing up, pacing a couple of steps before crouching back down in front of Lia again.

"Erm, after Aidan went down, Dean sort of advanced on me, then he stopped and raised his hands. On one of them this weird purple ball appeared with what looked like lightening around the outside. He then threw the ball at me, I managed to duck out of the way but the ball caught my arm."

"Where did the ball come from Lia?" Charlie asked.

"I don't know it just appeared on his palm and then he threw it at me. After the first one only hit my arm, he made one appear in each hand."

"How did he miss if you were lying on the floor?" Sam asked.

"I waved a tree branch into his stomach." Lia announced, smiling.

"Clever." David said, settling back down on the sofa. "However I do believe that the ancient battle between us and the evil family, which as you now know is the Foulds family has started. So as I discussed in our lesson, we need to start preparing for the battle and you guys need to start taking your magic more seriously."

They all looked around at each other, in various stages of concern.

"David, I think that is enough for tonight. You can have a nice magic-based evening tomorrow as I am going out with friends." Diane announced. "Come on Amelia, I'll give you a hand getting changed."

Lia left the room after her mum, the dogs followed her out and began to whine when Lia went upstairs.

"Mum, they are going to cry all night." Lia said, pausing on the stairs.

"The dogs are not allowed to sleep upstairs, Lia." Diane said.

"Just this once Mum. Please?" Lia begged.

"Just don't tell your father." Diane relented.

"Thanks Mum." Lia smiled. "Come on girls."

The dogs ran up the stairs, passing Lia and Diane. Once they got upstairs, the dogs went to lie down at the end of the bed where they could watch over Lia at night. Lia pulled off her jeans and replaced them with the pink checked pyjama bottoms. Diane picked Lia's discarded jeans and folded them up, placing them on the top of Lia's chest of drawers. Lia then turned round so her mum could help her get out of the jumper and into her pyjama top.

"Goodnight Lia." Diane said, giving her a hug as she turned off Lia's light and left the room.

"Night Mum."

It was Saturday, two days after the incident and Lia was curled up on the sofa in the small living room watching Riverdale on Netflix for the third time. She was getting a little bit bored but the second degree electrical burn was still very painful and consequently she still taking strong painkillers which prevented her from going out and she couldn't focus long enough to read anything.

"Lia, do you want anything to drink?" Ben asked, popping his head around the living room door.

"No, I'm fine, thanks Ben."

"Aidan is coming around in a bit, is that OK?" Ben asked, sitting down next to Lia on the sofa.

"Why wouldn't it be OK?"

"I don't know, just thought it would be best to check."

"How long until he gets here?"

"About 10 minutes."

Lia jumped up, being careful not to knock her arm.

"Where are you going?" Ben asked, as Lia dashed out of the room.

"I need to get changed, I'm not seeing Aidan for the first time since he asked me out in my pyjamas." Lia announced, starting up the stairs.

Lia entered her room, and quickly swapped from her pyjamas to her jeans, and one of her pink shirts. She looked at herself in her full length mirror, the look was not one of her best but she looked better than she had in pyjamas. She ran her hairbrush through her hair quickly but then getting dizzy, she sank back onto her bed.

"Aidan's here, been here about 15 minutes." Charlie said, entering her room.

"How long have I been up here?" Lia asked, struggling to sit up.

"Nearly half an hour." Charlie said, crossing the room to help his sister up.

"I guess I fell asleep." Lia mumbled, slightly confused.

"Pain killers are still taking their toll on you."

Lia nodded and began to head out of the room, leaning slightly on Charlie as she was still feeling a little bit dizzy. Once they got downstairs, Charlie let Lia go and headed into the office to do some work. Lia headed towards the main living room where the boys would be watching football.

No one looked away from the match when Lia poked her head round the door, so she headed back to the small living room to finish watching the episode of Riverdale.

"Hey." Aidan called, walking into the living room where Lia was curled up watching TV.

"Hi."

"How's the arm?" he asked, sitting down next to Lia.

"Not too bad. How are you?"

"I've had worse."

Aidan picked up Lia's right hand and sat there holding it in his for a couple of minutes. Lia stared down at their linked hands and waited for Aidan to say something.

"Do you want to go to the cinema next weekend?" Aidan asked, after a couple of minutes silence.

Lia nodded.

"Cool, I'll check the times and text you." Aidan said, getting back up.

Chapter Four

25th November 2017

"He wants to see Predator." Lia groaned to Heather and Siobhan, as they all gathered up in her bedroom.
Lia was supposed to be going on her date with Aidan later that day but she was having some reservations about the film they were going to see. She was also struggling with what she was supposed to wear, as her arm was still bandaged due to the burn but she had had her stitches out only the day before. Heather was stood in front of Lia's wardrobe, picking through her clothes, Siobhan was sat in Lia's desk chair and Lia was propped up on her bed.
"I'm sure it won't be as bad as you think." Siobhan soothed.
"The original was one of Sam or Ben's movie choices a few months ago, I swear it was one of the worst films I've seen."
"What's the film about?" Siobhan asked, after a few seconds.
"It's some sort of sci-fi horror film, where a space ship comes down and the aliens start taking people hostage and killing them. There are loads of quite gruesome killings and a dramatic rescue before the hero of the movie, played by Arnold Schwarzenegger, has an intense battle with the creature where he is nearly beaten but somehow manages to trap the alien and then it self-destructs somehow." Lia said, giving the film a scathing review.
"Definitely not a good date movie." Heather chimed in.
"It's a date with Aidan, just look on the bright side."
"True."
"How do your brothers feel about you dating Aidan?" Heather asked, throwing a top at Lia for her to try on.
"For the time being they all seem OK, I guess."
"Have you discussed with Ben, about dating his best mate?" asked Siobhan.

"I have asked him if he is OK with it and I know Aidan has had the same conversation but we haven't really discussed it in any detail."

Feeling slightly awkward and to put an end to the conversation Lia pulled on the top that Heather had passed her. Shifting the top into the right place, Lia then stood up to look in her mirror.

"I think this one is a bit much, we are only going to the cinema." she commented, pulling at the sparkly top to try and cover up her midriff which was bare.

"OK, try this one." Heather said, tossing Lia one of the tops that she had placed on the bed when she was going through Lia's wardrobe.

Lia passed the top she had just tried on, back to Heather who had taken a seat on the bed. Lia pulled on the pink striped one that Heather had just passed her.

"Too casual." Heather and Siobhan decided at the same time.

Lia passed it back to Heather and caught the next one she threw at her, Lia immediately threw the top back, wrinkling up her nose.

"I think I might have stolen that from Sam a few months ago." Lia explained.

"It's a cool t-shirt though."

"That's why I stole it but there is no way I'm wearing my brother's clothes on a date." Lia laughed.

Shaking her head, Heather added the t-shirt to the pile of discarded ones, then tossed Lia her next choice. Lia grabbed the it off of the floor, where it had landed and pulled it over her head. Just as she was pulling her top on, there was a knock at the door.

"Who is it?" Lia called, walking towards the door.

"Sam."

Lia opened up her bedroom door and let her brother in.

"We have a bit of time till the next match starts so we are planning to walk to the shop to get something for lunch, do you girls want anything?" Sam asked, glancing round Lia's room. "Did a hurricane hit?"

Lia pulled a face at her brother.

"I mean, seriously, there are clothes everywhere Lia." Sam continued dramatically.

"I am just sorting through my wardrobe, Heather and Siobhan are just giving me some second opinions." Lia commented, pushing her brother back towards the door when he started to step further into her bedroom.

"Do you want anything from the shop?" Sam asked, as he headed back out of the room.

"Can you get me some soup?" Lia asked.

"Chicken?"

"Yep."

"I'll see what bread there is as well. Do you two want anything?"

Heather and Siobhan shook their heads.

Once Sam had headed back downstairs, Lia shut her bedroom door and returned to standing in front of her mirror. The top she was trying on, was a simple black top with ruffles at the borders of the sleeves and with a slightly low v -neckline.

"I like this one." Lia commented, turning to check the back.

"Yeah, it's cute with the ruffles on but not really fussy, you could wear jeans and your good blue boots." Heather commented, rising off the bed to stand behind Lia.

Siobhan nodded her agreement.

"Excellent, that's tonight's clothes sorted then." Lia declared. "How are you guys doing with the History essay?"

"I've virtually finished mine." Siobhan answered.

"How have you nearly finished?" Heather asked shocked. "I've barely even started mine."

"I've just been working on it most evenings this week." Siobhan explained.

Lia was completely used to this sort of conversation, this had been the theme throughout their many years of friendship. Siobhan would get the work done as quickly as she could to ensure that she had plenty of time to get everything done and checked, whereas Heather forever left stuff to the last minute so it was always a bit of a rush to get everything done. Lia was usually more like Heather, although she would always have done extensive the research and made a plan well in advance, she just didn't tend to write the essay or complete the assignment until closer to the deadline.

"For once, I am in a similar boat to Siobhan." Lia commented.

"I'm doomed." Heather groaned, flopping down onto Lia's bed.

"What do you mean you're doomed?" Lia asked, sitting on the edge of her bed next to her friend's feet.

"Well, I'm clearly really behind if you've virtually written the essay and I've not started yet." Heather commented, dramatically covering her face with her hands.

"I'm only nearly finished because I haven't been in school all week due to this stupid cut on my arm and the ridiculous effect the painkillers have been having on me."

"That makes me feel a little better."

Laughing, the girls moved onto to discuss what had been happening that week at school, catching Lia up on all of the gossip. After about half an hour of chatting, there was a knock on Lia's door. When there was no immediate response there was a second louder knock on the door.

"I'm coming." Lia grumbled, crossing the room to open the door.

Ben, Aidan and Luke were stood on the other side of the door when Lia opened it.

"Sam's got the soup you asked for." Ben stated, once Lia had opened the door.

"Great, thanks."

Heather moved from behind Lia and walked over to Luke and to give him a quick kiss by way of a greeting.

"Have you two started your History essay?" Heather asked Luke and Aidan.

Luke looked marginally bewildered, as if he had forgotten that there was an essay, while Aidan shook his head.

"OK, now I feel much better." Heather commented, turning back to her friends. "However, I might head home now and see if I can make a start on getting through the essay."

"I've got a load of homework to do as well" Siobhan agreed, gathering up her and Heather's handbags.

"I'll see you guys on Monday." Lia said giving, both of her friends a quick hug goodbye.

"Call us tomorrow though." Heather called, as she walked down the stairs with Siobhan. "Luke! Are you coming?"

"Guess I will also be going." Luke sighed, before turning and following the girls down the stairs.

"That will be you two before you know it." Ben chuckled.

"Shut up!" Aidan said, punching Ben in the arm.

Laughing Ben, headed off downstairs, leaving Lia and Aidan awkwardly standing in the doorway to her bedroom. Aidan shifted slightly, so he could lean against the doorframe, causing Lia to take a slight step backwards. Aidan raised one eyebrow, questioning Lia's slight movement away from him. Lia shrugged slightly but did move half a step back towards Aidan. Watching Aidan, Lia lowered her arms from being crossed across her chest to let them hang down by her sides. Carefully, Aidan caught Lia's hands in his and pulled her gently towards him, standing virtually touching each other Aidan bent his head down and gently kissed Lia.

"HCK HMM!" Sam coughed, from his position most of the way up the stairs.

Lia and Aidan sprang apart at the sudden noise and both turned to look at Sam, who was smiling like an idiot. At Sam's grin, Lia blushed bright red and began to back into her room.

"Match is about to start." Sam commented, nodding at Aidan.

Aidan nodded back and then quickly headed back downstairs. Once he had passed Sam, he quickly turned round to catch Lia's eye and gave her a quick smile before jogging the rest of the way back down the stairs. Lia warily eyed-up her brother who had taken his time walking the rest of the way up the stairs and into Lia's bedroom doorway.

Sam started to laugh at the mortified look on Lia's face. Shaking her head, Lia gestured for Sam to come in. Lia sat down on the edge of her bed and hid her face in her hands while she waited for Sam to say something.

"Just be glad it was me who caught you." Sam commented, sitting next to Lia on her bed.

Groaning, Lia leant on her brother's shoulder and began to giggle at the situation. Sam swung his arm over his sister's shoulders and let her laugh for a minute.

"Anyway, I was actually coming up here to see if you wanted anything doing with your soup." Sam said, once Lia had stopped giggling and sat back up.

"I'll come down and sort it out, thanks, though."

"OK."

Sam stood up and held his hand out to help Lia get up off her bed. Once Sam had pulled her up off the bed, she followed him out of her room and downstairs. Once they had reached the bottom of the stairs, Sam walked into the living room to watch the match with the group of boys and Lia continued on to the kitchen.

Sam joined the lads in the living room, accepting the banter that was taking place as par for the course and settled himself in his usual chair to watch the football.

"You and Lia seem to be spending a lot of time alone together, Aidan." Jake stated. "Dog walks and private conversations."

"Problem?" Aidan asked mildly, flicking a glance over at Jake.

"Well I don't have a problem but you might if Sam or Ben catch you doing anything with their sister, we've all heard the stories." Jake laughed.

"I'm not worried, besides it's already happened." Aidan shot back with a grin.

"What?" Ben exclaimed.

"Yeah, I caught a bit of tongue action a few minutes ago

when I went to ask Lia if she needed anything doing with her lunch." Sam explained lazily.

"And Aidan's still breathing?" Carl asked.

"Yeah, figured I would wait until after their date tonight so I don't have to deal with her wrath, she can be bloody vicious when she wants. Ben and I have the battle scars to prove it." Sam joked.

"You've kept your date pretty quiet. What have you got to hide? Clearly Sam and Ben know." Jake teased.

"I can shout it from the rooftops if you want mate."

Before anyone else could comment, the match restarted on the screen and the boys all turned their attention back to the TV.

In the kitchen, Lia saw that Sam had left her lunch on the counter with a fresh roll next to it. After pouring the soup into bowl, she put it in the microwave for a couple of minutes and then put the kettle on to make a cup of tea. Lia quickly buttered the roll while she waited for the microwave and the kettle. Once her lunch was all ready, she placed it all on a tray and started to pick the tray up.

"You're not supposed to be carrying stuff yet." Charlie commented, taking the tray off Lia when it began to dip. "I'll take it up to your room."

Lia followed her brother upstairs.

"How did you know I would be eating in my room?" Lia asked, as they began walking up the stairs to the second floor.

"Easy, you never eat in the kitchen if you can help it, football's on in the main living room and Mum is in the other living room." Charlie commented, reaching the top of the stairs and allowing Lia to pass him.

"So? Why does that mean that I would be eating in my room?" Lia continued.

"You hate football, so it is unlikely that you would go in there plus it is really busy and Mum is doing the ironing while watching one of her shows, so your room was the only logical place for you to be eating." Charlie explained, placing the tray on Lia's desk.

After Charlie left, Lia quickly ate her lunch, whilst working on a bit more of her History essay. Leaving the tray on her desk, Lia picked her laptop up off the desk and went to work on her bed for a bit. Ignoring the clothes that were still all over her bed, Lia sat against her pillows and moved onto her English assignment regarding the metaphors used by Emily Bronte in Wuthering Heights and how they were used to emphasise emotions in the book.

After Lia had been working for an hour, her dad popped his head into her room.

"Do you want a cup of tea?" he asked, as he walked into the room.

"That would be great." Lia replied, lowering the laptop screen so she could talk to her dad.

Sitting in Lia's desk chair, David turned to look at his daughter.

"I'm a bit concerned about you going out tonight." David said, after a few seconds.

"Why? I'll be with Aidan."

"That's part of my concern and before you interrupt let me finish." David commented, waving his hand in a gesture to stop Lia as she began to interject. "I don't like the thought of you going on a date with anyone. I just don't like it but that's not the only reason why I don't like the thought of you going out. After what happened last week, I'm just not sure it's safe."

"I'll be in a public place so I don't think anything like what happened last week will occur." Lia commented, getting up from her bed.

"I still don't like the fact you are going out on a date." David commented, leaning back in Lia's chair.

Lia crossed the room and wriggled onto her dad's lap so she could give him a hug.

"I've got to grow up sometime Dad." She whispered, when her dad hugged her back. "And at least it's with Aidan, you like him."

"I'm rethinking that sentiment currently." David muttered,

as Lia scrambled off his lap. "You might want to tidy up in here a bit."

Lia remained standing as he her dad let the room, glancing round, she stared at the scattered piles of books, papers and clothes, covering the floor, bed, desk and other furniture. Sighing, she began by moving all of the various piles of clothes onto her bed so that they were all in one place. When David popped back into Lia's room, she was in the process of hanging her clothes in the walk-in wardrobe. David put the cup of tea on the small bit of available space of the desk, leaving Lia to continue tidying.

A couple of hours and a much tider bedroom later, Lia heard a sharp knock on the door, pausing mid dance, she quickly paused her music.

"Who is it?"

"Aidan."

Lia dumped the piles of papers she was in the middle of sorting out back on her desk and ran to answer the door.

"Hi." She said, opening the door.

"Hey. Can I come in for a sec?" Aidan asked.

Lia moved away from the doorway and let Aidan into the room, silently thanking her dad for the tip about tidying up. Aidan walked in and looked around the room, slightly bemused by the change in the room's appearance.

"I just wanted to talk about what happened earlier, you know when Sam appeared." Aidan started, sitting down on Lia's desk chair, while she settled on the edge of her bed.

"Kissing you then might have been a mistake." Aidan continued, as Lia blushed at the memory.

"Wha…wh…?" Lia stuttered confused.

"I err… what I meant to say was…" Aidan began.

Lia crossed her arms and legs, dropping eye contact with Aidan. He stood up and walked towards Lia's bedroom door, stopping just before leaving the room and turning back to Lia.

"I wanted to kiss you Lia, I've been wanting to kiss you since that evening in the woods, actually longer than that. I just meant that kissing you for the first time when any member of your family could walk up the stairs was a mistake." Aidan said, after staring at Lia for a few seconds.

Lia lifted her gaze up from the carpet, to meet Aidan's eyes, smiling she stood up and crossed the room to where he was stood. Standing on her toes, Lia quickly kissed Aidan, before backing away shyly.

"Well, I guess that settles that." Aidan declared. "I'm heading home, I'll swing back in about an hour."

"I'll see you later." Lia smiled.

Once Aidan had headed off downstairs, Lia quickly ran into her white, pink and purple tiled bathroom, so she could grab a quick shower before going out. Singing along with one of her playlists on the phone that was in her pocket, Lia switched on the shower. Making sure that she scrubbed off any dirt and grime from tidying, Lia tilted her head under the spray of water and let it rush over her for a minute before switching off the shower. Scrambling out, Lia wrapped one of her big, pink, fluffy towels around herself and then made a turban out of the smaller matching one, to dry her hair. With the music still playing, Lia headed out of the bathroom and into her bedroom to get dressed.

Continuing to sing, Lia quickly pulled on her underwear, before pulling out the expensive hair dryer to dry and style her light brown hair. Once she was satisfied that her hair was dry, she pulled it back into a loose ponytail to stop her hair falling in front of her eyes. Once content with her hair, Lia pulled on a pair of tight-fitted, dark blue jeans and the black jumper Heather and Siobhan had helped pick out earlier. She quickly applied a light layer of make up before checking herself out in the full-length mirror attached to the inside wardrobe door. Searching inside the wardrobe, Lia pulled out her nice, dark grey, wool coat, to keep her warm while she was out. Realising that the blue boots she picked out earlier wouldn't work with her coat, she carefully ducked into the wardrobe and pulled out a similar pair of grey boots and pulled them on.

"Aidan's here." Ben commented, pulling open his sister's door.

"Thanks, I'll be right down."

"You look nice." Ben assessed, giving her a once over.

"You sound surprised?"

"I'm just used to seeing you in t-shirts or pyjamas that's all."

"OK, well I guess I better head downstairs." Lia decided, giving herself one last critical look in her mirror and picking up her handbag.

Lia left her room, with Ben a few seconds behind her and headed downstairs. Lia paused halfway down the second set of stairs, suddenly feeling nervous about the date. Ben rested his hand on Lia's shoulder and gave it a quick squeeze before giving her a slight shove to get her the rest of the way down the stairs.

Aidan was waiting in the entrance to the living room, having a conversation with David and Charlie who were standing just inside the kitchen.

"Ah, there you are Lia!" David exclaimed, spotting his daughter as she came round the corner of the stairs.

Aidan glanced over his shoulder, before turning round to get a better look at Lia, Aidan's lips curved slightly before he walked towards her.

"You look amazing." Aidan stated, coming to a stop a short distance away from Lia.

"Thanks, you don't look so bad yourself."

"Shall we go?"

"Yep."

"Your curfew is 11, Amelia." David called, as Lia opened the front door.

"Got it." Aidan called back, closing the door behind him and Lia.

Aidan took Lia's hand as they walked down the driveway to go into town.

"So, Ben mentioned that you really like the Avengers movies." Aidan commented, as they turned onto the main road towards town.

"Yeah, I've been watching them with Sam over the last couple of years." Lia answered, glancing round at Aidan.

"Would you rather go and see the new Avengers movie rather than Predator?" Aidan asked.

"Are you sure?"

"Yeah, I would rather go to see a movie that you are interested in."

"Thanks."

For the remainder of the walk they stayed in comfortable silence, enjoying each other's company as they had done many evenings before. When they got to the cinema, Aidan pulled the door open and let Lia through. Lia waited for Aidan to finish holding the door for the couple that were coming up behind them and then joined the queue. Aidan paid for their tickets and then they headed over to the snack bar to get some popcorn and drinks. Once they had their refreshment they headed into the theatre where the film was playing and settled into their seats.

As the lights went down, Aidan wrapped his arm around Lia's shoulders and pulled her close so she could rest her head on his shoulder. Enjoying the sensation of having Aidan's arm around her, Lia shifted closer to Aidan and spent the movie with her head on his shoulder apart from the occasional times when she would bury her head in his chest when the movie got a bit gory or violent.

At the end of the movie, Lia gathered up their rubbish and followed Aidan out of theatre. Pausing briefly to dump the stuff in the bin, Lia lost sight of Aidan. Glancing round for Aidan, she spotted Dean Foulds and his sister Alice leaning against the wall by the toilets of the cinema. They both had narcissistic smirks on the pale, narrow faces when Lia looked at them and Dean conjured one of his energy balls and grinned as Lia shifted behind the bin. With a laugh, Alice clicked her fingers and blinked, then she and Dean vanished for a second before appearing on the opposite side of the corridor. Lia felt a rising sense of panic when she realised she would never be able to hide from Alice.

"Hey. There you are." Aidan stated, coming back round the corner to where Lia was standing.

"Sorry, I got a bit lost in the crowd."

"No problem."

Lia caught Aidan's hand as she rounded the bin to meet up with him, glancing over her shoulder she saw that Dean and Alice had vanished. Relaxing slightly, knowing that they weren't there, Lia turned her attention back to Aidan.

"I'll walk you back home." Aidan commented, as they walked out of the cinema.

Lia checked her watch and saw that it was much later than she thought and that she only had half an hour to get home.

"Thanks."

Keeping their fingers interlaced, Aidan began the walk from town towards Lia's house. They chatted about the film for a few minutes before lapsing into companionable silence enjoying the cold, bright evening and what Lia hoped was the beginning of a long term relationship with Aidan as she knew he was perfect for her.

Lost in thought, Lia walked straight passed her driveway until Aidan tugged on her hand pulling her to stop.

"Where are you going?" he teased, pulling her back towards him.

"Sorry. Got a bit lost in my own thoughts."

"What were you thinking about?" Aidan asked, turning to face Lia.

"Doesn't matter."

"Well, I'll tell you what I was thinking" Aidan said, pulling Lia against him.

Lia moved her hands so that they rested on Aidan's shoulders. Staring up at Aidan, Lia smiled slowly as Aidan lowered his head to kiss her. The kiss started slowly, but when Lia moved closer to Aidan he deepened the kiss. Stopping to breathe, Aidan rested his forehead against Lia's and held on to her for a few seconds.

"OK, I need to get you the last little bit of the way home." Aidan said, reluctantly moving away from Lia.

Lia followed Aidan up her driveway, and pulled her key out of her pocket. Pausing by the front door, she shifted her keys around in her free hand. Lia leant up to kiss Aidan again, resting her hand on the front door handle. As Aidan began to deepen the kiss, she felt the front door handle move down and the front door open.

"Time to come in now Lia." David said, pulling the door fully open, as Lia and Aidan broke apart.

Reluctantly, Lia let go of Aidan's hand and slid under her father's arm.

"Night Aidan." Lia said, turning back around as she entered the house.

"Night." Aidan responded, moving away from the doorway.

"Did you have a good time?" Diane asked, coming out of the living room.

"Yeah, it was amazing." Lia smiled.

Still smiling, Lia walked through into the kitchen to grab a glass of water. She was surprised to see all of her brothers sitting around the kitchen table.

"Is everything OK?" Lia asked, plopping down in the vacant seat next to Ben.

"Yeah, we were just talking." Sam explained.

"What were you talking about?" Lia asked, sipping on her water.

"Nothing." Sam replied.

"Oh really, so all three of you just happen to be sat in the kitchen talking about nothing."

"Yep." Ben said.

"Worst liars ever."

Ben laughed "Told you we should have planned this better."

"We were just discussing you and Aidan." Charlie explained, giving in before Lia could interrogate him, as he gave in more easily than his brothers.

"Oh?"

"Obviously, we are happy that you are happy and that you can finally stop drooling all over him" Sam explained, getting up from his seat, so he was standing the other side of Lia.

"We just know about Aidan's reputation." Ben continued.

"No." Lia said quietly.

The boys all looked at her.

"We aren't having this conversation." Lia declared, picking up her water and waltzing out of the kitchen.

Lia ran up the stairs to her room and slammed her bedroom door shut. She placed the glass of water on her desk and sank down onto her desk chair. Pulling her phone out of her handbag, she clicked the home button and saw that Aidan had sent her a text.

Aidan: Had a great time tonight. Want to go out for dinner this week? X

Lia: "Same here, sounds like fun xx"

Smiling Lia, placed her phone down on her desk and changed into her pyjamas. Picking up her laptop Lia walked over to bed and curled up against her pillows, she loaded up Netflix and settled into the episode of Grey's Anatomy that she was watching.

"Lia, it's Ben." Ben called, as he knocked on her door.

"Go away." Lia called back.

Ignoring Lia's request, Ben opened her door and walked into her bedroom.

"Pretty sure I said go away." Lia said, sitting up and clicking pause.

"I just want to talk to you." Ben commented, sitting down on the bed next to Lia.

"I know what you are going to say, you are going to tell me all about Aidan's dodgy history with girls and warn me against falling for him but I just don't want to hear it." Lia said, turning away from Ben.

Ben sighed and relaxed back against the wall, while he debated what to say.

"He's the only guy I've ever really liked Ben." Lia mumbled, turning back to Ben.

"I know and I think he likes you back but he has a bad habit of cheating on any girl he sees and I just don't want you to get upset." Ben explained.

"Let's leave this conversation here, it's only been one date."

"OK, how was the date?" Ben asked.

"It was great, film was fantastic and you know Chris Hemsworth was as fit as ever. The only problem was… oh crap I meant to tell Dad this bit!" Lia cried, scrambling over Ben to get off her bed and moving towards the door.

"Meant to tell Dad what, Lia?" Ben asked, following her out of the room.

"Dad! Dad! Where are you?" Lia shouted, as she hurried downstairs.

"I'm in the front living room." David called back. "What's the matter?"

Lia ran into the room and slid to a stop in front of her dad. Ben followed her into the room and took a seat on the sofa.

"What's the matter?" David asked.

"I meant to tell you when I got in but I was a bit distracted." Lia explained, plopping down onto the sofa before immediately bouncing back up.

"Lia, relax. What did you want to tell me?" David asked.

"I got separated from Aidan for a couple of seconds at the cinema. While I was looking for him I saw Dean and his sister, Alice, hanging around by the toilets." Lia blurted out.

"What happened?" David demanded. "Boys get in here!"

Sam and Charlie both came into the living room and sat on the sofa next to Ben whilst Lia settled into one of the chairs.

"Right Lia, finish explaining what happened at the cinema." David demanded, once everyone had settled down.

"Nothing happened, I saw them standing there, they were just watching me. I mean, Dean did create one of those energy ball things. Alice like clicked her fingers and blinked and then she and Dean appeared on the opposite side of the corridor" Lia explained. "How is that even possible?"

"It's called blinking, it is the power to think of a place and blink yourself there." David explained.

"What happened after Alice blinked herself and Dean to the other side of the corridor." Ben asked.

"Nothing happened, they just kept grinning and staring at me." Lia explained.

"They are trying to intimidate us." Sam declared.

"Well, I guess we just need to ensure that they can't do that." Ben announced.

"How?" Lia asked "They are so much stronger than us."

"No, they are just more disciplined than you guys have been. This is partly my fault, your mum and I decided that we would rather you guys not know about magic until you inherited your powers but I'm sure Joe Foulds has been plotting with his children for years" David explained. "We can add in an additional few hours to your group studies and some evenings I will work on your individual powers."

"Sounds like a plan." Sam agreed.

Lia nodded, whilst Ben and Charlie begrudgingly mumbled their agreement. Lia got up out of her chair and wandered through to the kitchen to put the kettle on. Diane came in shortly after her daughter and helped her out by getting down a few mugs whilst Lia finished making the tea.

"So your dad mentioned that he caught you and Aidan kissing by the front door." Diane observed.

"Yeah, he might have opened the front door when Aidan and I were saying goodnight." Lia commented, dodging her mum's eyes.

"Mmmhhmm… Aidan a good kisser?" Diane asked, at her daughter's blush.

"Amazing" Lia stated.

Diane laughed "That's always a good start."

"Yeah."

Lia poured the tea and picked up her mug to take up to bed with her but she paused by the kitchen doorway.

"Mum?"

“Yes?”
“Do you think I should be concerned about Aidan’s reputation?”
“I think you should trust your instincts.”
“Night Mum.”
“Night Sweetheart.”

Chapter Five

22nd December 2017

"Why don't we go on a double date over the holidays?" Heather proposed.

They were all waiting just outside the school, having finished for the Christmas break. Lia and Aidan were waiting for his dad to come and pick them up, while Heather and Luke were keeping them company. Aidan had his arm draped over Lia's shoulders and was keeping her close as it was freezing in the winter, whereas Luke and Heather were stood next to each other but not touching. Lia glanced up at Aidan at her friend's suggestion and he winked at Lia, indicating his acceptance of the plan.

"Sure, that sounds fun." Lia said, smiling at her friend.

"What are you thinking?" Aidan asked.

"Just something fun like bowling and dinner." Heather suggested.

"Hmm." Luke managed half heartedly.

"Not bowling." Lia declared.

"How about ice-skating?" Heather suggested, grinning at Lia.

"Heather." Lia mock warned Heather, with a matching grin on her face.

Heather laughed at her friend's response but nodded her acceptance at Lia's lack of willingness for her chosen activities, she knew that Lia was useless at physical activities but she enjoyed teasing her.

"Here's my dad." Aidan announced, as his father's slightly battered blue Corsa pulled into the school grounds.

Lia untangled herself from Aidan's arms and hugged her friend goodbye, before she picked her rucksack up off the floor and slid onto the backseat of Mark's car. Aidan watched until Lia was settled in the car, before he got in the passenger's seat and shut the door.

"No Carl?" Mark asked, before he pulled away.

"No, he didn't bother coming in today." Aidan explained.

"OK. So what are you two up to today?" Mark queried, as he left the school premises.

"Lia's coming over for a bit before we take the dogs out." Aidan told his dad.

"As long as that is alright with you?" Lia added.

"Of course." Mark assured her.

"Thanks."

"You planning to have dinner at ours tonight?" Mark asked.

"I think I'm stopping at Lia's for dinner, Ben and I have some plans tonight." Aidan explained.

"That's fine. Let me know if you are going to be back late." Mark said.

Aidan nodded at his dad, before turning round in his seat so that he could face Lia. Aidan watched an intense look appear on Lia's face as she chewed on her bottom lip, engrossed in something on her phone. He smiled at the intensity of her focus while she was unaware of her surroundings. Suddenly Lia looked up and her eyes collided with his. Lia's eyes widened with confusion, before a faint blush spread across her face causing Aidan's smile to widen. Lia glanced down at her lap but quickly glanced back up at Aidan and met his grin with a soft smile of her own.

"Everything OK?" Aidan asked, indicating at Lia's phone which kept vibrating in her hand.

"Oh, it's nothing, my brothers and I are just having a chat about dinner as Mum and Dad have been invited out tonight." Lia explained, with a shrug.

"What's the discussion so far?" Aidan asked.

"We have agreed that we will get a takeaway but now we have to pick something we all agree on." Lia laughed.

"Anyone suggested pizza." Aidan enquired.

"Ben has." Lia commented, glancing back down at her phone.

"What did you suggest?" Aidan asked, when Lia remained staring down at her phone.

"Erm Chinese but pizza also sounds good." Lia mumbled.
Lia: Aidan votes pizza as well
Ben: Yes
Sam: But I really want Indian
Charlie: I still vote Thai
Ben: No-one else likes Thai
Charlie: Fine pizza then
Lia: I'm happy to have pizza
Sam: Eugh! Fine! Pizza it is
Ben: Yes... Tell Aidan thanks
"Ben says thanks, pizza won in the end." Lia said, looking up from her phone.
Aidan smiled and nodded before turning back round in his seat as they pulled into his street. Lia put her phone back into the front pocket of her bag before picking up both her bags and getting ready to get out. Lia unstrapped her seatbelt when the car came to a stop and slid across the backseat, Aidan took the bags off Lia as she climbed out. Aidan linked fingers through Lia's as they made their way up his drive to the house.
"Buster! No!" Mark yelled, as Buster burst out of the house when he opened the front door.
Aidan slid in front of Lia just in time to take the brunt of Buster's overenthusatic welcome jump, he stumbled slightly at the weight of the dog but managed to stay upright.
"Buster! Get down." Aidan moaned, pushing his dog back onto all fours.
Lia laughed, as Buster tried to get raound Aidan to jump at her and say hello. After a few seconds, Aidan managed to grab Buster's collar and pulled him into the house, with Lia trailing slightly behind them. Aidan pushed Buster into the kitchen and shut the baby gate, to keep him in, while Lia pulled the front door shut.
"Just once, I would like to have you come around and not nearly be mauled by my over-excited dog." Aidan groaned, as he walked over to Lia.
"Oh, I love your dog, you know that. Him jumping at me

doesn't bother me." Lia laughed, wrapping her arms around Aidan's waist and resting her forehead on his chest.

"What are we going to do over the Christmas break?" Lia asked, tilting her head up so Aidan could kiss her.

"Oh, I have a few ideas." Aidan teased, walking Lia backwards into the living room.

Pushing Lia slightly, so she fell onto the sofa, Aidan then followed her down and wrapped his arms tightly around her. Lying entwined together, Aidan kept kissing her until they were both completely breathless. After a few minutes, Aidan sat up, pulling Lia up with him and let her slide onto his lap. Once Lia was settled comfortably on his lap, Aidan grabbed the remote and switched the TV on then relaxed against the back of the sofa, holding Lia tightly. Lia rested her head on Aidan's shoulder and settled down to watch TV.

After a little while, Aidan shifted Lia off of his lap and stood up. As Aidan went into the kitchen, Lia continued her casual study of the living room. When Aidan's mum had suddenly left a couple of years ago Mark, Aidan, Ben and Sam had spent the next couple of school holidays redecorating the house. Where the house had been filled with pictures and knick knacks, against a background of pale, neutral tones, it was now much more minimalistic and painted in much bolder colours. The sofas were black leather, centred on the 72 inch curve screen TV and game consoles which had pride of place in the living room. Whilst it wouldn't have been Lia's choice of décor, as she preferred more girly colours and fabrics, she did appreciate how much it suited Mark and Aidan.

"Hi Buster." Lia cooed, when Buster came wandering into the living room, wagging his tail.

"Don't let him jump up at you." Aidan called from the kitchen.

"He's fine Aidan, he's on his best behaviour, aren't you?" Lia said, making a fuss of Buster, who was sat at her feet.

After a few minutes, Aidan came in carrying two steaming

mugs of tea. Lia stood up to take one of them out of Aidan's hand and smiled at him over the top of it.

"Thought you want might want a cup of tea." Aidan said, sitting down on the sofa.

Lia took a sip of the boiling hot drink before putting the mug on the coffee table and curling up against Aidan's side. Aidan wrapped his arms around Lia and sat playing with her hair while they watched more TV.

After The Big Bang Theory had finished its second episode of the evening, Aidan switched off the TV and the couple shifted apart slightly.

"Time to go and get Betty and Veronica." Lia yawned, as she got up from the sofa.

"Yep, I just need to grab a few things from my room before we go." Aidan said, as he also got up from the sofa.

"OK, I'll wait here with Buster." Lia decided.

"You can come up if you want." Aidan grinned.

"You sure?" Lia asked.

"Come on." Aidan said, laughing as he caught Lia's hand and tugged her out of the room.

After a slight hesitation Lia followed Aidan out of the living room and upstairs to his room. Lia paused just outside Aidan's room and glanced around not sure if she should enter. Looking round, she took note of the posters that were covering the walls featuring: Blink 182, Nirvana, Green Day and Rage Against the Machine. After studying the walls, she moved her gaze onto the chestnut chest of drawers and matching wardrobe. In one corner of the room stood a couple of Aidan's guitars which was the most uncluttered area. Lia continued her survey by moving to examine the carpet before briefly glancing at Aidan's unmade bed.

"Everything OK?" Aidan asked, turning round so that he could look at Lia who was still stood just outside his bedroom door.

"Yeah I'm fine, I just realised that I haven't been in your room before." Lia muttered, staring at her feet as she moved one of them around in circles.

"What do you mean?" Aidan asked, crossing back to Lia.

"It's just a little bit strange." Lia whispered.

"There's nothing to be afraid of." Aidan assured her. "Just relax."

Lia looked up from her keen study of Aidan's charcoal grey carpet, so that she could focus on the concerned look in Aidan's eyes. Aidan wrapped his arms around Lia's waist and pulled her close and rested his cheek on the top of Lia's head. After a few seconds, Lia shifted so that she could return his embrace, Lia lifted her head to meet Aidan's lips. Aidan started by kissing her lightly but Lia deepened the kiss. As the kiss continued, Aidan began walking backwards until he was sat on his bed with Lia straddling his lap. Lia made a minor noise in shock when Aidan's hands slid under her jumper and over the bare skin of her back.

"Everything OK?" Aidan asked, pulling away slightly.

"Yeah, I've just never done this before." Lia whispered, staring over Aidan's shoulder.

"What do you mean?" Aidan asked.

Lia shifted herself off of Aidan's lap so she was sat next to him on the bed. Lia linked her fingers on her lap and focused on them, while debating what she was going to say to Aidan.

"Erm. So, I guess that I have never been particularly serious with any of the guys that I have dated before." Lia whispered.

"Oh." Aidan managed, realising what Lia was saying.

"Yeah." Lia muttered sadly.

For a couple of minutes Aidan and Lia sat in silence right next to each other but not touching while they digested what Lia had just said and how it impacted their relationship.

"I won't pressure you to do anything you don't want to do." Aidan announced, after several minutes.

"That's the thing Aidan, I don't know what I do and don't want to do." Lia admitted.

"We can take this as slowly as you want." Aidan told her.

"Are you sure?"
"Absolutely."
"Thank you."
"Right, let me grab my gloves and then we can go get Betty and Veronica." Aidan announced, getting up from the bed but running a hand over Lia's hair as he did.
Lia nodded but remained perched on the edge of the bed while Aidan rifled through one of his drawers until he located some fingerless gloves and yanked them on. Once Aidan had his gloves on, he reached out and helped Lia to her feet. Walking back downstairs, they pulled their coats on and Aidan helped Lia wrap her scarf around her. Lia then picked up her school bags while Aidan clipped on Buster's lead.
"See you later, Dad." Aidan called, as he pulled open the door.
Aidan linked his left hand through Lia's right hand and then they set off towards to Lia's house. Buster led the couple on their walk, running slightly ahead and tugging on the lead when he felt that the couple were walking too slowly.
"Are we OK?" Lia asked, after a few minutes.
"Of course." Aidan responded, mildly surprised.
"I just don't want what we talked about in your room to cause any problems between us." Lia admitted.
"It won't." Aidan assured her.
Aidan gave Lia's hand a quick squeeze and they continued on their walk to Lia's house. At the bottom of Lia's drive, Lia pulled her hand out of Aidan's so that she could search through her handbag until she found her keys at the bottom of her bag. Lia quickly unlocked the front door, then Betty and Veronica came running up to her and jumped up causing her to stumble back into Aidan.
"Down girls." Lia giggled, as she pushed at the dogs.
Betty immediately sat down in the doorway while Veronica tried to get past Lia so she could greet Aidan and Buster.
"Veronica! Sit down!" Lia ordered, while pulling gently

on her collar until she sat down. "You want to come in while I get myself ready?"

"Sure. Do I need to leave Buster outside?" Aidan asked.

"No, he'll be fine." Lia told him, as she walked into the house passed the dogs, who were still sitting in the doorway.

Aidan followed Lia into the house and let Buster off his lead, so that he could play with Betty and Veronica. When Lia dashed upstairs so she could get changed, Aidan walked into the back living room where he found Ben, Sam and Jake engaged in an intense battle on the Playstation.

"You're here early." Ben observed, as Aidan sat down on the sofa next to him.

"Lia wanted to get changed before we go and walk the dogs." Aidan explained.

"Yeah, she has some thing about not wearing some of her jeans when she goes out to walk the dogs." Sam groaned.

"Why?" Jake asked.

"Must be some sort of girl thing I guess." Sam muttered.

"Ridiculous." Jake mumbled.

"Agreed." Ben stated.

"I hear you are staying for dinner Aidan?" Sam enquired.

"Yeah." Aidan responded.

"Plans with Lia?" Jake asked.

"Nope, plans with Ben." Aidan told him.

"I think I would rather hang out with Lia." Sam laughed.

"Me too." Ben quipped.

"Hi." Lia said coming into the room, having been upstairs for twenty minutes.

"What the hell have you been doing upstairs?" Ben asked, glancing over his shoulder to his sister.

"Problem?" Lia asked, perching on the arm of the sofa next to Aidan.

"You ready to go?" Aidan asked, resting his hand on Lia's leg.

"Yep." Lia chirped, standing up. "See you guys in a bit." Aidan followed Lia out of the living room and clipped the leads on the dogs while she zipped up her coat and pulled on her gloves. Once they were both ready, Aidan passed Lia Betty's lead before he opened the door and headed out. Aidan took her free hand and linked their fingers as they set off towards the woods.

"What are you up to this evening?" Aidan asked, after a few minutes.

"Erm I haven't decided yet, probably just to relax with some movies or a good book." Lia responded thoughtfully. "What are you and Ben up to tonight?"

"We are thinking of having a jam session, it's been a while since we played together." Aidan told her.

"Yeah, you two haven't been hanging out as much." Lia observed.

"Yeah, it has been a while." Aidan suddenly realised.

"Is it because of us?" Lia asked.

"No it's not. I have started spending more time with you but I still see Ben a lot." Aidan commented. "Besides I like spending time with you."

"I like spending time with you too but I don't want to come between you and Ben." Lia stated.

"What do you mean?" Aidan asked.

"You and Ben have been friends forever, I don't want to be the reason that you two stop hanging out." Lia announced, striding away from Aidan.

"Lia, calm down." Aidan laughed.

"Why are you laughing?" Lia demanded, whirling back around.

"Ben and I haven't stopped hanging out. Just because I now spend more time with you, doesn't mean that I have stopped seeing Ben. There's no reason to get upset." Aidan explained, taking Lia's hands.

"You have to promise that our relationship won't come between you and Ben." Lia begged, squeezing Aidan's hands.

"I can't make that promise." Aidan whispered.

"Please Aidan, please promise me that you won't let our relationship come between your friendship with Ben. It's important to me." Lia said, leaning against Aidan's chest.

"Lia, I understand why you want me to make the promise but I don't want to put Ben in an awkward position. Ben is your brother, you come first with him, so he gets to decide what happens to our friendship, if our relationship ends." Aidan explained, hugging Lia to him. "The last thing I want though is for this to end."

"Same here, I won't make you promise that but you do need to spend more time with Ben." Lia decided.

"OK." Aidan agreed.

Feeling somewhat mollified, Lia eased back from Aidan and settled back into the walk. Swinging their entwined hands Lia continued their walk with a small smile until Aidan pulled her back to him so he could kiss her lightly on the lips.

"Are you sure that you want me to hang out with Ben tonight?" Aidan asked, as he continued to kiss Lia intermittently.

"No, but I'm going to let you do it anyway." Lia mumbled, kissing Aidan back.

"OK." Aidan sighed, having glanced at his watch. "Come on, let's get this walk finished."

"OK." Lia agreed.

Aidan placed his arm over Lia's shoulders and pulled her close to him as they trailed around the woods after the dogs. Every now and then they would stop to kiss then continue to walk. At the end of the trail, the dogs stopped and waited patiently for their owners to catch up to them. Lia and Aidan put the leads on the dogs quickly as they walked hand in had back up to the Taylors' house. Just as they got to the edge of the drive Diane and David were pulling out. Spotting Lia and Aidan, Diane slowed the car down to a stop.

"Your brothers have just ordered the pizzas." David said, when Lia poked her head through the open car window.

"OK." Lia commented.

"We won't be home until after midnight." Diane said to Lia.

"No funny business." David announced, addressing both Lia and Aidan.

"No sir." Aidan agreed.

"Don't worry Dad. Have a nice evening, I'll see you in the morning." Lia told her dad, with a smile.

"Bye Sweetie." Diane and David chorused, as they rolled the window up and continued to reverse out onto the street.

"Well, your parents have spoken." Aidan joked, as they continued up the drive.

"Yeah, no funny business." Lia muttered, wrinkling up her nose.

"Come on Lia, it's a little funny." Aidan laughed, tugging on her hair while she unlocked the door.

Lia turned round resting her hand on the door handle and fake scowled at Aidan. He let out another laugh before he grabbed Lia and crushed her to him. Squeezing Lia tight, Aidan then released her just enough for him to lean down and kiss her. Lia tilted her head allowing Aidan to change the angle and the kiss gained more passion until the dogs barked causing them to break apart.

"I think the dogs want their dinner." Lia stated, with a wry smile.

"Yeah, they don't seem to be impressed." Aidan agreed, grinning as Veronica wiggled her way between him and Lia.

Lia shook her head at Veronica, before turning back round and opening the door. The three dogs all charged past Lia into the house and skidded to a stop in the kitchen.

"We were beginning to take bets on who would get here first, you guys or the pizza." Sam called, from the living room.

"You guys take the scenic route?" Jake asked, joining in.

Aidan rolled his eyes at the comments coming from the living room, making Lia smile as she put their coats and shoes away. Once all their stuff was in the cupboard, Lia walked through the kitchen into the utility room and pulled the dog food out of the cupboard while the dogs danced around her.

"Need a hand?" Aidan asked, from the doorway.

"No, I think I've got it." Lia said, through gritted teeth as she poured liberal helpings of the dog food into three bowls.

Once she had put the dog food away, Aidan reached round her, grabbed the dogs' bowls and took them through to the kitchen to place them on the floor for the dogs. Aidan let Lia passed him and followed her into the living room. Lia curled up in the corner of the sofa as Aidan sat down next to her and rested his hand on her legs.

"What are the plans for the evening?" Lia asked.

"Jake and I are having an all-night gaming competition, Ben and Aidan are spending the night in the summer house and Charlie is planning to spend the evening in his room." Sam told her.

"So the front living room is free?" Lia asked.

"Yeah." Sam grunted.

"Great."

With that, Lia bounced off the sofa and ran up to her room, banging the bedroom door open, she slid to a stop in front of the double bookcase in her room. Leaning down to the second from bottom shelf, she pulled out her DVDs of Dirty Dancing and 10 Things I Hate About You, then headed back out of her room. Just as she was leaving she grabbed her blanket off the chair and quickly ran downstairs. Lia heard someone knock on the door, as she reached the bottom of the stairs. She watched Ben pay for the pizzas and take a huge pile of food from the delivery man.

"Ordered you a chicken pizza, no mushrooms and some brownies." Ben told her.

Lia dropped her DVDs and blanket off in the front living room, before heading into the kitchen where Ben had dumped the food.

"Charlie! Food's here!" Sam yelled, as he walked out of the kitchen carrying two pizza boxes and a pile of sides into the back living room.

Lia grabbed her pizza and brownies from the kitchen,

where Aidan and Ben were stood eating slices. Back in the front living room, Lia flicked on the TV and settled down for a night of chick flicks. Once she had eaten a couple of slices, Lia curled up on the sofa and pulled her blanket over her. Humming along with the songs in Dirty Dancing, Lia happily worked her way through the brownies. At the end of the film, Lia gathered up her boxes and took them through into the kitchen. She poured some water into the kettle and prepared a mug for a cup of tea. While she waited for the kettle to boil, Lia decided to pop out to the summer house to see how Ben and Aidan's evening was going. Pausing by the window, Lia listened to Ben and Aidan playing together, she smiled as they played a couple of Blink 182 songs and then decided that she would leave them to it and head back into the house. She did, however, remember her conversation with Aidan from their dog walk and sent Ben a quick text.

Lia: Can I talk to you later? X

Having sent a text to her brother, Lia finished making herself a cup of tea, then headed back into the living room to watch 10 Things I Hate About You. Curling back up on the sofa, Lia began watching the film while she drank her drink, but after about 30 minutes she fell asleep.

"Hey Princess, wake up." Aidan said, shaking her slightly.

"Aidan?" Lia mumbled sleepily.

"Hey, I just thought I would let you know I'm staying over tonight as it's now after midnight." Aidan told her, sitting down on the sofa next to Lia who immediately sat up. "I'm going to crash on Ben's floor don't worry."

Lia leant her head sleepily against Aidan's shoulder and began to drift back off to sleep.

"Lia, why don't you head up to bed?" Ben suggested, coming into the room.

"Mmm… kay." Lia agreed sleepily.

Ben eased his sister to her feet and then directed her towards the door. Lia followed her brother's suggestion and slowly wandered up to her room, stopping to pet the three dogs who were sleeping at the bottom of the stairs.

Once in her room, Lia changed out of her clothes and tossed them towards the washing basket, she then yanked on her dark blue checked pyjama bottoms and a pale blue long sleeved top before heading into the bathroom to clean her teeth. When she came out of her bathroom, Ben was sprawled on her bed waiting for her.
"Hi." Lia said, plopping down on the bed next to him.
"You said you wanted to talk." Ben yawned.
"Yeah I want you to promise me something." Lia said.
"Sure."
"You have to promise that no matter what happens between me and Aidan you will still be his friend." Lia told him.
"That sounds good in theory but if he hurts you, I don't know if I could be his friend if that happened." Ben commented.
"Sure you can, you would simply comfort me and for a little while meet at Aidan's rather than here." Lia decided.
"You seem to have thought this through." Ben observed.
"It means a lot to me."
"Fine, I promise." Ben agreed begrudgingly.
"Thank you." Lia said smiling.
"See you in the morning." Ben said, getting up off Lia's bed and heading out of the room.
"Night Ben." Lia echoed.
Ben disappeared out of sight but left Lia's bedroom door open. Lia sighed and shook her head before sliding off her bed and crossing her room to shut the door. As she reached the door, the top of Aidan's head appeared coming up the stairs.
"Hi." Lia said.
"Hey."
"Everything OK?" Lia asked, as Aidan reached the top of the stairs.
"Everything's fine, I just thought I would bring you a cup of tea."
"Thanks." Lia said, taking the mug from Aidan.
For a few seconds they stood smiling at each other, Aidan

then took the mug back out of Lia's hands and placed it on the floor. He then slid his arms around Lia's waist and leant down to kiss her. He intended the kiss to be a light goodnight kiss but that intention went out of the window when Lia leaned into him and deepened the kiss.

Breathing hard, Lia pulled away slightly but remained wrapped in Aidan's arms enjoying his strength and the sensation of being completely safe with him. After a few seconds, Aidan leant down again and gave Lia a quick kiss before letting go of her and heading downstairs.

"Night Princess." Aidan called, with a wink before he vanished out of sight.

"Night."

Chapter Six

2nd January 2018

"Right, so you guys have almost mastered your telepathy." David declared, as he was finishing up his magic lesson for the day. "Your powers are strengthening, as you can tell from the fact you can now move heavier objects and you can move them further."

Pausing, David glanced at his children who were sitting around the edge of the table focusing on what he had to say. Since Lia had seen Dean and Alice at the cinema, David had increased the magic lessons to twice a week and throughout the Christmas period he had been working with them on their powers every day.

"Whilst I want you to keep practising your telekinesis, it will now no longer be the main focus of our lessons. I now want to focus on teaching each of you how to use your elemental powers, I will start on individual lessons next week."

"Why are we having individual lessons?" Lia asked.

"Because you each have control of an individual element, I want to start helping you channel that element separately before we focus on how they work when you are all together." David explained.

"How do you want to do the individual lessons?" Charlie asked.

"I'll have one evening a week with each of you to start off with and we can work on tapping into your specific element." David decided. "We can work out who has which night later on today."

With that, David began packing up the various items he had been using to teach the lesson. The siblings headed back into the house and dispersed once inside. Charlie and Ben went upstairs to their rooms, Sam headed into the main living room and Lia settled herself in the smaller living room, where she had been reading earlier on in the day before the magic lesson.

Curling up at one end of the sofa, Lia turned the TV back on and found a rerun of the Big Bang Theory to use as background noise whilst she continued to reread To Kill a Mockingbird for the sixth time. After a few minutes, Betty and Veronica wandered into the living room and settled down: Betty by Lia on the sofa and Veronica in the middle of the room.

Happily engrossed in her book, Lia jumped at the sound of someone knocking on the door, while both dogs bolted out of the room to the front door. Uncurling her legs, Lia got up from the sofa and followed the dogs out of the room. The dogs were waiting impatiently by the front door, wagging their tails and whining to see whoever was at the door. Lia managed to wriggle past and pull open the front door just as Aidan was lifting his hand to knock again.

"Hi" Lia said shyly.

"Hey."

"Do want to come in?"

"If you don't mind."

Lia pulled the door fully open, stepping back so that Aidan could enter the house. After Aidan had shut the door, he crouched down to pet Betty and Veronica as they were starting to jump up, begging for attention. Patting the dogs on their sides, Aidan stood back up and followed Lia into the living room. Lia paused before she sat down and turned to face Aidan.

Aidan glanced back at the door before sliding his hand around Lia's waist. Lia took half a step forward so she was standing almost touching Aidan, keeping one hand on the small of Lia's back, Aidan used his free hand to tilt Lia's head up towards him as he bent down to kiss her. Lia leant closer and wrapped her arms around Aidan's waist to lean into the kiss.

"Hck hmmm!" David coughed, from the doorway.

Lia and Aidan sprang apart and turned to look at David.

"Hi David, didn't see you there." Aidan managed.

"Is everything OK Dad?" Lia asked, tugging down her

jumper which had ridden up slightly.

"Everything is fine Lia. Afternoon, Aidan." David commented.

David nodded and left the room, sighing Aidan sank down onto the sofa then tugged Lia down after him, when she remained standing.

"Oh! I forgot to mention." David declared, walking back into the living room. "As long as you two are doing 'this' you must be in one of the communal rooms. You are not to spend any time alone together in any of the bedrooms."

Lia and Aidan glanced at each of other and then back to David.

"Is that understood?"

"Yes." Lia and Aidan said in unison.

David left the living room again, Lia propped her elbows on her knees and buried her face in her hands to hide the blush that was spreading up her face, after a few seconds she began to giggle uncontrollably.

"You know I'm beginning to think that your dad no longer likes me." Aidan commented, leaning back on the sofa.

"I'm sure it's nothing personal." Lia mumbled, from inside her hands.

"For the last month and a half, he has glared at me every time he is in the same room as me." Aidan continued.

Lia sat back up and swivelled slightly to face Aidan.

"You seem really worried about that." Lia observed.

"I am, David has never had a problem with me, I've been coming around here since I was five." Aidan continued.

"He doesn't like any guy I date." Lia offered, by way of explanation. "So trust me, it is nothing personal and you know he likes you."

"How many other guys have you dated?" Aidan asked, changing the subject.

"Wow, that's the point you picked up on."

"How many?" Aidan teased, picking Lia up and depositing her on his lap.

Lia giggled as Aidan tickled her and tried to squirm off his lap. After a few seconds, Lia managed to wriggle free,

Aidan successfully captured her and pinned her arms above her head with one hand. Leaning down, Aidan captured Lia's mouth with his, slowly he released Lia's arms, allowing her to wrap them around his shoulders. Aidan's hands skimmed down Lia's back and over her butt, as he pulled her closer to him. Lia groaned at the intimate nature of what they were doing then squirmed against him as he slid his hands up under her top and stroked her bare skin with his thumbs. Suddenly Aidan broke off the kiss, breathing hard, he moved to sit up, pulling Lia up with him.

For a few minutes, the couple just sat and stared blankly at the TV.

"Wow." Aidan managed. "I've known you forever Lia and as a result I know how innocent you are. If we keep doing this then it's going to lead to something I don't know if you are ready for."

Confused, Lia backed up and shifted so she could look at Aidan, who wouldn't meet her eyes.

"What do you mean?" Lia asked.

"I know you have been on a few dates over the past couple of years but that none of them have been anything serious." Aidan continued.

"And?" Lia queried.

"I've had more experience with girls than you have had with boys." Aidan muttered, shifting uncomfortably under Lia's gaze.

"But I've never felt anything like this." Aidan observed, looking away from Lia's gaze.

"Is that a good or a bad thing?" Lia all but whispered.

"It's intense." Aidan answered. "And I don't want to do anything that you aren't ready for."

Lia started to ask a further question when there was a knock on the door and dogs started to bark.

"I'll be right back." Lia said, fleeing the room.

Grabbing the dogs' collars, Lia pulled them away from the door so that her dad could answer the incessant knocking at the door.

"Good afternoon Mr Taylor. My name is Edward Thompson-Carter of the London Thompson-Carters." The perfectly polished, well dressed, blonde gentleman announced from the doorway.

"Erm, nice to meet you" David replied. "How can I help you?"

"I am here to talk to you about your daughter, Amelia Elizabeth Taylor." Edward continued.

"What about Lia?" Ben asked, appearing from the kitchen, sliding past Lia who was somewhat hidden by the door.

"Ah, you must be one of the brothers. Are you Benjamin, Charles or Samuel?" Edward asked.

"I'm Ben, why are you here about Lia?" Ben demanded.

"Let's cool this down a notch." David suggested, as the boys started to square up to each other.

Edward nodded and Ben shifted, allowing Edward to enter the house.

"Why don't you come take a seat in here?" David suggested, directing Edward away from Lia, who was still slightly behind the door, holding the dogs who were growling quietly.

"Everything OK?" Aidan asked, coming up behind Lia.

"Yeah, everything's fine." Lia responded absently.

"Who was at the door?"

"Just some guy from London, wanted to talk to Dad."

"OK."

"Are we OK?" Lia asked leading Aidan back into the living room.

"Yeah, we are fine."

"Are you sure?" Lia continued.

"Yeah." Aidan said, quickly kissing Lia but pulling away before Lia could react.

"Lia?" Ben called, coming into the living room.

"Hmm."

"Can you come into the other living room?" Ben asked.

"Sure."

"I'll hang out in here." Ben stated, taking Lia's seat on the other side the sofa to Aidan.

Lia walked through into the other living room, where Edward was sitting in one of the chairs and her dad was sat on the sofa opposite him.

"Hi." Lia mumbled, as she came into the room.

"Good afternoon, you must be Amelia, my name is Edward Thompson-Carter."

"Nice to meet you." Lia said sitting down next to her dad.

"Edward is here on a long-term family quest." David explained.

"Long-term family quest?" Lia enquired.

"Yes, your great, great, great grandfather promised my great, great, great grandfather that once there was a girl born in your family, then our families would join together."

"What?" Lia gasped.

"In order to fufill this agreement, I must insist that we start dating immediately."

"I think this is something that Lia needs to think about." David interrupted.

"This is a long-standing agreement between our families." Edward warned.

"That may be the case but in this century there is freedom of choice." David stated carefully.

"I will be back tomorrow and I don't want to be disappointed." Edward announced, getting up from his chair and strolling out of the door.

"Christ almighty." David sighed, when he heard the front door shut.

"Dad, what's this all about?" Lia asked, curling up in a corner of the sofa.

"I don't know but you don't need to worry about it. I'll fix this." David declared. "When your mum gets back from the shops, let her know I'm in the garage."

Lia nodded absently before hugging her knees to her chest. Ben walked in from the other living room followed closely by Aidan and Sam.

"Mr London left?" Ben asked, flopping down in one of the chairs.

"Yeah, he'll be back tomorrow though." Lia mumbled, shifting into a sitting position and resting her head on her knees.

"Everything OK?" Aidan asked, wrapping his arm around Lia and hugging her against him.

"He wants us to start dating and some old pledge between families that promises me to him." Lia explained, lifting her head up from her knees and resting it on Aidan's shoulder.

"What?" Aidan and Sam exclaimed together.

Lia dropped her head back onto her knees when Aidan lifted his arm off her shoulders and groaned.

"What did Dad say?" Ben asked.

"He told Edward that I needed to think about it, then Edward made some sort of thinly veiled threat before leaving." Lia told the group.

"Where's Dad now?" Sam asked.

"He went to the garage for something."

Ben and Sam got up and left the room to go to find their dad, Lia heard Sam go upstairs and assumed it was to go fetch Charlie.

"What are you going to do about Mr London?" Aidan asked.

"Nothing."

"Nothing?"

"Yeah nothing! I don't want to date him, I'm dating you." Lia exclaimed, lifting her head up from her knees.

"As long as that is what you want." Aidan commented, leaning back on the sofa.

"Dammit Aidan!" Lia snapped.

"What?"

"Why are you making this so hard?" Lia demanded.

"Making what hard?" Aidan asked.

"You keep making these cryptic remarks." Lia cried. "Do you want to keep doing this?"

"Doing what?"

"Seeing me?"

"Of course I want to keep seeing you. Christ Lia, why

would you think that I didn't want to be with you."

"Earlier I asked you whether what you were feeling for me was a good or a bad thing and all you said was that it was intense. Then I tell you some other guy wants to date me and all you say is that it's my choice."

"Crap, Lia I'm sorry." Aidan said gently.

When Lia didn't respond, Aidan shifted off the sofa to crouch down in front of Lia and was shocked to see that she was crying.

"Lia, I'm sorry." Aidan repeated, resting his hands on Lia's knees.

Lia wiped at the tears on her cheeks and tried to smile when Aidan caught her hands. He got to his feet and pulled Lia up after him and wrapped his arms around her. Holding Lia close Aidan stroked her back to comfort her as he could still feel her crying.

"Lia, please stop crying, I hate seeing you cry."

"I'm stopping."

"Lia, Ben's going to kill me if he sees you crying." Aidan whispered into Lia's hair.

Lia pulled away from Aidan and wiped her cheeks again but this time she did manage a watery smile.

"OK, I'm going to run home and grab Buster. How about we take the dogs for a long walk?" Aidan asked.

"That sounds like a plan." Lia smiled.

"OK, I'll be back in about 45 minutes."

Aidan began to leave but Lia pulled him back and kissed him. Aidan wrapped his arms around Lia and kissed her passionately, trying to pour everything he felt about her into the kiss.

"OK, if we are going to walk the dogs, I need to fetch Buster." Aidan said, when they stopped for air.

"OK, go get Buster." Lia said, leaning up for one more kiss, as they walked out of the living room.

Lia shut the front door after Aidan left and leaned back on it, smiling. Gathering herself, Lia got up from against the door and walked through to the garage.

"How is it going in here?" Lia asked, as she opened the

door to the garage.

"Well, we have found some information about the Thompson-Carter family but so far there is no reference to anything about marrying off a daughter." Charlie commented, not looking up from the book he was reading.

"But they are a Wiccan family?" Lia asked.

"Yes." David agreed.

"You don't have to date him just because he said so, Lia." Ben commented, getting up to rub his sister's shoulders.

"But what if it is something to help us with the Foulds family?" Lia asked.

"We can sort that out without you having to date someone you don't want to date Lia." Ben reassured her.

"Yeah, we've started to master our powers now, the Foulds family won't know what hit them." Sam agreed.

Lia smiled at her brothers' support, knowing that they would try their hardest to find out about the agreement and that they would see if there was a way to prevent her from having to date Edward.

"Try not to worry about this Lia." David said.

"OK, well Aidan is swinging back in a little bit so we can take the dogs out but I can help out for a bit." Lia said, sitting down in one of the arm chairs and opening one of the books Charlie had on his pile, to find out more about the Thompson-Carter family.

"How long till Aidan comes back?" Ben asked, pulling the book out of Lia's hands.

"About thirty minutes."

"Ok well, you can read up on any historic promises of marriage later." Ben told her, pulling her up to her feet. "Go relax for a little bit and maybe wash your face."

Seeing nods from her other brothers and Dad, Lia left the garage and wandered into the house. She paused in the kitchen and got herself a glass of water, which she took upstairs. Up in her bedroom, Lia pulled out her ipad and looked up Edward on Facebook. She learnt that he was nineteen years old and that he was currently working at his dad's office whilst taking a couple of years off before university. She flicked through a few of his photos and smiled in appreciation of his looks, even though his pictures were vain and staged.

"Hello!" Diane called, from the front hall.

"Hi Mum!" Lia called, as she left her room to go and help her mum put away the food shopping.

"Where are the boys and your dad?" Diane asked.

"In the garage, some guy from London turned up earlier today and told us that there is some historic family agreement that the first girl born in our family is supposed to marry into their family, so he wants to start dating me now." Lia explained in a rush.

"Well, that's not what I expected." Diane commented, staring at her daughter who was still putting away the shopping.

"It's not the afternoon that I had envisioned either." Lia agreed.

"I take it you have no interest in dating him?" Diane observed.

"No, I'm with Aidan." Lia stated.

"And if Aidan wasn't in the picture." Diane asked.

"It doesn't matter, I love Aidan." Lia protested.

"What?" Sam exclaimed, coming into the kitchen.

"I love Aidan, I don't want to date anyone else." Lia said, turning so she could lean against one of the kitchen cabinets.

"Well, that was fast but I guess not that surprising." Sam commented.

Before Lia could say anything else there was a knock on the door, Lia pushed herself away from the cabinets and went to answer the door.

"Hi." Lia smiled, as she opened the door to Aidan "Hi Buster!"

"Who are you more excited to see me or Buster?" Aidan teased, when Lia bent down to pet Buster.

"Buster obviously." Lia joked, standing back up and quickly kissing Aidan.

"You ready?" Aidan asked, running his hand down her

back.

"Yep, just let me grab my coat and the leads." Lia said stepping back into the house.

Lia grabbed her coat out of the hall cupboard and quickly pulled it on. She took the dogs' leads out then crouched down and snapped them on the dogs' collars, ready to set off.

"I'll be back in a bit." Lia called, as she shut the front door.

Lia placed both leads in her right hand so she could hold Aidan's hand with her left. In comfortable silence, Lia and Aidan walked for a few minutes. Once they reached the entrance to the woods they let the dogs off their leads so they could run around. Once the dogs had run off, Aidan slid his arm over Lia's shoulder so he could kiss her and then he set off, keeping Lia close.

"So, do you want to do something tomorrow?" Aidan asked.

"What are you thinking?" Lia asked.

"Well, I just want to hang out. I want to spend time with you." Aidan explained.

"Let's go out for lunch." Lia suggested.

"Sounds like fun."

"Looking forward to it."

"Lia, I've known you for years but sometimes I feel like I don't know you." Aidan said, after a few minutes of walking in silence.

"What do you mean?" Lia asked, pulling away from Aidan so she could look at him.

"I just feel like there are things I don't know about you." Aidan explained. "After you told me about that Edward guy and some old family promise I walked home thinking about all the things I don't know about you. Things I should know, we've been dating for two months and I've known you for years but I don't even know your favourite film."

Lia laughed and hugged Aidan.

"So, you are worried because you don't know my

favourite film?" Lia teased, grinning up at him when he hugged her back.

"Among so many other things." Aidan said, kissing Lia on the forehead.

"OK, well at lunch tomorrow we can play twenty questions." Lia joked.

"Lia, I want to get to know you." Aidan groaned.

"My favourite film is Grease." Lia told Aidan kissing him. "And I know your favourite film is the Fast and Furious."

Aidan laughed and swung Lia round in a circle. Once he put her back on the ground, he wrapped his arm back round her shoulders and began their walk again.

"I'm starting twenty questions now." Aidan teased Lia.

"Go for it."

"Hmm, OK, I'll start with some easy questions, favourite colour?"

"Blue or silver."

"OK, favourite animal?"

"That's a hard question." Lia laughed.

"How is picking your favourite animal a hard question?" Aidan asked.

"Because I love animals, I have so many favourites it's hard to choose just one."

"OK, so what are your top five?"

"OK that's a bit easier, dogs obviously" Lia started, bending down to pet Betty, who had wandered over to Lia. "Pandas, dolphins, tigers and polar bears, I could go on and on."

Aidan laughed.

"What's your next question?" Lia asked.

"I'm thinking. There are a lot of things I want to know about you."

"We've got loads of time to get to know each other."

"You already know loads about me. How do you know so much?" Aidan asked.

"Like you said we've known each other a long time and as you always came round to hang out with Ben and Sam, I was often in the background." Lia explained.

"I'm paying attention now." Aidan assured her.

"I would hope so." Lia laughed.

"I mean it Lia, I'm paying attention." Aidan insisted.

"I know you are." Lia smiled. "Aidan, I meant what I said earlier I'm only interested in dating you."

"We are going to make this work."

"Aww! Isn't that cute?" Alice Foulds cooed.

"Alice, it's good to see you again." Aidan said, coolly, pulling Lia close.

"I was wondering why you had stopped calling, now I see why." Alice snarled, continuing to advance towards Aidan and Lia.

"You two dated?" Lia asked, pulling away from Aidan

"We went out on like two dates." Aidan told Lia. "Go away Alice!"

"No, no. I want to talk to your perfect little girlfriend." Alice told Aidan, and with that she waved her hand towards Aidan which sent him flying into a tree.

"Aidan!" Lia shouted, starting to run towards him.

"Oh no you don't." Alice told her stepping in front of her and stopping her in her tracks. "We need to have a little conversation."

"I'm not interested in talking to you." Lia announced, trying to get round Alice.

"Well, then just listen… my ancestors had control of the elements first. It's written in all our family history books and your relatives stole them so I'm going to get them back. Then I'm going to win Aidan back as he was my boyfriend first, soon you will just be a little bump in the road of mine and Aidan's story." Alice told her.

"Not a chance." Lia retorted.

"Want to see what happens when you go against me." Alice suggested.

With that, Alice waved her hands and sent Lia flying in the opposite direction to Aidan, Lia landed in a pile of dead leaves but sprung back up. Lia raised her hands, pulling a load of thorny branches with her. Using every ounce of her strength, she flung the thorns directly at Alice's face.

Alice screamed as the branches hit her, then she clicked her fingers and vanished but not before sending another wave of invisible energy at Lia, causing her to fall over the roots of some nearby trees.

"Lia?" Aidan called, groggily.

"I'm over here." Lia called back.

"Are you OK?" Aidan asked, as he scrambled through the bushes to where Lia was sprawled on the floor.

"Yeah, I just fell over and twisted my ankle." Lia partially lied, wincing as Aidan helped her to her feet.

"What happened?" Aidan asked.

"What do you mean?"

"Well, one second I was standing next to you and the next I'm flying through the air." Aidan explained. "And then when I landed, I could hear you and Alice arguing. I swear I heard you talking about powers."

Lia fell silent, unsure of what to say, she knew she wasn't supposed to tell anyone about magic but she didn't want to lie to Aidan.

"What did she mean?" Aidan asked.

"I can't talk about it." Lia managed after a few seconds.

"What do you mean you can't talk about it?" Aidan probed. "What happened to being honest with me and helping me get to know you?"

"Aidan. Please don't." Lia whispered.

Aidan sighed, frustrated with Lia's lack of response, he removed the arm that was supporting Lia leaving her to limp along after him. Betty wandered over to Lia and nudged her hand in a doggy gesture of support. Lia rested her hand on Betty's head and walked along aside her, trailing behind Aidan and the other two dogs.

At the end of the trail, Lia caught up with Aidan to put the leads back on Betty and Veronica for the rest of the walk home.

"I'll come round tomorrow." Aidan announced, as they reached the bottom of Lia's driveway.

"I'll see you tomorrow." Lia echoed, as Aidan started to walk the rest of the way to his house.

Watching Aidan walk away, Lia trailed up the driveway to the back door so she could let the dogs in. Letting them back off their leads she checked both their feet for mud before allowing them into the main house from the utility room.

"Aidan not come back with you?" Diane asked.

Lia shook her head and then headed out to the garage.

"Dad?" she called, walking into the garage.

"Over here." David called down, from his position levitating at the top of the bookcases.

"Can I talk to you?" Lia asked, sitting down in one of the arm chairs.

"Sure." David said, floating over to his daughter and pulling out a chair so he could sit down opposite her.

"While Aidan and I were walking the dogs we bumped into Alice…wait don't interrupt. She was waiting for us in virtually the same place as when we bumped into Dean recently. She did this thing with her hands, forcing this invisible wave of energy into Aidan which sent him flying. After that, she started going on about how my powers were supposed to be hers, before knocking me over, then she clicked her fingers and just vanished." Lia blurted out.

"They are certainly making it known that they want our powers." David pondered.

"That's not the bit that I wanted to talk to you about. Aidan overheard Alice when she said she wanted my powers and he wants to know what Alice was talking about." Lia explained.

"Ah, what did you say?" David asked.

"I told him I couldn't talk about it and then he got annoyed because earlier we were playing twenty questions and working on being honest but I couldn't be." Lia continued. "Dad, I don't want to lie to him."

"I know you don't but it's important that you keep this a secret."

"Dad, please can I tell him." Lia tried. "You always told us that we need to be honest with people and now you are telling me to lie to Aidan."

"On this one occasion, I am asking you not to lie necessarily but to avoid telling Aidan the truth about magic, it's to protect you and your brothers."

"But it's Aidan, Dad. We've known him forever." Lia pleaded.

"Amelia, that's enough." David snapped. "You are not to tell him and that is final."

"Dad please, I'm in love with him." Lia begged.

"No, now that's the end of this discussion, go and get ready for dinner."

Lia stomped out of the garage and into the house. Pausing in the hallway she pulled off her coat and gloves that she had yet to take off, shoving them in the cupboard. She stopped in the downstairs bathroom to wash off any dirt from the woods and then headed into the dining room, to set the table ready for dinner.

Chapter Seven

3rd January 2018

"Eugh!" Lia groaned, as she woke up once again that night. Although she could see it was daylight, she felt like she had only been asleep five minutes, she pressed the home button on her phone and saw that it was only 8.30am.

Sighing, Lia tried shifting positions, only to realise that she needed to go to the toilet, she kicked off the quilt and shoved herself out of bed. Having gotten up, she decided that it wasn't worth trying to go back to sleep, so she pulled on her dressing gown and slippers before wandering downstairs. When she entered the kitchen Sam, Charlie and her mum were all sat in the kitchen, eating their breakfast.

"Morning Lia. We weren't expecting you up so early." Diane greeted her daughter.

"Couldn't sleep." Lia mumbled, pouring herself a cup of tea and sliding onto one of the chairs.

"What's up?" Sam asked.

"Just kept having these weird dreams." Lia explained.

"You were quiet yesterday at dinner." Charlie observed.

"I had a lot on my mind."

"Does it have to do with Mr London?" Sam asked.

"No." Lia groaned, suddenly remembering Edward's visit the day before and feeling restless, got up from her chair.

"Lia? Where are you going?" Diane asked.

"I'm going to get dressed, I'll take the dogs out this morning." Lia said, leaving the room.

Diane followed her daughter up to her bedroom and stopped her just before she could close the door.

"I hear you and your dad had a bit of an argument yesterday." Diane commented, sitting down on Lia's bed.

"It doesn't matter." Lia sighed.

"Talk to me, Lia." Diane insisted.

"It's silly and it doesn't matter." Lia argued.

"If it's upsetting you then it does matter." Diane countered.

"We argued about keeping my stupid powers a secret from Aidan." Lia told her mum, giving in.

"I take it your dad won't let you tell him."

"No, and it's so stupid because he already sort of knows, thanks to Alice Foulds." Lia blurted out.

"Lia, in this case I think your father knows best. He's the one with the powers." Diane decided.

"It's not fair." Lia cried.

"Your dad only wants what is best for you." Diane reminded her daughter.

"But if I keep this secret from Aidan he'll end it between us. Mum he means so much to me, I love him." Lia argued.

"I know you do, but just think about your dad and your brothers before you do anything." Diane told her daughter, as she stood up. "Better hurry up and get dressed to walk Betty and Veronica."

Lia pulled on some jeans and a warm jumper, before running back downstairs.

"Betty! Veronica! Walk!" She called, as she reached the bottom of the stairs.

Shoving her feet into her walking boots, she pulled on her coat and gloves then snapped on the dogs' leads.

"I'll be back shortly."

Lia hurried down the drive and turned onto her usual dog walking route.

"Hello Amelia." Edward said, getting out of his matt black Lexus LS, which was parked at the bottom of the Taylors' drive.

"Good morning."

"Where are you off to this fine morning?" Edward asked, falling into step with Lia.

"Just walking the dogs." Lia commented, stopping at the entrance to the woods to let the dogs off their leads.

Despite being off their leads, the dogs both stayed by Lia's side, growling softly at Edward.

"You walk your dogs in the woods?" Edward asked, staring warily at the entrance to the trail.

"Yep."

"Well, I was hoping to have a word with you, without your family around, would you like to go somewhere more civilised and get a cup of coffee?"

"I can't I'm afraid, I need to walk the dogs." Lia explained, gesturing to the dogs who were stood next to her.

"Well, can I talk to you later?" Edward persisted.

"I can't. I've already got plans with my boyfriend." Lia said, trying round Edward to the entrance of the woods.

"You have a boyfriend?" Edward exclaimed.

"Yes, his name is Aidan." Lia told Edward.

"I hadn't planned on you having a boyfriend." Edward muttered absentmindly.

"Well I do." Lia huffed.

Edward shook his head and walked slowly back to climb in his car. Lia waited until he drove away before turning and walking into the woods. The dogs remained by Lia's sides for a few minutes, before they headed slightly in front of her but keeping her in sight. Lia walked slowly round the woods, debating what she was going to say to Aidan when they had lunch later today.

As she came up to the corner where Dean and Alice had ambushed her, feeling nervous, Lia whistled for the dogs. They both ran back to her. Lia rested one hand on each of the dogs' heads as she rounded the corner and was relieved when there was no one standing there waiting to attack her. Removing her hands from the dogs' heads she allowed them to go ahead.

At the end of the trail, Lia called the dogs back so she could put their leads back on. As she was finishing putting their leads on, Buster ran up to her and jumped straight up, knocking Lia over.

"Hi Buster." Lia laughed, as she reached up to pet Buster, who was now standing over her.

"Lia?" Aidan called.

"Morning." Lia replied, from her position sprawled under Buster.

"Buster get off her." Aidan grumbled, pulling his dog away from Lia. "Are you alright?"

"I'm fine."

Lia gingerly got back to her feet and picked up Betty and Veronica's leads, as she had dropped them when Buster had knocked her down.

"This is a nice surprise." Aidan commented. "Normally it's Sam or Charlie who I bump into in the morning."

"I felt like getting some fresh air." Lia replied. "The dogs are primarily my responsibily and I was up early, so it seemed best that I walked them this morning."

"Hmm."

"What's that supposed to mean?" Lia demanded.

"You and Ben hate getting up in the mornings." Aidan commented mildly.

"Well today is different." Lia retorted.

"That's crap." Aidan muttered under his breath.

"How?" Lia countered.

"You hate mornings! You prefer spending the morning in bed asleep and when you do wake up, you usually spend a chunk of the morning in your pyjamas." Aidan declared.

"Guess you do know some things about me." Lia quipped.

"That's not funny." Aidan told her, walking away from her.

"Sorry, you're right, I'm not a morning person." Lia mumbled, giving in.

"It's fine." Aidan sighed, walking back to her.

"I woke up early this morning and went for a walk to clear my head before I spoke to you." Lia explained.

"Oh."

"Do you still want to meet up later?" Lia asked.

"I don't know to be honest with you." Aidan admitted.

"Please." Lia whispered.

"We are just going to end up in a fight, Lia." Aidan told her.

"You can't know that." Lia begged.

"Yesterday you refused to answer a simple question, how do I know that you're not going to keep clamming up whenever you feel like it." Aidan continued.

"It's not like that. If you come round later we can talk properly and I promise to be as open as I can. Please."

"I'll think about it." Aidan said, walking away.

Lia slowly walked back up the rest of the way to her house. She wiped down the dogs' muddy paws and let them in the house. Rather than following the dogs, Lia continued into the back garden and sat down on the garden swing.

"You're going to freeze out here." Ben called, heading over to Lia, his coat over his sweatpants.

"I just needed a little bit of quiet." Lia explained, pushing the swing with one foot.

"Want to talk about it?" Ben asked, sitting down next to her.

"Aidan wants me to tell him about our powers." Lia mumbled, leaning into her brother's side.

"Oh."

"I don't know what to do." Lia said, starting to cry.

Ben put his arm around his sister and held on while she cried.

"It's OK Lia, we will come up with a solution." Ben told her, when she had stopped crying.

"Dad told me that we are not allowed to tell him about magic." Lia sniffled.

"I'll talk to Dad." Ben reassured her.

"Why are you so invested in this?" Lia asked, wiping her eyes.

"Two reasons, first, Aidan has been my friend for so long, he's practically a third brother by now and the second reason, is I like seeing you smile." Ben explained.

"I smile a lot of the time." Lia said confused.

"It's a different kind of one, I noticed a lot over the Christmas break." Ben offered. "You started doing it a lot when your phone bleeped, then when we had our usual pre-Christmas buffet on Christmas Eve, I noticed the same smile when you and Aidan were talking in the corner. I put two and two together and realised that Aidan was the reason."

"I'm in love with him." Lia admitted to Ben.

"Then we need to get this sorted." Ben said, standing up and pulling Lia with him. "Let's go inside before we freeze."

Lia followed her brother into the house where they were greeted by Sam, who was waiting for them in the hallway.

"You two were outside a while." Sam stated, as they were putting their coats away.

"We had some stuff to talk about." Ben told his brother.

"Stuff to do with Aidan?" Sam enquired.

"Yes, why?" Lia asked.

"He called while you guys were outside, said he'd tried both your mobiles." Sam told them.

"I'll call him back." Ben announced.

Lia nodded and then left her brothers to head upstairs to her room, she bumped into Charlie on the first set of stairs.

"You OK?" he asked.

"Yeah, I'm just tired." Lia told him. "I'm heading upstairs to take a short nap."

"See you later."

Lia continued upstairs to her room and curled up under the blanket on her bed. She checked her phone and saw that she had missed two calls from Aidan. Knowing that Ben would call him back, she dropped him a quick text.

Lia: Everything ok xx

The response came in almost straight-away.

Aidan: Spoke to Ben be round in a bit

Lia: Ok xx

Lia looked at the set of texts she had received and noted that Aidan had not signed off the texts like he had been doing for the last two months. She closed her eyes and flopped back on her bed, pulling her blanket tight around her.

"Lia, it's Ben." Ben called, as he knocked on her door.

"Come in." she called back
"I just spoke to Aidan, he's coming around in a bit. I'll talk to him when he first gets here, if you want." Ben commented, sitting by Lia's legs.
"I don't know what's best in this situation." Lia admitted.
"I'll talk to him, see if I can't smooth things over for you." Ben assured her. "Charlie said you were thinking about taking a nap. Try that, it might make you feel a bit better." Ben patted Lia's leg as he stood up, he shut her bedroom door on his way out and left her curled up on her bed. Lia remained curled up and read through all the text messages that she and Aidan had sent each other over the last two months. They had texted virtually every night, even though they had seen each other virtually every day, either for a date or a dog walk.
"Knock knock." David said, pulling open her door.
"Hi Dad." Lia sighed, sitting up.
"What are you up to?" David asked, crossing the room to his daughter.
"Just trying to take a nap." She lied, hiding her phone under her blanket.
"You still upset about yesterday?" David asked, sitting down on the edge of Lia's bed.
"Yes, I just hate keeping this a secret from Aidan." Lia told her dad.
"Ben agrees with you."
"I know we spoke about it earlier."
"I don't think that telling Aidan is a good idea." David sighed.
"I know you don't but Ben trusts him and Ben trusts him with me. Dad that must count for something!" Lia exclaimed.
"It does. I've been thinking and against my better judgment, I have decided to let you and Ben make the decision whether or not you tell Aidan."
"Really?"
"Yes, but I must insist that you speak with Sam and Charlie before you make your final decision." David told

her.

"I will, thanks Dad."

David nodded and walked out of the room.

Lia uncurled her legs and quickly sent Ben a text.

Lia: Is Aidan here yet? X

Ben: No

Lia: Can you grab S & C and meet me in living room? X

Ben: Done

Lia pulled off her blanket and walked downstairs to talk to her brothers. As she walked into the main living room to join them, she stopped to pet Betty, who had come to meet her at the bottom of the stairs.

"What's up?" Sam asked, as Lia took her usual spot at the edge of the sofa so she could curl up.

"I had an encounter with Alice Foulds last night." Lia began.

"You had a what?" Sam demanded.

"Why is this first time you are mentioning this?" Ben exclaimed, at exactly the same time.

"OK, calm down." Lia told them. "I will be honest, I was so preoccupied with Aidan that I completely forgot about Alice, although she is the reason that I'm in this mess with Aidan."

"Tell us what happened, Lia." Charlie quietly demanded.

"I was out with Aidan yesterday and as we turned the corner at the top of the woods, Alice was just there, waiting. She did this thing with her hands that sent an invisible wave of energy into Aidan, which sent him flying. Then, she started going on about how my powers were supposed to be hers before knocking me over. Then she clicked her fingers and just vanished. The real problem was Aidan overheard her talking." Lia explained, using the same explanation as she had with her dad the day before.

"You need to tell us when you see any of the Foulds." Ben told her.

"I will, I was just so confused and upset about everything that happened with Aidan because he kept asking me what Alice was talking about when she mentioned powers.

When I couldn't tell him he got really mad." Lia explained.

"What are you going to do about Aidan?" Sam asked.

"Well, that's actually what I wanted to talk to everyone about." Lia mumbled. "Both Ben and I want to tell Aidan about magic."

"He's like another brother." Ben chimed in, "It doesn't feel right keeping this a secret, not now he partially knows."

"There's no way Dad will let you tell him." Charlie announced.

"Actually, Dad has said it is up to us. We all need to be in agreement but we can tell Aidan about magic." Lia continued.

The room fell into silence while they all thought about what they were going to do.

"I take it you two really want to tell Aidan." Sam said eventually.

Lia nodded.

"Don't you?" Ben asked.

"I don't see Aidan not knowing as a problem." Sam commented.

"Why don't you see it as a problem?" Ben asked.

"I just don't see what the big deal is." Sam countered.

"Is there a problem between you and Aidan?" Lia asked Sam.

"No, I'm just having trouble adjusting to him being around all the time and I'm concerned about what happens when you break-up."

"What if we don't break up?" Lia asked.

"It's still not a big deal if Aidan doesn't know." Sam argued.

"It is a big deal to Lia, if she feels it's going to ruin things with Aidan. Christ, don't you have someone you want to tell!" Ben demanded.

"Guys, lets think about this rationally!" Charlie interrupted.

"What do you want to do Charlie?" Lia asked.

There was a knock at the door before Charlie could answer Lia. Ben threw a furious look at Sam before he stalked out of the room to open the front door.

"Hey Aidan, come on in." Ben greeted his friend.

"Thanks."

"We are all in the living room." Ben told Aidan, steering him into the room.

"Aidan." Sam greeted him warily.

"Sam, Charlie." Aidan echoed.

Lia smiled at Aidan when he looked over at her but it soon dropped, when Aidan didn't smile back. Locking her fingers together, she breathed in and out slowly, worrying about what to do next. Aidan sat down on the chair furthest away from Lia, so Ben came and sat down next to her, he squeezed her knee in a gesture of silent support.

"You were a bit cryptic on the phone." Ben said to Aidan.

"Needed to talk to you guys in person."

"Well, we are all here." Sam said sarcastically, gesturing around the room.

"Sam." Ben warned.

Sam sunk back onto the sofa cushions but continued to glare around the room.

"I'm sure Lia spoke to you and told you how our walk was once again interrupted by a member of the Foulds family." Aidan started.

"She has." Ben confirmed.

"Well, yesterday, Alice said something strange and when I asked Lia about it she clammed up." Aidan continued.

"Right?" Sam questioned.

"Well, I want to know what the hell is going on and why the Foulds family have it in for you guys. I've seen one of the four of them, a couple of times when I've been out with Lia." Aidan said.

"What do you mean you have seen them a couple of times when you have been out with Lia?" Ben asked. "Lia, you never mentioned this."

Lia stared at Aidan wordlessly. He hadn't mentioned this to her. She hoped that she meant enough to Aidan that having an ex-girlfriend or her family appear would have been worth a mention.

"Lia didn't know. I thought it was to do with me until yesterday." Aidan admitted.

"But you want an explanation from me about something private, when you didn't bother to tell me you thought your ex and her family were stalking you." Lia stated quietly.

"It wasn't important." Aidan argued.

"It wasn't important?" Lia repeated.

Aidan shoved his hands in his pockets as he stood up from his chair, he glanced around the room looking for support, only to be met by angry or disappointed looks.

"Lia?" Aidan managed.

"I would have told you everything." Lia whispered shocked. "But you still get to pick and choose what is and isn't important for you to tell me."

With that, Lia fled from the room straight up to her bedroom and slammed the door shut. Seconds later she heard a knock on the door.

"Lia, it's Aidan."

"I don't want to talk at the minute."

"I do."

"Fine!" Lia shouted, yanking her door open.

Aidan winced at the look of fury that Lia sent him.

"OK, I screwed up." Aidan admitted, holding his hands up.

"You made me feel like crap for having one secret but you were hiding all sorts, weren't you!" Lia yelled.

"It's not like that, Lia." Aidan protested.

"Then what is it like? No wait, I'll tell you what it's like. I was so surprised when you asked me out as it's all I had been thinking about for years. Yes, I had a huge crush on you. I told my brothers that you could change, that you wouldn't cheat on me or hurt me and that somehow we would make this work. So here I am Aidan, completely and utterly head over heels in love with you and you don't trust me in the slightest."

"Lia."

"Save it, I don't want to hear it."

With that, Lia slowly shut her bedroom door in Aidan's stunned face, before sinking onto the floor to cry.

On the other side of the door, Aidan raised his hand to knock on Lia's bedroom door but couldn't bring himself to do it. Instead, he turned and walked back downstairs to where Lia's brothers waited.

"I take it that didn't go well." Ben observed, when Aidan came into the living room and sank down on the sofa.

"She's so angry, she wouldn't let me say anything." Aidan dejectedly admitted.

"I warned you not to hurt her." Ben responded.

"I was trying not to." Aidan protested. "I didn't tell her about Alice and her family following us because Alice meant nothing to me, we literally went on three dates."

"You wanted Lia to be completely honest with you, so you should have known she would expect the same from you." Sam stated.

"Well, she was completely honest upstairs." Aidan told them.

"What do you mean?" Charlie enquired.

"She told me she is in love with me, after announcing that she's had a crush on me for years."

Charlie breathed a sigh of relief, while Sam and Ben exchanged worried glances.

"What did you say back?" Ben asked.

"I didn't say anything and she just slowly shut the door on me."

"You need to leave now." Sam declared.

"What?"

"Leave." Sam repeated.

"I told you not to hurt Lia, I think you might have just destroyed her." Ben said carefully. "Lia is the most caring, giving person in the world but she is also guarded with her emotions. She doesn't like letting people in, unless she trusts them implicitly. She's just completely opened herself up to you and you saying nothing will have hurt her. So yeah, you need to leave now."

In disbelief, Aidan stood up and shrugged into his leather jacket, as he left the room he felt Charlie following him.

"Ben will come around." Charlie assured him, as he went upstairs.

"What about Lia?" Aidan asked, opening the front door.

"She's probably already forgiven you." Charlie observed. "But better to give her some space."

With that, Aidan left the house. Up in her room, Lia watched from behind the curtains as Aidan walked down the drive. Once he had turned the corner and was out of sight, she let out the breath that she had been holding. Steeling herself for the next set of tears that threatened, Lia opened her laptop and opened her diary that she kept hidden.

"Amelia, it's lunch time." David called, through his daughter's door after she had sat locked in her room alone for a couple of hours.

"I'm not hungry." Lia replied.

"OK."

With that Lia was left in peace again, sitting cross-legged on her bedroom floor she picked up the collection of Disney movies she wanted to watch and crawled over to her bed. Wrapping herself up in her blanket, she put the Aristocats DVD into the laptop and settled down to watch in bed. An hour into the movie, Ben came into her room with a cup of tea.

"Thanks." Lia said, pausing the movie

"How you feeling?" Ben asked.

"Stupid." Lia mumbled.

"What are you watching?" Ben asked, wisely deciding to change the subject.

"Aristocats, my favourite Disney movie."

"I personally prefer Toy Story and the Pixar movies." Ben commented, moving Lia's laptop onto his lap so he could watch the film with her.

"I'm watching The Little Mermaid next." Lia told him, resting her head on Ben's shoulder.

"Cool, Disney Movie marathon." Ben observed.

"I pick the movies." Lia responded absently.

Ben pressed play and settled down to watch some films with his sister. Part way through The Little Mermaid, Ben's phone bleeped, he checked his phone and saw he had texts from Sam and Aidan.

Sam: You with Lia?

Aidan: Sorry... Is Lia ok?

Ben checked on Lia, who had fallen asleep about 20 minutes into the Little Mermaid and confirmed that she was still asleep, before he sent Aidan a text back.

Nows not the time Ben text back to Aidan

Up in her room watching Disney Films he told Sam

Sam: What film you watching?

Ben: The Little Mermaid... Lia's picking the films

Sam: Suggest The Jungle Book and come downstairs to watch

Ben laughed silently at his brother. They all had different tastes in films, so apart from the compulsory family movie night once a month, they rarely watched movies together but Disney movies were a bit different, particularly if Lia was upset as they would all join in to watch.

Ben: Tell C, I'll get L

"Lia wake up." Ben said, gently shaking his sister.

"Huh? What?" Lia mumbled startled.

"We are going downstairs to watch the Jungle Book." Ben told her, putting her laptop on the edge of her bed.

"I'm not in the mood for company." Lia groaned.

"Tough, family Disney movie marathon." Ben stated, picking Lia up to cart her and her blanket out of her room.

"If we are watching the Jungle Book, then we are watching Lady and the Tramp next." Lia decided.

The siblings settled in for the evening to watch Disney films and order Chinese takeaway. About 9 o'clock Lia's phone bleeped, checking it, she saw that Aidan had messaged her.

Aidan: Can we talk?

Lia: I don't have anything left to say x

Aidan: Lia please, I need to talk to you

Lia: I'll call you later… with the brothers atm x
Aidan: Ok
At the end of Big Hero 6, Charlie's pick, Lia stood up.
"I'm really tired, I'll see you guys in the morning." Lia told her brothers, as she left the room.
"Night." They chorused distractedly, as they continued their debate as to whether they should watch Wall-E.
Lia slipped into the kitchen and made herself a cup of tea before heading upstairs. Shutting her bedroom door, Lia pulled her phone out of her pocket and called Aidan.
"Hi." He answered almost immediately.
"Hi." Lia echoed.
"I missed you walking the dogs earlier." Aidan told her.
Lia remained silent, unsure of what to say.
"Are you there?" Aidan asked.
"Yeah, I'm still here." Lia replied, after a few second pause.
"What you said earlier, I wasn't expecting it." Aidan admitted.
"I know."
"I didn't know you felt like that."
"I know, I didn't mean to spring it on you. Where do we go from here?" Lia whispered.
"I don't know." Aidan admitted.
On that admission, Lia pulled the phone away from her ear unable to listen anymore, clutching the phone in her hand as tightly as she could. She could hear Aidan calling her name, so she moved the phone back to her ear.
"Lia are you there?" Aidan asked.
"I'm still here."
"Good."
"Good?"
"OK, not good, I was just glad you were still on the phone."
"Aidan, just say whatever it is you need to say." Lia told him.
"I can't." Aidan muttered.
"You can't what?"

"I can't do this but I can't end it either." Aidan admitted.

"You want to end this?"

"I don't know, I'm confused Lia. In one breath you are hiding stuff from me but in another you're saying you love me."

"Aidan."

"I'm sorry."

On that note, Lia hung up the phone unable to hear anymore. She quickly pulled on her pyjamas and got into bed where she just lay there, staring at the ceiling until she fell into a dreamless sleep.

Chapter Eight

4ᵗʰ January 2018

Lia moved as quickly as she could through the midday crowds in the town centre, looking around, trying to find Aidan. She wanted to talk to him after their telephone call and say how sorry she was for hanging up the phone. She had agreed with her brothers, that due to the circumstances she would not tell Aidan about their powers for the time being but that didn't mean she couldn't try and regain Aidan's trust to make their relationship work.
At the bottom end of town, Lia spotted Aidan with a few of his friends, including Matt, Luke and Carl. Lia paused when she saw Marie and Sophie joining the group. Moving so she was slightly hidden, she decided to wait until the girls moved on. Gasping, Lia's jaw dropped when she saw Sophie lean close to Aidan and kiss him. Rooted in her spot, Lia felt the familiar sting of tears in the back of her eyes as she watched Aidan rest his hand on Sophie's hip.
Turning away, Lia fled back through town and ran back to her house as quickly as she could. Blinded by tears, Lia struggled to get her key in the lock to open the front door. After four unsuccessful attempts to open the door, she simply sank to her knees and sobbed.
"Lia? What are you… Are you OK?" Ben asked, horrified to find his sister crying uncontrollably by the front door.
When Ben crouched down to check on Lia, she curled up against him and kept on crying.
"I'm just going to open the door." Ben told his sister, as he let her go.
Ben quickly opened the front door before bending down to pick Lia up. Kicking the door shut, Ben carried his sister into the living room, startling Sam who was watching the football.
"What happened?" Sam asked.

"I don't know, I just got home and Lia was outside the front door crying." Ben told Sam, as he sat down with Lia on his lap.

"Lia? Can you tell us what happened?" Sam asked.

Lia wiped at the tears which continued to stream down her face but she did try to sit up on Ben's lap.

"Does this have anything to do with the Foulds family?" Sam continued, when Lia didn't answer as she continued to sob uncontrollably, her body shaking with every breath.

Lia shook her head and continued to swipe at the tears that just would not stop.

"Aidan." Ben sighed.

Lia nodded and hiccupped as she continued her attempts to stop crying. At Ben's faint shove she slid off his lap so that he could stand up.

"I assuming this has something to do with your conversation yesterday." Ben observed, pacing up and down the living room.

"I wanted to say I was sorry for hanging up on him yesterday." Lia managed between sobs.

"When were you on the phone with him?" Sam asked angrily.

"After I went to bed, he wanted to talk but part way through I thought he was going to end things so I hung up." Lia explained, through her sobs.

"So when you went to town today, did you have another fight?" Sam asked.

Lia shook her head and curled up into the corner of the sofa.

"I'm guessing he ended things when you saw him today then?" Ben guessed.

"Well it's over but I never actually spoke to him." Lia's voice broke. "When I saw him in town he was with Sophie so I hid behind a corner to wait for her and Marie to leave but I guess the joke was on me because what I actually saw was them kissing."

Starting to cry harder again, Lia hugged her knees to her chest, and remained motionless on the sofa. After a minute or two of crying, while her brothers looked on, both furious and horrified, Lia's phone started to ring. When she saw that it was Aidan trying to call her, she declined the call and sat up straight. Once the phone had stopped ringing, she saw that Aidan had texted her a couple of times.

Aidan: Sorry about yesterday xx

Aidan: Can we talk? Xx

Aidan: Everything ok? Xx

Aidan: Lia? Xx

Steeling herself against the remainder of her tears, Lia shoved her phone into her pocket, ignoring all the texts. Standing up and taking a couple of deep breaths, Lia walked through into the kitchen to make a cup of tea. Busying herself in the process of making the tea, Lia ignored the knock on the door.

"Aidan? What are you doing here?" Sam asked, as he answered the door.

"I just want to talk to Lia, is she here?"

"No."

"Can I come in and wait?"

"Not today." Ben declared, walking out of the living room to stand next to Sam.

"She's here isn't she?" Aidan observed. "Lia!"

"As far as you're concerned, she's not home." Ben told him.

"Look! I just want to talk to her, to tell her I'm sorry." Aidan protested.

"I told you not to hurt her." Ben growled.

"We had a bit of a fight, I get that she's upset but please let me come in and talk to her."

"She walked into town earlier to talk to you, she saw you with Sophie." Sam commented.

"How could you cheat on Lia?" Ben asked "Particularly after everything she told you yesterday."

"I'm sorry. Just let me see her, I can explain."

"Even if I thought you had a decent explanation, there is no way I would let you anywhere near her at the moment."

Ben told him.

"Lia? Please can you come out and talk to me!" Aidan begged.

Ben glanced back into the kitchen to see if Lia had moved into Aidan's line of sight but seeing that she hadn't, he turned back to his friend and shook his head.

"If she wants to talk to you, I'll let you know but for now you really need to leave." Ben encouraged his friend.

"I just need five minutes." Aidan tried. "Lia, please come out!"

"Goodbye Aidan." Sam said, shutting the door.

Once the door was shut Lia came out of the kitchen, into the hallway. Both dogs immediately ran up to her and whined. Lia knelt down and put one arm around each dog for comfort, Veronica licked Lia's face while Betty nudged her chin.

"What are you going to do?" Ben asked Lia.

"I don't know." Lia admitted. "You need to go after him though."

"What?" Ben exclaimed.

"We made a deal Ben, you need to stick to it."

"I'm not sticking to that stupid deal, not after he cheated on you." Ben argued.

"You promised me. Now you need to go after him." Lia continued.

"What promise did Ben make?" Charlie asked, coming down the stairs.

"He promised me that no matter how badly things ended between me and Aidan, he would try and remain Aidan's friend." Lia told her brothers.

"Why did you make him promise that?" Charlie asked.

"Because they have been friends forever and I didn't want to come between them." Lia explained, getting up from her crouched position on the floor.

"Ben just go after him, Lia won't drop it." Sam groaned.

"Go!" Lia told him. "I'll sort myself out."

With that Ben grabbed his jacket and headed out after Aidan. He was surprised to find that Aidan was still near the edge of the driveway.

"What do you want?" Aidan demanded, when he saw Ben.

"Lia made me promise that your relationship wouldn't interfere with us two being friends." Ben explained. "I'm trying to keep my promise."

"Yeah, she wanted to me to make the same promise but I chose not to." Aidan observed.

Aidan sighed and shoved his hands into his pockets, mirroring Ben's stance.

"How did we end up in this mess." Ben observed.

"It's my fault, I'm sorry."

"I'm so angry at you for upsetting Lia and making her cry." Ben admitted.

"I know, and trust me, I'm even more angry at myself."

"Why did you do it?" Ben asked.

"It was a stupid mistake."

"That's not good enough." Ben told him.

"I know. Do you think she will ever talk to me again?"

"She's too forgiving for her own good, so I imagine she will."

The two boys fell into silence and remained standing at the bottom of driveway for a few minutes.

Back inside the house, Lia watched them from her bedroom window, nodding when she saw Ben and Aidan shake hands before Ben headed back into the house. Deciding to move on from her drama with Aidan, Lia changed into her checked pyjama bottoms and a long sleeved T-shirt before heading to the garage to brush up on her magic.

A couple of hours later, Lia was surrounded by a number of different spell books and had also been back into the house so she could grab her laptop to do some further research. One of the main areas that had caught her eye were the passages that covered the power of empathy. This had caught her attention, as she had noticed that recently she could often get glimpses of how people she was close to were feeling.

"Lia, Mr London is here." Ben announced, coming into the

garage. "What are you doing?"

"I'm moving on." Lia told him.

"Great, you are moving on with magic." Ben groaned.

"No, I am simply choosing to focus my attention elsewhere."

"Whatever! Anyway Mr London wants to talk to you." Ben repeated.

"I'm coming." Lia said, shutting the book she was reading and getting up.

Lia walked through the house and found Edward sitting at the kitchen table having a conversation with Charlie.

"Edward, Hi." Lia said, as she came into the kitchen.

"Good evening Amelia." Edward greeted her.

"How can I help you?" Lia asked, sitting down next to Charlie, opposite Edward.

"So, Charles and I have just been discussing the promised destiny of us being together." Edward announced, once Lia was settled into her seat.

"Oh?" Lia queried.

"Edward brought us some of the documents from his family's history, I have just been looking through them and there are references to a promise between our families that a male and a female will be joined in destiny." Charlie explained. "However, I am still looking for anything that we have in our family's history that confirms the promise."

"It says quite clearly here in black and white that our families are destined to be joined together." Edward interrupted, pointing to some of the documents that were on the kitchen table.

"That's only your family's side of the promise, I want to see what our documents say." Lia protested.

"Why are you being so stubborn?" Edward growled.

"I'm not being stubborn I'm being practical, I don't see why I have to take your and your family's word for some centuries old agreement that, for all I know, you made up on the spot and these documents are fake." Lia argued.

"So, you don't trust my family's honour?" Edward yelled.

"I don't know anything about your family and its honour."
Lia retored.

"Have you been looking into this promise?" Charlie asked
suddenly.

Lia gave Charlie a look that conveyed her lack of interest
in finding out any more about their ancestors' vows
between them and Edward's family. Charlie gave a faint
look at the documents but Lia's barely detectable head
shake, prevented him from pressing the issue any further.

"I was hoping that I could persuade you to go out for
dinner with me." Edward told her, when he realised that
Lia was not going to budge from her position.

"Today's not a good day." Lia quipped.

"Plans with the boyfriend?" Edward enquired.

"No, no plans, it's just not a good night." Lia told him.

"That's a shame, I was hoping to introduce you to my
cousin Emily. She's recently moved here and is looking to
make some new friends." Edward continued.

"Edward spoke to me about this before you came in, I'm
going as well." Charlie interjected.

"Well, I suppose I could go, as it's just making new
friends." Lia mumbled thoughtfully.

"Excellent, I will let Emily know, then come back in an
hour and we can go for dinner." Edward announced,
getting up from the table.

"I'll walk you out." Charlie commented, getting up from
the table and walking out of the kitchen with Edward.

"Did I hear you agree to go to dinner with Mr London?"
Sam asked. "You were literally in tears over Aidan this
morning."

"I'm going to meet his cousin Emily." Lia told him,
swinging round in her chair to face Sam. "Not to mention,
Charlie is coming with me."

"So, not a date then?" Sam continued.

"No, I'm not interested in him that way and like you said
it's far too soon after Aidan" Lia agreed.

"Just be careful." Sam warned, as he left the kitchen.

Sighing, Lia got up from the kitchen table and headed out

of the kitchen to go upstairs but she paused, just as Charlie shut the door to Edward.

"I'm not sure that this is the best idea." Lia told her brother, when he turned to look at her.

"Why not?" Charlie asked.

"I just don't think it's a good idea to go out with Edward when I'm not even sure what is going on between me and Aidan." Lia explained.

"It's just meeting his cousin." Charlie whined.

"Two days ago he turned up on our doorstep and announced that we need to start dating immediately." Lia commented.

"Was that really two days ago?"

"Yes."

"Oh, it feels like longer."

"A lot has happened since then."

"Let's go and meet his cousin tonight and you can also tell him that you are not interested in dating him. You never know maybe he will agree to be your friend."

"OK, but if this gets remotely date like then we are leaving."

"OK."

Charlie walked back into the kitchen while Lia stood at the bottom of the stairs for a few more seconds, before heading upstairs. Rather than heading up to her room, Lia walked over to Ben's room and knocked on the door.

"What?" Ben yelled.

"It's Lia, can I talk to you for a sec?" Lia yelled back.

"Come in."

Lia opened her brother's door, as Ben turned down the music, he had been playing at full volume.

"What's up?" Ben asked, when Lia perched herself on the edge of his desk chair.

"I think I'm about to do something horrible." Lia told him.

"About to do?"

"Yes, I've agreed to meet Edward's cousin Emily for dinner."

"That sounds like fun. What's the problem?" Ben asked,

confused.

"Edward is going to be there."

"You and Aidan literally broke up this morning!" Ben exclaimed.

"I know, I know!" Lia cried.

"Christ, Lia! Why would you agree to date Edward?" Ben yelled.

"I didn't agree to go on a date with him, I agreed to meet his cousin for dinner, Charlie's coming too." Lia protested.

"The guy wants to date you Lia, he will try anything." Ben continued to yell. "How could you be so gullible?"

"I'll just get Charlie to cancel, I don't want to date him, I still love Aidan." Lia admitted.

"No, go and meet his cousin. You need a friend you can talk to about your powers." Ben told her. "But tell Edward you aren't interested."

"What about Aidan?" Lia whispered.

"That will be between you and him."

Lia got up out of Ben's chair and continued the rest of the way up to her bedroom, stopping briefly for a quick shower. In her room, she swapped her pyjama bottoms for a pair of jeans then slid her feet into her high-heeled black boots and zipped them up. Pulling open her jumper drawer, she got out four jumpers and went to the mirror to decide which one she wanted to wear. As she was pulling her pink striped jumper over her head, Lia heard her phone ring. She walked over to her desk and checked her phone, she saw that Aidan was calling her. She stared at the phone until it stopped ringing as she couldn't bring herself to answer the call.

Lia placed her phone in her handbag and made sure that she put it on vibrate so it didn't ring loudly during dinner. Running her brush through her hair, Lia sat down on her desk chair so she could check her appearance and then slammed her hairbrush down.

"What did your hairbrush do to you?" Diane asked, coming into Lia's bedroom.

"Nothing." Lia muttered.

"What's the matter?"

"Nothing." Lia repeated.

"You don't normally slam your hairbrush around." Diane commented, coming to stand behind Lia and resting her hands on Lia's shoulders. "Talk to me Lia."

"It's silly, I'm just annoyed at myself for agreeing to go to dinner with Edward." Lia muttered angrily.

"Why did you agree?" Diane asked.

"Because I'm stupid and gullible."

"Explain?"

"Edward asked me to dinner and I said no but then he started to tell me how he wanted his cousin to meet people. She's just moved here, so like an idiot, I agreed to go."

"Why does agreeing to go and meet someone's cousin make you an idiot and gullible?" Diane asked.

"Because I have no interest in Edward. I mean yesterday I was dating Aidan and now I'm going to dinner with Edward. Who does that?"

"So the problem is Aidan?" Diane observed.

"I want to be with him even though he cheated on me and I can't be honest with him. He's the guy I want to be with." Lia continued, getting frustrated again by the situation she found herself in.

"So what are you going to do?" Diane asked her daughter.

"Well, I'm going to meet Edward's cousin because I've stupidly agreed to go and I'm going to tell Edward that I'm not interested in dating him then hope for the best." Lia told her mum, picking her hairbrush back up and yanking it through her hair, before putting it back down again.

"Be careful Lia." Diane warned.

When her mum left the room, Lia picked her brush up again and ran it through her hair again and again. After a couple of minutes, Lia put it back down on her desk but more gently this time. Staring at her reflection for a few minutes, Lia got up off her chair and pulled her handbag up off the floor and began to gather up all of the bits and pieces she needed. Once she had her purse, lipstick and keys, she pulled her phone back out. She pressed the home button and saw that over the afternoon she had missed six calls from Aidan. She unlocked the phone and moved to the call log, her fingers hovered over Aidan's name as she debated calling him.

Before she got a chance to decide whether or not she was going to call Aidan back, there was a knock on her bedroom door.

"Lia?" Charlie called, from the other side of her bedroom door.

"Come in." Lia called back.

"Are you nearly ready?" Charlie asked, entering her room.

"I'm just sorting out my handbag, then I will be ready." Lia told him, putting her phone down on her desk, walking across her room to pick up a mini hairbrush and placing it in her bag.

"Lia, are you OK?" Charlie asked, watching as Lia wandered around her room fiddling with various bits and pieces.

"I'm just not sure this is a good idea." Lia mumbled, picking up her perfume, sniffing it, then putting it back down.

"What's not a good idea?" Charlie asked, leaning against Lia's doorway.

"Going out with Edward tonight." Lia mumbled.

"It's just dinner Lia, it's not a big deal. Besides I'll be there and we are meeting his cousin." Charlie told her.

"It just doesn't feel right." Lia continued to mumble.

"What doesn't feel right?" Charlie asked exasperated.

"Going out with Edward, I'm still in love with Aidan." Lia announced, flopping down on her bed.

Charlie sighed and stared at his sister as she sat on her bed, looking confused and miserable. Not saying anything, he left the room and walked downstairs to get Ben.

"You need to come and talk to Lia." Charlie announced, opening Ben's door.

"Why?" Ben asked, looking up from his guitar to his brother.

"Because she's being ridiculous, she says that she can't go

to dinner with Edward because she is still in love with Aidan."

"It's her choice Charlie, you can't make her do anything."

"It's dinner!" Charlie cried.

"She's had a tough day, she has every right to be confused." Ben told his brother, in a warning tone.

"She can't sit around and mope." Charlie continued. "It will be good for her to make friends with Edward and his cousin."

Sighing, Ben put his guitar down on the edge of his bed and swung his legs off. Shaking his head, he followed Charlie up to Lia's room. The boys knocked on Lia's open door and walked into her room. Ben hurried over to Lia'when he saw that she was crying silently on her bed.

"Hey, why are you crying?" Ben asked, wrapping his arm around Lia.

"I don't know what I'm doing!" Lia cried.

"That's OK. It's been a tough day but you don't need to do anything." Ben reassured her.

"I'm supposed to be going to dinner but all I can think about is Aidan, what am I supposed do?" Lia sobbed.

Ben sat hugging his sister while she cried, Charlie stood awkwardly in the doorway watching. After a few minutes, Charlie pulled his phone out of his pocket and messaged Edward.

Charlie: Really sorry but something has come up we can't make it tonight.

"I've cancelled dinner." Charlie said, walking over to his sister and patting her shoulder.

"Thank you." Lia managed between sobs.

Edward: Oh that's a shame. I was looking forward to dinner as was Emily.

Charlie: I'll see if we can rearrange.

Edward: That would be greatly appreciated.

"Edward has said he is fine to rearrange dinner." Charlie said, once Lia had stopped sobbing.

Lia lifted her head off of Ben's shoulder and turned to face Charlie.

"Let's leave talking about this until tomorrow." Ben suggested.

"I have been researching the vow though." Charlie protested.

"Why?" Ben growled.

"Because it needed doing." Charlie explained.

"You don't believe in any of this, why would you research something you don't believe in?" Ben countered.

"Edward has been telling me a lot about the promise and living with powers, as we bumped into each other in town yesterday and we have been speaking a bit." Charlie continued.

"Eugh!" Ben moaned.

"What have you learnt Charlie?" Lia asked quietly.

"There is an agreement between the two families that we will merge but there is nothing in the agreement that says the girl has to be from our family so there is a potential way round this." Charlie announced.

"That's why you agreed to go to dinner with Edward and his cousin." Ben suddenly realised.

"Yes, I was hoping that I could persuade Edward that we could still keep the promise but that he and Lia did not need to be the ones to fulfil it."

"So this is where we are all hanging out tonight." Sam observed, walking into the room and settling himself down on Lia's desk chair.

"We were just chatting about the promise and Charlie here is thinking about taking one for the team." Ben told Sam.

"Oh?" Sam enquired.

"Turns out Lia may not be the only girl in the two families." Ben grinned.

"Wow." Sam managed.

"Thank you Charlie." Lia managed, wiping at the tears that were still falling.

For a little while the only sound in the room was Lia's sniffles, as she continued to try and stop crying. The boys shifted uncomfortably but none of them moved to leave the room, they would never leave Lia upset.

"Who's up for a takeaway?" Sam asked, once Lia had settled down.

"We had one yesterday." Charlie stated.

"So? Mum and Dad are out again tonight, Lia is the only one of us who can cook and let's be honest she's in no state to cook, therefore takeaway is our best option." Sam declared.

"I vote Indian." Ben added.

"Or we could get pizza." Sam suggested.

"Pizza sounds good." Ben agreed.

"We can't have takeaway two nights running." Charlie continued to argue.

"There is no rule that says you can't order a takeaway two nights running and anyway weren't you originally planning to go out for dinner tonight." Ben observed.

"I would have had a proper meal not a pizza though." Charlie continued.

"You don't have to have a takeaway if you don't want to. You could go and raid the freezer and see what we have in there." Sam suggested.

"Lia, what do you want?" Ben asked, suddenly realising that she had not entered the dinner conversation.

"I'm not really that hungry." Lia said.

"You need to eat though." Charlie told her.

"Charlie you are acting like an old woman." Ben snapped.

"She can't just wallow in self pity because Aidan cheated on her." Charlie argued.

"Charlie! Leave her alone." Sam yelled.

"Can you all please go away?" Lia groaned. "I just want to be left alone."

Sam grabbed Charlie's arm and dragged him out of the room before he could protest or argue about anything else. Ben remained seated on Lia's bed, ignoring her request that they all leave. Lia slid into a ball on the edge of her bed and curled into herself.

"I said go away." Lia grumbled, when Ben relaxed against her pillows and stretched his legs out in front of him.

"I'm comfy." Ben responded.

"Ben please, I just need a little bit of time to myself to process this." Lia moaned.

"That's fine, process away, you won't even know I'm here." Ben said mildly.

"Ben, all I want to do is curl up in bed, watch girly movies and cry." Lia continued.

"How about we watch Disney movies again?" Ben suggested.

"I'm not in the mood for Disney today."

"Lia, I don't really want to leave you when you are upset." Ben tried.

"Ben, I just need a little bit of time to myself. I promise I will text you if I want company." Lia assured him.

Sighing, Ben levered himself off Lia's bed realising that maybe Lia needed a little bit of time to herself and that she would come around when she was ready.

"I'll bring you a slice of pizza." Ben said as he left the room.

Chapter Nine

5th January 2018

Lia was sat wrapped in her blanket at her desk, she had finally worked out how she wanted to write her Law essay and was typing away, trying to get it finished before she went back to school. She had woken up at six o'clock that morning and remained sat at her desk, since getting her first cup of tea that morning. Charlie had brought her a second cup when he got up at eight and her mum had brought her one up about ten minutes ago but primarily, she had been alone all morning. She picked up the drink and took a sip, as she paused in her essay, glancing down at her copy of the English Legal System and flicking to another page, that she had tabbed for quotes when she first started planning the essay.

"Go away." Lia called, at the knock on her door.

"Is everything OK?" her dad asked, through the door.

"Yeah, I'm just busy." Lia called.

"We are all a bit concerned." David continued, but he made no move to open her door.

Sighing, Lia picked up her tea and walked to open her bedroom door, slowly she gestured for her dad to come in.

"Your brothers told me that you and Aidan broke up." David stated, sitting down on Lia's bed.

Lia sank down onto her desk chair and took a mouthful of tea, then nodded at her dad.

"How are you doing?" David asked.

"Honestly, it sucks and I'm confused, I feel sick and I just want to curl up in a ball and cry." Lia admitted.

"Is there anything I could do to make it better?" David asked.

"Not at the moment." Lia told him. "I just need a little bit of time by myself to help process this."

"OK, but we are all here for you when you are ready." David assured, getting up from Lia's bed and heading back out of the room.

"Thanks Dad."

Lia pulled her blanket back around herself and settled herself down to continue to type up the essay. Putting her headphones in her ears, Lia settled on Adele to listen to while she was working, it suited her mood better than some of the other music that she liked to listen to. Tapping along with the music, she finished off her 2000 word essay and sent it down to the communal printer, located in the office. Wrapping the blanket tightly around herself, Lia got up and left her room. She moved very slowly down the stairs, creeping as quietly as she could past her brothers' rooms and continuing down to the ground floor.

A few steps from the bottom of the stairs, Betty and Veronica ran into the hallway to bark their greetings at Lia.

"Hi girls." Lia said, sitting down on the last stair so that she could pet the dogs.

Lia remained with the dogs sitting at the bottom of the stairs for a couple of minutes while she listened to the sound of FIFA being played in the back living room and tried to work out who Sam and Ben had round. Realising that it was just a couple of their college friends, she patted the dogs on their heads and she stood up continuing on her way into the office. The printer had run out of paper after the first page of her essay, so she pulled open the top drawer of the desk and replace the paper in the printer. She settled herself onto the desk chair to wait for the essay to finish printing and glanced out of the bay windows, when she heard a knock on the door.

Seeing that it was Edward, Lia ducked under the desk to avoid being spotted by him. She stayed in her hiding place while Ben opened the door.

"Good afternoon, Benjamin." Edward stated, once the door had opened.

"Sup?" was Ben's response.

"I was hoping to see if Charles and Amelia were free for lunch." Edward continued, undeterred by Ben's lack of enthusiasm.

"Charlie is working on a Biology project and I don't know where Lia is." Ben told him, blocking the door so Edward couldn't just waltz in.

"Oh, because I have been talking with Charles today and he led me to believe he would be free for lunch and that Amelia was here." Edward retorted.

"OK, well I will go and see what Charlie is up to but I don't think Lia's home. I think she went out for a bit." Ben said, finally letting Edward in. "Why don't you go into the front living room and I will get Charlie for you."

Checking that Edward was sat down, Ben turned and shut the door to the office, winking at Lia as he did. Lia heard Ben run up the stairs and then a few moments later she heard him come back downstairs with Charlie. Easing herself out from under the desk, Lia sat crosslegged on the floor, hidden from the window and began to proofread her essay. Having read through the essay three times, marking it with red pen and highlighters, Lia was thrilled to hear Edward and Charlie leaving for lunch.

"If you see Amelia please let her know she is welcome to join us, I know Emily would be thrilled to meet her before she starts at their school on Monday." Edward said to Ben, as he opened the door.

Lia didn't hear Ben's response as it was muffled by the sound of the door opening. Once the door had shut, Lia waited a minute before crawling out of the office so as not to get caught by Edward as he left the house.

"Thanks." Lia said to Ben, as she stood up.

"Not a problem. That guy is persistent." Ben commented, as Lia started up the stairs.

"What do you mean?" Lia asked, turning to face her brother.

"He doesn't give up. I have never met anyone who keeps getting so blatantly lied to, who will just keep coming back." Ben explained.

"He'll get the point eventually." Lia stated thoughtfully.

"I hope so, otherwise I'm going to have to start using the

old 'she's washing her hair' line." Ben joked.

"That's awful." Lia sighed, before she continued on her way back upstairs.

Back in her bedroom Lia sat down at her desk and reloaded her essay on her laptop, before clicking the itunes icon on the ribbon at the bottom of her computer and randomly shuffled her playlist to listen to while she was working. Singing along, Lia began to make the amendments to the essay that she had been working on downstairs. When she had finished she once again sent it downstairs to the communal printer.

Getting up from her desk, Lia headed out of her bedroom. This time she didn't creep downstairs but she did try to make her footsteps as quiet as possible. The dogs ran up to her when she got to the bottom of the stairs so she paused to pet them before she continued on her way into the office and grabbed her essay off the printer. This time rather than heading back up to her room, Lia went in search of her mum.

"Mum!" Lia called, heading into the front living room.

"Kitchen!" Diane called back.

Lia turned around and headed into the kitchen, where her mum was doing some of the washing up and her dad was hunting through the freezer for something.

"Are you feeling better?" David asked, when Lia came into the kitchen.

"Not really, but I have plenty of stuff to keep me occupied." Lia told him.

"What do you need?" Diane asked, drying her hands on the tea towel beside her.

"I've just finished my Law essay and was hoping you wouldn't mind giving it a once over." Lia explained.

"Not a problem."

"Thanks."

Lia placed her essay on the kitchen table so her mum could read it when she was ready and then began to make a pot of tea for them both. The boys and her dad tended to drink coffee or soft drinks. Leaving the drink brewing for a few minutes, Lia let the dogs out into the back garden as they were hovering around the back door. Lia watched as the dogs ran around outside, barking at the birds and squirrels who were perched on the fence. Betty came back into the house quite quickly but Veronica remained outside barking at something on the other side of the gate.

"Veronica!" Lia yelled, when Veronica ran round the corner of the house.

Veronica did not come back immediately so Lia slipped out of her slippers and into the pair of trainers that she left by the back door.

"Veronica!" Lia yelled, as she walked to the gate. "Come here!"

"Amelia?" came Edward's voice, from the other side of the fence.

"Edward? Hi." Lia managed, catching hold of Veronica's collar.

"I was hoping you would be around when I dropped Charles back off." Edward called, as Lia began dragging Veronica back into the house.

Sighing, Lia shut the back door as the dogs were now back inside and she didn't want to let too much cold air into the house. She saw that her mum had poured her a cup of tea and left it on the kitchen counter for her. Picking up the mug, Lia walked slowly from the kitchen towards the front door where Edward and Charlie were just coming inside, closely followed by a petite brunette.

"Amelia, it's good to see you again." Edward stated, when he spotted Lia standing by the stairs.

"Hi Edward." Lia said.

"This is my cousin Emily." Edward said, dragging the petite girl to stand next to him.

"Nice to meet you." Lia said, smiling at the girl.

"It's nice to meet you too, Edward's been telling me a lot about you."

"Oh." Lia managed.

"I was hoping that you and Emily would become friends, as she is going to start going to school with you on

Monday." Edward interrupted.

"Oh cool, what will you be studying?" Lia asked.

"Why don't we go and sit down?" Charlie suggested.

Lia nodded and directed Edward and Emily into the front living room, as Sam and Ben were continuing their group FIFA matches in the back one. Lia settled herself at one end of the sofa and Charlie sat down next to her. Emily and Edward both sat down in the chairs on the other side of the room.

"So, what subjects are you taking?" Lia asked, once everyone was settled in the living room.

"I'm taking both English classes and History." Emily answered.

"I take English Literature, it will be nice to have a friendly face in the class, none of my other friends take it." Lia explained.

"Anyone who I recognise will definitely make the first day easier." Emily admitted.

"I think we are moving onto Shakespeare's The Taming of the Shrew for the next few weeks." Lia told her.

"What were you studying before?" Emily asked.

"Our big topic was Wuthering Heights but we also dipped into some of the poetry aspects for a couple of weeks as a bit of a break. Have you read Wuthering Heights?"

"I love the Bronte sisters, I've read all their books." Emily exclaimed.

"Really?" Lia asked.

"Yeah, I love the darker nature of the Bronte's books." Emily explained.

"Fair enough. Ms Barter will love you, she's also a big fan of the Bronte sisters." Lia commented.

"Do you like their books?" Emily asked.

"I find them a bit hard to read, although I have read Wuthering Heights a couple of times I've also read Jane Eyre but that's about all I can manage." Lia admitted.

"Do you like reading?" Edward asked.

"Yes, I love to read. I just prefer books that use more modern English." Lia explained.

"What is your favourite book?" Edward probed.

"To Kill a Mockingbird is one of my favourite books and lots of thrillers but I also love the Harry Potter novels, they are part of my childhood." Lia offered.

"Do you not find the Harry Potter books offensive?" Edward asked horrified.

"No, they are wonderful stories that make me smile." Lia commented, feeling mildly affronted.

"You are an idiot, reading those books, they are just moronic. They make a mockery of our heritage. Books about magic should not be allowed, they show us as outcasts and unable to move on from the past." Edward announced.

"Are you actually kidding me, you turned up at mt door announcing that we need to start dating because of some centuries old promise that for all I know could very well be made up. Yet you are complaining about works of fiction showing us in an unfavourable light because they don't move on from the past." Lia queried, standing up.

"Edward I think it's time to go." Emily stated, standing up.

"You don't have to." Charlie offered.

"I feel Lia and I need to have a conversation about our destiny." Edward announced.

"I'm not interested." Lia declared, walking out of the living room.

Lia slammed the door as she left the room and then stalked into the back-living room, where Sam and Ben were holding a gaming competition with a group of friends. Lia glanced round and noted that only Matthew had come around from the group that were still at school. She got a quick pang of guilt for causing problems with her brothers' friends but shaking it off, Lia walked over to where Ben was lounging on a bean bag on the floor, cheering Liam on as he was playing against Sam. Tapping Ben on his shoulder to get his attention, Lia inclined her head towards the door and silently asked him to come with her.

"What's up?" Ben asked, as Lia closed the door to the living room so they weren't overheard.

"Edward is in the other living room with Charlie. He has just started to insult me over my choice of books and is now insisting that we talk about that stupid destiny thing." Lia muttered.

"Why is that a problem?" Ben asked.

"I don't like the way he talks to me, it's insulting but also I don't want to have to talk about that promise. I'm not interested in him and he's just going to insist that we are destined to be together."

Ben laughed and shook his head but he headed towards the front living room, regardless of his personal opinion on the situation, he was going to give Lia a hand. Lia trailed after him, making sure that Ben was positioned slightly in front of her but not completely hiding.

"Everything OK in here?" Ben asked, as he walked into the room.

"Your sister is being a bit melodramatic and unreasonable." Edward explained, before anyone else could answer.

"Oh?" Ben enquired.

"I was just explaining that she should be ashamed of herself for reading those moronic Harry Potter books. Then I wanted to have a conversation about our future together and she stormed out of the room. This is not the impression of Amelia that I wanted my cousin to have." Edward declared.

"In her defence, Ed, you did call her an idiot and yell at her." Emily interjected.

Edward turned to glare at his cousin who shrunk back in the chair and hugged her arms to her chest. Turning back to Ben, who was looking mildly amused, Edward darkened his glare in an attempt to intimidate him.

"I think you are going to have a lot of problems dating Lia, if you think that is unreasonable." Ben half laughed.

"Why?" Edward hissed, moving so he stood directly in front of Ben only to realise he could not tower over Ben who was 6ft 2in to Edward's 5ft 10in.

"Well, she is quite prone to slamming doors and stomping

out of rooms. It's a truly frustrating habit of hers but completely unbreakable." Ben continued on cheerfully.

"I'm sure I will be able to control her once we are together." Edward declared.

"I'm sorry! What did you just say?" Lia interrupted.

"This is what I have been trying to talk to you about Amelia. Once we have engaged in the proper courtship and been married, you will be my wife and I will look after you. You won't have to want for anything. All I must ask is that you refrain from such childish temper tantrums and we will be so very happy together." Edward announced.

"You are out of your mind!" Lia stated, before leaving the room again.

"Emily, as lovely as it was to meet you and I wish you could stay longer, I must ask you and Edward to leave now." Charlie said.

Emily nodded slowly then quickly gathered together her coat and handbag, Edward remained where he was and continued to glare at Ben, who was blocking him from following Lia.

"Move!" Edward demanded, shoving at Ben.

Ben moved slightly but grabbed the top of Edward's arm and used Edward's momentum to propel him out of the living room, towards the front door. Ben started to lose his grip so was grateful when he spotted Sam standing on the bottom step, preventing Edward from being able to follow Lia upstairs.

"I thought I heard Charlie ask you to leave." Sam said mildly, when Edward tried to shove him off the stairs.

"I will leave once I have finished my conversation with your sister!" Edward snarled.

"Ed!" Emily exclaimed.

"Be quiet!" Edward shouted, bringing the group of lads out of the back living room at the sound of all the commotion.

"Everything OK?" Jake, one of Sam's best mates asked.

"Yes, this guy just doesn't seem to know when he has worn out his welcome." Sam commented, gesturing at

Edward, who was silently fuming at the bottom of the stairs.

Glaring at all of the people who were now stood staring at him in the hallway, Edward half growled before he marched past Ben, Charlie and Emily to storm out of the house. Emily started to follow him out but before she got to the bottom of the drive, Edward had sped away.

From her bedroom window Lia spotted Emily standing in the middle of the drive, so she quickly ran downstairs and out of the house.

"Do you want to come back in?" Lia asked, as she stopped just behind Emily.

"Oh no, I don't want to be any trouble."

"It's not a problem, please come inside." Lia said, when Emily turned to face her.

"I don't want to impose, I know Edward has upset you and your brothers." Emily insisted.

"That was Edward, not you." Lia stated "Charlie seemed to like you and I was enjoying talking to you before Edward interrupted us"

"Are you sure?" Emily asked, looking uncertainly at the ground.

"Yeah, it's no problem." Lia insisted, propelling Emily back towards the house.

"I'm really embarrassed." Emily admitted, when Lia opened the front door.

"Why?" Lia asked, pausing as she stepped in the door.

"Ed made such a scene." Emily explained.

"So?"

"It just makes me feel quite awkward."

"If people felt awkward every time a scene was caused in our house, no one would ever come round. Trust me, it's nothing we haven't seen before." Lia told her, as she walked through to the kitchen.

"Isn't this a bit different though?" Emily asked, following Lia into the kitchen.

"Well, it's the first time someone has announced that they will be able to control me but other than that, no, it's like ninety percent of the other scenes that happen." Lia smiled. "Would you like anything to drink?"

"Can I have a glass of water please?"

"Sure."

Lia grabbed two glasses out of the kitchen cabinet and filled them up with water, then sat down across from Emily at the table.

"Can I ask you a question?" Lia asked, after watching Emily fiddle with her glass for a few minutes.

Emily looked up and nodded cautiously. Lia glanced around the room checking that they were alone in the kitchen.

"I know that Edward has some sort of magical power, do you have powers too?" Lia asked, whispering and leaning forward so that she couldn't be overheard.

Emily also glanced around the room and leant forward before nodding.

Lia leant back in her chair and took a sip out of her glass, while she thought about what Emily had confirmed and what questions she wanted to ask her. Both girls sat in silence for a few more minutes until Emily's phone rang in her handbag.

"Hello." Emily said, answering the phone.

"I'm still with Amelia." Emily said after a few seconds.

"OK, I'll see you in a few minutes." Emily told the person at the other end of the phone. "Edward is on his way back here to pick me up."

"That's fine. I'll just go get Sam and Ben, if you don't mind." Lia said, getting up from her chair.

"I understand, I can wait outside." Emily said, standing up and pulling her coat back on.

"No, you don't have to wait outside. I just don't particularly want to talk to him but one of my brothers will wait with you."

With that, Lia left the kitchen and walked next door into the living room where the eight boys were sprawled on every available seat in the room, playing FIFA. Walking to stand in front of the TV, Lia put her hands on her hips while the boys glared at her.

"Get out of the way!" Sam yelled.

"I need your attention." Lia retorted, shifting so she blocked more of the TV.

Glaring at her, Sam threw the controller at Jake who was sat next to him. Convinced that she had both her brothers' attention, Lia moved so that Jake and Phil could continue the game of FIFA that was currently being played.

"What now?" Sam groaned, as they all approached the living room door.

"Edward is on his way back to pick Emily up, I was hoping that one or both of you would wait with her in case he comes to the front door." Lia explained.

"I can't believe that posh prat forgot his own cousin." Sam muttered.

"Sam!" Lia admonished.

"Sorry, I just don't like him, he's a twat." Sam continued.

"We'll wait with Emily." Ben reassured his sister. "Why don't you say bye to her and then head upstairs, so you aren't hanging about when he gets here."

"Thanks." Lia said, as she darted back into the kitchen. "Sam and Ben are going to wait with you."

"Are you sure it isn't a problem, I know that Edward isn't their favourite person." Emily asked.

"They'll get over it." Lia assured her.

"Thanks Amelia." Emily said.

"Call me Lia, Amelia is what I get called when I'm in trouble." Lia told her smiling.

"OK, thanks Lia. I guess, I will see you on Monday at school." Emily commented, as they walked out of the kitchen.

"Yeah, I'll see you on Monday." Lia repeated, as she began to head up the stairs.

Lia was most of the way up the second flight of stairs when she heard a knock at the door. Pausing so she didn't make any noise, she waited until she heard the front door close again before she decided to edge back downstairs to talk to Charlie. Knocking on Charlie's closed door, Lia waited for him to open up.

"Charlie?" Lia called, when Charlie didn't open the door straight away.

Lia knocked again on Charlie's door and then again a little bit louder. Sighing when he didn't open the door, Lia turned away and headed back up to her room. She checked her watch as she was walking up the stairs and saw that it was nearly half past five. Shaking her head, she put on her dog walking jeans and a pair of thick fluffy socks, then pulled an oversized jumper over the top of her long-sleeved t-shirt that she was wearing. She then picked up her phone and texted Ben and Sam to see who was going to walk the dogs with her. She smiled at the debate that she knew would be going on downstairs.

Sam: It's my turn

Lia: Meet you downstairs in 2 minutes

Sam: Ok

Lia shoved her phone in the pocket of her jumper, grabbed her scarf and gloves off her cushion and headed downstairs. Once she had all her layers on, she got the leads out of the cupboard and clipped them onto the dogs' collars. She leant on the banister as Sam pulled his coat on and yanked the door open.

"Come on." Sam said, as he headed out.

"Wow, you're grumpy today." Lia commented, as she walked past Sam with the dogs.

"We have people round Lia." Sam retorted.

"We always have people round." Lia countered.

"That's not the point." Sam argued.

"What is the point?"

"It's just, oh never mind."

"No, tell me." Lia said, as they turned into the woods.

"It doesn't matter Lia, I'm just annoyed." Sam sighed.

"But what are you annoyed about? Is it helping me with the dogs?" Lia asked, bending down to take the leads off the dogs and let them run around.

"No, it's just the situation." Sam told her.

"What situation?" Lia continued.

"The one with you and Aidan and Edward and the whole stupid magic stuff. I mean it's never ending!" Sam blurted out.

"So, you are annoyed because we are all witches and I'm having guy trouble?" Lia asked.

"Well, it sounds ridiculous when you put it like that, doesn't it?" Sam observed, kicking at the ground.

"A little bit." Lia admitted.

"Well, let's just get the dogs walked." Sam decided.

Lia fell into step behind Sam and wandered along in silence, glancing around at all the rustling in the bushes. She was concerned about another encounter with the Foulds family whilst out with the dogs. She flinched at the sound of some twigs snapping around the next corner and sped up so that she was stood directly behind Sam.

"You OK?" Sam asked, glancing behind him.

"Yeah, I just thought I heard something." Lia told him.

"Don't wander off." Sam told her, pausing so he could wait slightly out of sight in case another person came around the corner to attack them.

Lia edged closer to the trees and headed a little way back down the path. She grabbed the dog's collars to prevent them from jumping at Sam if he needed to defend them. The bushes closest to the corner began to rustle more urgently, causing Lia to back further into the bushes and trees while Sam moved into a slightly crouched position so he could react quickly in the event of an attack.

Lia gasped, as she was suddenly pounced on by a large ball of fur and fell back into the bushes behind her. She smiled when she realised that it was Buster who was pinning her down. She managed to wriggle one hand out from underneath Buster and petted him then pushed him away, so she could clamber to her feet. Sam walked over and gave Lia a hand brushing the dirt off once she was on her feet. Lia rested her hand on Buster's head to stop him from jumping up at her and also to steady her. She knew that Aidan would be coming round the corner in a minute or two as she could hear him calling for Buster. Sam moved closer to Lia, as did Betty and Veronica, effectively forming a protective barrier for when Aidan appeared.

"Buster, there you are." Aidan said, just as he came round the corner. "Oh, hi Sam, Lia."

"Aidan." Sam snarled in greeting.

"How are you?" Aidan asked, turning to face Lia.

"I'm OK." Lia muttered, staring at her feet.

"I've been trying to call you." Aidan continued, moving slightly closer to Lia only to be blocked by Sam.

Lia continued to stare at her feet shifting her weight from foot to foot, avoiding Aidan's intense gaze.

"Lia, I need to talk to you, please hear me out." Aidan begged.

"What is there to say Aidan?" Lia whispered, bringing her gaze up to meet his.

"I just need to talk to you. I want to talk about what you said outside your bedroom the other day, you told me you loved me, we can't just not talk about that." Aidan begged.

"Aidan, I don't think that this is a good idea." Sam interrupted, before Lia could respond.

"I get that you are trying to protect Lia, Sam, but I just need a few minutes to talk to her, please." Aidan tried.

"Aidan" Lia managed.

"OK, I think this is enough." Sam interrupted, moving so he was once again between Lia and Aidan.

Tugging on Lia's hand, Sam whistled for the dogs and began to quickly continue the walk leaving Aidan to stare after them.

"Are you OK?" Sam asked, after a few minutes of dragging Lia at his brisk pace.

Lia nodded and swiped at the tears that remained on her cheeks.

"What are you going to do?"Sam asked.

"About what?" Lia asked.

"About Aidan?" Sam said, continuing to walk round the last bit of the woods.

"I   don't   know."   Lia   admitted.

Chapter Ten

8ᵗʰ January 2018

"Amelia, you are going to be late!" David yelled up the stairs to Lia, who was in her bathroom getting ready for the first day back at school after the Christmas holidays.
"I'm coming." Lia yelled back, giving her reflection one last critical glance.
She had taken a bit longer to get ready that morning as she was nervous about seeing Aidan again. They hadn't seen each other since the evening in the woods and she wanted to make sure she looked as good as she could. Walking quickly back into her bedroom, she pulled on a pair of stiletto heeled boots and grabbed her book bag off her bedroom floor. Picking up her note pad and the Law textbook that was open on her desk, she shoved them into the bag and ran downstairs.
"How are you always the last one ready?" Sam asked, pushing himself off the wall he was leaning against.
"I'm not always last." Lia retorted, pulling on her gloves as they walked out of the house.
"True, Ben is last occasionally but most of the time it's you, which by the way, makes no sense as you are the only family member who does not share a bathroom." Charlie observed, as they all climbed into the Taylor family people carrier.
This was the first day for their new morning routine. Lia had decided that she didn't feel comfortable getting a lift with Aidan, they had all agreed that they would try and adjust, so David would now drive them all in the morning, dropping the boys off at college, then take Lia to school. There were still a couple of problems at the end of the day but they would plan that out depending on what time they all finished and when David had meetings with his clients.
"I'm the only girl." Lia retorted, fastening her seatbelt.
"That's not a reason to be the last one ready every day."

Sam commented.

"I have more to do in the mornings than you do." Lia protested.

"Does this really matter?" Ben groaned, from the seat next to Lia.

"Someone got up on the wrong side of the bed." Sam smirked, turning to face his brother.

"Get stuffed." Ben retorted, shoving his jacket against the window and closing his eyes.

"You got in late last night Ben." Charlie observed.

"I was out." Ben mumbled, not bothering to open his eyes.

"Who with?" Sam asked.

"What's it to you?" Ben asked, still not bothering to open his eyes.

"Just curious." Sam muttered, turning back round in his seat.

"Christ." Ben sighed.

The car journey continued in silence. Lia pulled out her phone and read through the conversation that Siobhan and Heather had been having that morning that she had been a part of in the beginning but had abandoned when she had realised that she was running late. The conversation had moved on from what to wear and where they were meeting that morning.

Heather: Do we have History today? X

Siobhan: Yes x

Lia: Is there any chance we could move seats a bit? X

Siobhan: Not a problem x

Heather: You still not talking to Aidan? X

Lia: Not yet... it's still really fresh x

Siobhan: Is the new girl taking History? X

Lia: I think so but I can't remember x

Siobhan: Did you ask? X

Lia: I know she's taking both Englishes x

Heather: You got distracted, didn't you lol x

Lia: Haha! x

Siobhan: Lol typical x

Smiling, Lia put her phone back in the front pocket of her

bag and then went through to check that she had everything she needed.

"If you've forgotten something Lia, you'll have to do without." David commented, watching his daughter searching.

"I've got everything, I think." Lia commented, catching her dad's eye in the rear view mirror.

"No one comment." David demanded.

"What?" Sam said, pulling his headphones out of his ears.

"Never mind, I just don't need another stupid squabble this morning." David told his son.

"Is everything OK, Dad?" Charlie asked.

"Yes, everything is fine." David ground out.

"Seriously Dad, what's up?" Ben piped up, opening his eyes and sitting up a bit straighter in his seat.

"There is nothing wrong, I just have a headache and don't need any more of your petty squabbles this morning, so let's continue the rest of the journey in silence." David then turned on the radio to prevent any further discussion.

Lia exchanged a look with Ben, who shrugged before pulling his headphones out of his bag and tuning the world out. Lia glanced at Sam and Charlie, who had also put their headphones in. Realising this must be part of their morning routine, Lia routed around in the front pocket of her handbag until she pulled out the tangled pink wires of her headphones. Ben saw Lia's headphones and shook his head, before he pulled them out of her hands and untangled them for her. Once they were free, he passed them back to her and settled back against his seat. Lia plugged her headphones into her phone and began scrolling through the collection of music she until she found Little Mix and selected their Glory Days album. Once she had the album on shuffle, Lia logged onto Facebook and scrolled through the usual selection of selfies, complaints and grumbles. Liking a few posts from a couple of her friends and a variety of cute animal pictures and videos, she came out of the App when she saw that Emily had sent her a message.

Emily: Can I meet you somewhere before school starts? X
Lia: I'll meet you by the front gate x
Emily: Thanks, I'm a bit nervous x
Lia: Why? x
Emily: I get nervous when I have to meet new people x
Lia: I wouldn't worry most of the people are friendly x
Lia: I'll be with my two oldest friends when we meet up, that will give you three people you know before you start x
Emily: Thanks x
Lia: I'll be there in about 15 mins x
Emily: Ok see you soon x

As Lia finished off her text exchange with Emily, David pulled up outside the college, so that Ben, Charlie and Sam could get out of the car.

"I'll be here at 4." David called, before Ben could slam the door shut.

The boys all acknowledged this with either a nod or hand gesture, Lia scrambled over the back of the middle seats so she could get out more easily when they got to her school. Once Lia had her seatbelt on, David pulled away from where he had stopped and headed towards the school to drop Lia off. Lia continued to listen to Little Mix and smiled to herself when No More Sad Songs and Shout to my Ex came on one after the other, giving her a bit of a boost before she got to the school gates.

"I'll pick you up shortly after half three." David told Lia, as they came to a stop in front of Siobhan and Heather. "Try not to be too late."

"Thanks Dad." Lia called, as she scrambled out of the car.

"Hi." Lia called to her friends once she was out of the car.

Siobhan and Heather waved and watched as Lia got the strap of her bag caught on her head as she walked over to them. On a half laugh, Siobhan came forward and helped Lia with her bag before she tripped over.

"How have you survived this long?" Heather asked, laughing once Lia was finally organised.

"I have you." Lia retorted with a smile. "Oh, that reminds me, I told Emily that we would meet her here, so she

doesn't have to go in by herself."
"That was nice of you." Siobhan observed.
"I am nice." Lia laughed.
"You keep telling yourself that." Heather teased.
"Oh, there's Emily." Lia said, waving at Emily as she got out of the dark grey Audi A7.
"Wow, that is an impressive car." Heather whispered.
"Since when are you interested in cars?" Lia asked, turning to look at her friend.
"Luke likes checking out cars and apparently it's starting to rub off on me." Heather commented, with a half laugh.
"Hi." Emily said, pausing close to the group.
"Hi, I'm Siobhan." Siobhan started, gesturing to herself. "This is Heather and you've met Lia, I believe."
"Yes, it's nice to meet you." Emily said smiling.
"Nice to meet you too." Heather said "Do you know what subjects you are taking?"
"I'm taking English Literature, English Language and History." Emily replied.
"That's good, we all take History, so we can catch you up without too much trouble and I'm sure Lia has spoken to you at length about English Literature." Siobhan started cheerfully, as they headed into school.
With Siobhan looking after Emily, Lia fell into step with Heather, who was glancing around to see where Luke was. The girls stopped by their lockers and agreed to meet back there at break time. They had different classes first and Emily had a meeting with the head of sixth form to sort out the details of her joining mid-way through the year.
Dumping her History and Law textbooks in her locker, Lia pulled out her notebook that she used for her English class and headed off towards her first lesson of the day.
"Lia!" Luke called, jogging over to her with Matthew trailing behind.
"Hi." Lia smiled, when they both reached her.
"Where are you off to?" Luke asked.
"I've got English." Lia stated, gesturing towards the classroom she had been heading for.

"Do you have a second?" Matthew asked.

"I don't, I can't be late." Lia told them, trying to edge past them to her class.

"It will just take a second." Luke said, blocking her escape route.

"It will have to be later, I have English and I can't be late." Lia insisted.

"OK but can we talk after?" Matthew asked.

"I suppose so, I have a free period after this." Lia said warily.

With that, Luke and Matthew nodded and let Lia duck into her class, just before it began. Sliding into her customary seat towards the back of the class, Lia quickly pulled out her pad and pens so she was ready.

"I trust everyone had a good break and is back and ready to learn." Ms Barter announced, moving to the front of the classroom.

"Excellent, for the next eight weeks we will be focusing on Shakespeare's The Taming of the Shrew because, as you all know we must study one Shakespeare text for this course." Ms Barter continued. "We will each have a role in the play and will read our various parts over the course of the next week in an effort to make this a more enjoyable experience."

Ms Barter then passed out the copies of the play, that were sitting on her desk and watched as the class began to flick through it.

"For today's class, I will be going through the synopsis of the play and starting to pick who will read each character." She announced, when the class began chatting amongst themselves.

Falling back into relative silence, Ms Barter began to give a detailed review of the play. Starting with the prank played on the drunk tinker and that the play itself was a story inside a story, before going into detail about the schemes that the male characters came up with to get Bianca and to tame Katherina. After talking about the play for about 40 minutes, Ms Barter finished her detailed overview of the play and began to write the name of all the characters down on the board.

"OK, does anyone have a preference on who they would like to be?" Ms Barter asked, turning back to the class.

Callum, the flamboyant but well meaning Drama student put his hand up immediately. "Can I please be Petruchio?"

"Of course."

At that moment there was a knock on the classroom door, Ms Barter scowled slightly at the interruption before calling for whoever was knocking to enter. The door opened and in marched the head of sixth form, Mr Mallory, followed by Emily.

"Sorry for the interruption." Mr Mallory boomed out in greeting.

"Not a problem."

"I just wanted to introduce you to your newest student, Emily Carter, she is joining us for the remainder of this year."

"It's nice to meet you, please have a seat."

Emily nodded and walked quickly over to sit at the desk behind Lia. Reviewing the class, Mr Mallory nodded, then turned on his heel and left the room.

"OK, where were we?" Ms Barter asked, once the door had closed.

"We were just splitting into characters." Vanessa volunteered.

"OK and have you got any preference on who you would like to read?" Ms Barter asked.

"Yes, my New Year's Resolution is to challenge myself more so I would like to play Hortensio." Vanessa announced.

"Whatever you would like to do is fine with me." Ms Barter mumbled, turning back to the board to write Vanessa's name next to Hortensio.

"Amelia, would you like to volunteer?" Ms Barter asked, picking on Lia because she had been teaching her for a few years and knew that Lia wouldn't volunteer unless asked.

Lia glanced up from her pad, where she had been doodling

in the margins, she glanced around the class and saw that everyone was staring at her. Putting her pen down, she reviewed the notes that she had made while Ms Barter had been giving her overview.

"Erm… Bianca." Lia managed, after a few seconds.

"Excellent." Ms Barter said, writing Lia's name on the board. "OK, Joe is there any character you would like to play?"

Once all the roles were given out, Ms Barter allowed the class to pack up after telling them that they would be starting the reading in the next class on Wednesday.

"Emily, may I have a word?" Ms Barter called, as the class began to walk out.

"I'll wait outside." Lia told Emily, before she shut the door behind her.

Once outside, Lia took a deep breath remembering that Matthew and Luke wanted to talk to her during her free period. Lia pulled out her phone and texted Heather to see if she could find out what this talk was about, before meeting up with the boys.

Lia: Do you know why your bf wants to talk to me? X

Heather: He hasn't said anything to me x

Lia: Oh! He ambushed me with Matt just before my English class and all but demanded to talk to me x

Heather: Give me a sec, I'm with him I'll find out x

Trusting Heather's ability to get any details out of her boyfriend, Lia put her phone back in the front pocket of her bag and waited for Emily to finish off her conversation with Ms Barter. After a minute or two, Lia felt her phone vibrate indicating a text had just come in.

Heather: Luke won't tell me what this is about but has said I can come with if you want x

Lia: Please x

Heather: No problem x

Lia: I'll meet you by the lockers in a min just waiting for Emily x

Putting her phone back in her bag, Lia glanced up at the door as it opened and Emily came out looking particularly worried.

"Is everything OK?" Lia asked.

"Yeah, I just hadn't thought about the amount of work that I will need to catch up on. That's just for one class, I haven't even been to the other classes yet!" Emily cried.

"It's OK, I'll help you catch up in English Lit and all of us take History, so you can easily catch up in that." Lia reassured her.

"It's just a lot of pressure." Emily admitted.

"I'll help in anyway I can." Lia promised. "Do you have a lesson now or are you free?"

"I have English Language." Emily said, looking at the timetable she had neatly placed in her diary.

"OK, well that's right next door. We are meeting by our lockers at break if you want to join us." Lia said.

"That would be good." Emily managed.

"OK, I'll see you in a bit." Lia called over her shoulder, as she headed off towards the lockers to meet up with Heather and Luke.

When Lia walked into the main hallway where their lockers were, she paused as she saw Aidan waiting with the group. Heather spotted Lia before the guys did and broke away, so she could catch Lia before she got to them.

"I'm so sorry." Heather whispered, when she reached Lia.

"Did you know he was going to be here?" Lia whispered back.

"No, I had no idea. I should have guessed though as this is about the only thing that Luke would keep a secret from me." Heather sighed.

Lia remained silent and didn't make a move to join the boys, who by now had noticed her. Heather kept her hand on Lia's arm in an effort to comfort her. Lia continued to stare at the boys, until Luke broke away from the other two and walked the few metres to where the girls were standing. Heather shifted her position, so that she was standing next to Lia and glared at Luke when he stopped in front of them.

"What were you thinking?" Heather hissed at Luke.

"Aidan asked me to help him talk to Lia." Luke explained.
"And you just agreed to it?" Heather continued.
"He just wants to talk to her Heather, it's not a big deal." Luke insisted.
"Yes, it is a big deal." Heather insisted.
"How is it a big deal?" Luke asked.
"Because it's upsetting her. I told you that she was upset about what had happened and you have just ignored me." Heather told him.
"He's my friend, Heather." Luke pleaded.
"And Lia's mine." Heather retorted.
Shoving his hands through his hair, Luke shook his head before turning around and stalking over to where Aidan and Matthew were now staring at him.
"I didn't mean to cause a fight between you and Luke." Lia whispered, once Luke was a safe distance away.
"It's OK." Heather reassured her.
"What do you want to do?" Heather asked, after a few seconds of silence.
"I suppose I should go talk to him." Lia managed, squaring her shoulders slightly.
"I'm right behind you." Heather told her, as they walked slowly over to where the boys were still standing.
Once they had reached the boys, Luke and Matthew moved so that they weren't crowding the conversation, whereas Heather remained right next to Lia with her hand on the small of Lia's back in a gesture of support.
"Hi." Aidan said, smiling at Lia.
"Hi."
"I was hoping to talk to you in private." Aidan said, glancing at Heather.
"Heather is staying." Lia told him.
"Come on Lia, this is between us." Aidan said.
"I'll listen to what you have to say but Heather is staying." Lia insisted.
"You are being ridiculous." Aidan ground out.
"How?" Lia asked.
"Because you're acting like you need to be protected from

me!" Aidan yelled.

"There's no need to shout at her, Aidan." Heather told him, when Lia backed away from him slightly.

"I don't even know why you are here." Aidan said, lashing out at Heather.

"I'm here because Lia wants me to be." Heather said, standing her ground despite Aidan towering over her.

"There is no need for you to be here, this is nothing to do with you." Aidan growled.

"Aidan." Lia said warily.

"Look, I just need to talk to you and I can't do it with an audience." Aidan explained, turning to her.

Lia remained silent, as Aidan fixed her with a furious glare.

"Fine, seeing as you want your friend here, I might as well just say everything I need to say now as you'll clearly run back and tell her everything after we're done." Aidan snapped, feeling trapped, he wanted to tell Lia how he felt but couldn't do that in front of anyone yet so went with the opposite approach. "I think you are acting like a child, hiding behind your friend and your brothers. Honestly, you need to grow up. You can't just throw things away when you don't get what you want, although you clearly think that that's the way the world works. I'm so glad that we are no longer together because dating you was the single worst decision I have ever made."

Lia bit down on her lower lip to prevent herself from crying at Aidan's cruel words and leaned into Heather when she hugged her. Blinking to clear the tears that had started to form, Lia nodded at Aidan.

"Well, I'm glad everything is out in the open." Lia stated, before she turned and fled the hallway with Heather only a second behind her.

Standing outside in the courtyard, Lia wrapped her arms around herself and let the tears that had been forming roll down her cheeks. Heather hugged Lia and held her tight while she cried. After a couple of minutes the tears stopped and Lia straightened up. Swiping at the last of the tears on her cheeks, Lia met Heather's eyes and managed a small smile.

"He's a jerk, Lia." Heather told her.

"How am I supposed to face him at school everyday?" Lia asked, as she stared round the courtyard in disbelief.

"By relying on your friends. Once I tell Siobhan, Callum, Jessica, Kate and Emily what's just happened, there is no way that he will be able to get within 10 feet of you." Heather announced.

"I'll help keep him away." Luke said, coming out from around the corner.

"I'm sorry, I should have listened to you." Luke told Heather, before turning to Lia "I'm so sorry, I never would have asked you to come and talk to him if I had known that he was going to say that."

"Can we talk about this later?" Heather snapped.

"Heather." Lia gasped.

"I just want to focus on you right now, Luke can apologise later." Heather explained.

Luke nodded his acceptance and wandered off back inside, while Lia leant back against the wall behind her. Heather dropped her hands from Lia's shoulders and pulled out her phone.

"What are you doing?" Lia asked.

"I'm texting a few of our friends to help keep Aidan away from you." Heather explained, as she typed rapidly into her phone.

"Thanks Heather."

"Anytime." Heather assured her. "Do you want to head back inside? It's freezing out here."

"Sure."

Lia pushed herself up from the wall and trailed after Heather. Inside, Heather glanced over her shoulder at Lia and then decided to head towards the library as there was less chance of bumping into Aidan or any of his friends than if they went to the canteen or the common room.

"Heather, Lia wait up." Callum called, spotting them as he headed out of the theatre.

"Do you mind?" Heather asked.

"Not at all, I could do with some of his enthusiasm." Lia said, smiling at Callum when he joined them

"How was your break?" Callum asked, as they walked into the library.

"Good, yours?" Heather asked, sitting down at the closest table.

"Yeah, pretty good." Callum replied.

"You ready for this term's performance piece?" Callum asked.

"I'm still trying to pick what I would like to do, there is so much to choose from." Heather admitted laughing.

Leaving her friends to talk about their Drama class, Lia got up from the desk where she was sitting and headed over to the fiction section of the library. She strolled around the few aisles of books, picking up a book occasionally and reading the blurb before putting it back. Frowning slightly, she picked up a book she hadn't seen before, the red cover and title Don't Tell catching her attention. Reading the blurb, she decided that this was her sort of book, part crime thriller and part romance. Walking back over to where Callum and Heather were still chatting happily, Lia settled herself back into her chair and began to read.

Lia jumped when the bell rang signalling the end of her first free period and that break was about to start, she had been engrossed in what she was reading.

"I'm just going to get Siobhan and Emily, I'll be right back." Heather told her, when Lia looked up at her slightly confused.

"Heather told me that you and Aidan broke up over the Christmas break." Callum said matter of factly, when Heather left the library.

"Yes, we did and according to him, dating me was the biggest mistake he has ever made." Lia mumbled sadly.

"He said that?" Callum gasped scandalised.

"Yep." Lia muttered.

"Well that's a load of bull, isn't it?" Callum declared.

Lia glanced up at him and smiled.

"Well it is. Have you seen some of the tramps that he has dated in the past, honestly he should be worshipping the ground you walk on, babe." Callum continued.

"Oh my God, Lia! Heather just told us what happened with Aidan." Siobhan exclaimed, running over and hugging Lia.

"I was just saying that she is far too good for him anyway." Callum assured Siobhan.

"Oh, she really is." Heather agreed.

On this note of agreement, Siobhan sat down in the seat next to Lia, with Heather opposite and Emily next to Callum.

"So Emily, how has your first couple of hours in this complete dump been?" Callum asked, turning his attention to Emily.

"It's a bit different to what I am used to." Emily admitted, staring round the library.

"Where did you live before?" Siobhan asked.

"In London." Emily replied.

"Whereabouts in London?" Callum enquired.

"Kensington."

"Oh wow! Did you ever meet any one famous?" Callum asked.

"Did you go shopping all the time?" Heather asked.

"Why did you move up here?" Lia asked.

"I saw the occasional famous person but never spoke to any of them. We did do quite a bit of shopping. I moved up here because my grandmother wanted to get away from the city and she needs someone with her." Emily stated, answering all the questions as quickly as she could.

"So, how has everyone else's first day been?" Lia asked, sensing that Emily was feeling a bit uncomfortable.

"Pretty much the same as every other day we are at school." Heather muttered.

"Oh come on Heather, it's not that bad." Siobhan laughed.

"It really is, so far today I've been bored stupid for an hour in Biology, watched an absolute jerk yell at my oldest friend and my boyfriend is an idiot." Heather argued.

"OK, so maybe this has not been the best start to the term for you and Lia but it can only go up from here." Siobhan continued. "Emily, please tell me you have had a good start to the day."

"Not really, I've just found out how much work I need to catch up on for both Englishes and I still have to find out about History." Emily said.

"I promised Emily that we would help her catch up in History." Lia commented.

"Yeah, we could have a girly night in with movies and we can go over all of our notes." Siobhan cried.

"You should watch Ten Things I Hate About You." Callum commented.

"Why?" Emily asked.

"Well, we are studying the Taming of the Shrew in English Lit and Ten Things I Hate About You is loosely based on it, so technically it counts as studying." Callum explained.

The bell went signalling the end of their short break. Lia picked up the book she was reading as she had another free period, while the rest of her friends began to scramble to get to their various classes. Settling back in, Lia was almost immediately absorbed in the story and didn't notice when Aidan came up to her.

"Lia." Aidan said, tapping her on the shoulder.

Lia jumped and threw her hands up, causing all of the books on the shelf in front of her to come crashing down onto the floor. Lia spun round to face Aidan, before immediately spinning back round to see the damage she had caused.

"What the hell?" Aidan gasped, staring at the books.

Sensing that Aidan was momentarily distracted, Lia quickly slid from the desk and ran into the girls toilets, where she locked herself in one of the cubicles until she felt a bit calmer. Focusing purely on her breathing, Lia sank down onto the lid of the toilet and rested her head on her hands. After a few minutes she began to feel a little calmer, however when she checked her watch she saw that she still had another 40 minutes to kill before her friends would be with her. Carefully sliding her phone out of the front pocket of her bag she sent a quick message to Ben.

Lia: Having a bad day

Ben: ??

Lia: Had a fight with Aidan and then managed to send a whole load of books flying ☹

Ben: Avoid Aidan.. I'll talk to him later

Lia: Thanks

Chapter Eleven

"Are you sure that you are OK to come round?" Emily asked Lia, for the fourth time that day.
"It's not a problem." Lia assured her, glancing behind her at her new found friend. "My dad has agreed that it isn't problem."
"I'm sorry, it's just that Edward got really cross with me for bothering you on a Thursday, as it's normally your craft training day." Emily whispered, as they crossed the school carpark to where Emily's grandmother's car was waiting for them.
"Emily, I mean it. It's not a problem and you don't need to worry about it." Lia repeated.
"OK." Emily sighed, giving in as she opened the car door and slid in.
"Hi Grandma." Emily chirped, as she got in the car.
"Good afternoon Mrs Carter." Lia said in greeting, sliding into the car next to Emily.
"Good afternoon girls, and Amelia, please call me Maureen." Mrs Carter greeted the girls as they buckled up their seatbelts. "How was school today girls?"
"It was fine." Emily told her.
"Did you learn anything exciting?" Maureen continued to ask.
"Not particularly, two hours learning about language diversity, followed by an hour of Taming of the Shrew, then an hour about the War of the Roses, then an hour on how America gained dominance through economic change and development." Emily said, outlining her day.
"So which of those topics are you two looking into tonight?" Maureen asked.
"The Taming of the Shrew. We are looking at the Katherina final speech and its meaning. So Lia and I are just doing some research together before we have to write

our essay." Emily explained.

"How are you planning to approach this?" Maureen asked.

"I am planning to approach this from the character development point of view. She starts off being unwilling to do what any man says, but by the end of the play, she tells the other women the importance of obeying their husbands." Emily explained.

"What about you Amelia?" Maureen asked.

"I have been focusing on the play's impact on feminism, as this is one of the more important issues that we are facing at the moment." Lia explained.

"Have you always been interested in feminism Amelia?" Maureen asked, glancing at Lia through the rearview mirror.

"Growing up with three brothers has taught me to appreciate the importance of being able to stand your ground and ensure equal treatment for both sexes. My brothers have all been taught that men and women are equal. So yeah, I guess I've always had an appreciation for feminism." Lia offered.

"Hmmm." Maureen responded.

Lia shifted in her seat, feeling slightly uncomfortable under Maureen's stern look through the rearview mirror, so dropped her gaze from the mirror to her feet. The next ten minutes of the car journey continued in silence with only the sound of the indicator interrupting it, every couple of minutes. Maureen pulled the car onto the drive, ensuring that she left plenty of room for another car.

"Is someone coming to visit Grandma?" Emily asked, glancing at the space between the wall and her grandmother's car.

"Edward is coming up for a week or two." Maureen told Emily, as she got out of the car.

"Oh, I didn't know." Emily gasped, glancing over at Lia, who was now focusing on looking for something in her bag.

Lia looked up and met Emily's gaze, Emily mouthed that she was sorry. Nodding, Lia pulled her bag onto her shoulder and climbed out of the car to follow Maureen into the house. Emily gathered up her bag, then followed her grandmother and Lia in.

Once inside the house, Lia and Emily took off their shoes and hung their coats up on the coat pegs, before picking their bags up and heading through into the dining room where they would study for the next couple of hours. After they had been reading for a while, staring at the dialogue from the play highlighting various passages that would help the two of them write their essays, Maureen came in to the dining room to place a plate of biscuits on the table and pass both girls a cup of tea.

"Thank you, Grandma." Emily said, as Maureen left the room.

"Are we allowed to use other texts to back up our points in the essay?" Lia asked, sipping on her tea as she leafed through the play.

"I'm pretty sure we should be able to." Emily commented.

"Good, I have a couple of ideas of how I want to write my essay." Lia stated.

"That's good. I know at least a couple of the passages I want to use but I have no idea how to start the stupid thing." Emily commented, pushing her copy of the play away from her.

"Have you tried writing out some bullet points and seeing if you can arrange your beginning from those?" Lia asked.

"What would that do?" Emily asked.

"It would allow you to see what you want to say and therefore you might be able to write an introduction based on those points." Lia explained.

"Where did you learn that?" Emily asked.

"It's something that my mum taught me a couple of years ago, I use it on any of my essays that I don't know how to start." Lia commented.

"Does it work?"

"Sometimes, other times it just gives me an idea of what not to do."

Before Emily could ask another question, the sound of a

car engine interrupted her train of thought. Lia shifted in her seat and glanced towards the door, preparing herself for Edward's impending arrival. Watching for him out of the corner of her eye, Lia picked her pen back up and attempted to make it look like she was busy studying, hoping that it would prevent Edward from coming in when he spotted her. He had been back in London for the last six weeks but that hadn't stopped him from calling and texting her, requesting that they meet up when he was back in town.

"Edward, Edward, come in, come in." Maureen cooed, as she opened the door almost immediately after Edward had knocked.

"Hello Grandma." Edward greeted her, coming into the house.

"You are in luck my dear, Emily is in the dining room studying with Amelia." Maureen advised him.

"Hello Emily. Amelia it is lovely to see you again." Edward said, coming into the dining room where the girls were sat.

"Edward, I didn't know you were coming." Emily commented, glancing up at her cousin.

"Well, I established that it was your half-term next week so I felt it was a good time to visit you and Grandma." Edward replied mildly, as he continued into the dining room.

"Oh, well, it's a lovely surprise." Emily murmured, turning her attention back to the play in front of her.

"I wasn't expecting to see you today Amelia." Edward stated, sitting down in one of the chairs next to Lia.

"Emily and I have a big essay to write over half-term, so we thought it would be good to have a planning session together." Lia explained, gesturing at all the stuff on the table.

"I was under the impression from Charles, that your father liked to conduct his tutorials on a Thursday evening." Edward commented, staring intently at Lia.

"He lets us have the occasional lesson off, if we have

school work to do." Lia responded mildly.

"Surely learning your craft is more important than having a little planning meeting with your friend." Edward retorted.

"I would disagree." Lia continued, using the same mild tone.

"Has your father not taught you the importance of your role in our world?" Edward hissed.

"He has explained our family's history to me and I have read a few of the books that have been kept by our ancestors. Whilst I appreciate that our family had some influence on the Wiccan community in the past, I'm not sure that this is the case nowadays." Lia offered.

Clearly frustrated, Edward slammed his hands down on the table before taking a number of deep breaths and storming out of the dining room. Once Edward had left the room, Lia sighed and leant back in her seat, with her eyes closed. Sensing Emily's concern, Lia opened one eye so she could look at her friend, who was staring at the door that Edward had just closed.

"Sorry Em." Lia said, when her friend turned back to face her.

"It's not your fault." Emily whispered.

"Do you want me to leave?" Lia asked, watching Emily's face.

"No, I like having the company but I understand if you feel you should because of Edward." Emily said.

"I'll stay for a bit longer but I don't think I'll stay for dinner tonight, if that's OK?" Lia asked.

Emily smiled and nodded. Sensing Emily's relief that she wasn't going to abandon her, Lia picked her pen back up and continued working on the mind map that she had started just before Edward had arrived. Using a number of different coloured pens and highlighters, Lia managed to get the mind map to show the basic themes that she wished to cover in her essay, a comparison of Katherina with her sister at the beginning of the play and also between Katherina at the beginning and end of the play.

"I thought you were meant to be planning an essay not doodling." Edward sneered, making Lia jump as she hadn't registered that he had come back into the dining room, let alone that he was standing behind her.

"I often use mind maps to help with my essays." Lia retorted, trying to keep calm.

"That is a complete waste of time." Edward told her.

"Ed, you can't say that." Emily piped up.

"Why not? It's completely obvious that this has no educational value, its just a stupid picture." Edward retorted, picking up Lia's mind map and showing it to Emily. "How would something like this be a useful tool for studying?"

"It tells me the themes I plan to use in my essay and I can add any details that I wish, whenever I need to." Lia snapped.

"Doodles should not be used as plans." Edward stated patronisingly.

"Why does it bother you how I plan my essay? Lia asked.

"The way that you plan something shows the sort of person that you are. This sort of ridiculous doodle clearly indicates that the person who made it is unorganised and unstructured. Not the sort of person who I am destined to spend the rest of my life with." Edward explained to Lia, as if she were a child.

"This is how I plan a lot of my essays so clearly we aren't destined to be together because I am quite a disorganised person." Lia commented cheerfully.

"I thought you said that you had studied the books that have been written by your ancestors!" Edward exploded.

"I have." Lia replied, batting her eyes in mock innocence.

"Then you must realise that it is our destiny to be together. I am up here for the next seventeen days, let's go out for dinner and then you will see that we are meant to be together." Edward declared, almost desperately.

"I'm not sure that is a good idea." Lia started.

"It's an excellent idea, it will be the beginning of our relationship." Edward interrupted, looking pleased with himself.

"Edward, please listen to me. I am not interested in dating you and therefore I don't think that going out to dinner with you is a good idea." Lia protested.

"Why do you keep saying that you aren't interested in dating Edward?" Maureen asked, bustling into the dining room.

"Because I'm not." Lia stated. "Thank you for letting me study here this evening but I think it's best if I head home now."

Lia quickly began to gather her things and shoved them into her bag in a haphazard manner. Sliding out of her chair, Lia grabbed her phone off the table and jammed in her passcode.

"How are you going to get home Amelia?" Maureen asked.

"I'm just texting my mum now, to see if she can come and get me." Lia stated, scrolling through her texts until she found the conversation with her mum.

"Oh, there is no need to put her out, I'll take you home." Edward announced, trying to be charming.

"Edward, I really don't think this is the best idea." Emily interrupted, before anyone else could voice an opinion.

"Nonsense Emily, your friend has to get home and Edward is being the perfect gentleman offering to drive her home." Maureen told her granddaughter.

"I really don't want to impose. You have only just arrived Edward, you should be spending time with your family." Lia commented mildly, trying hard not to start another fight.

"It's no bother at all Amelia." Edward advised, placing his hand on her arm just above the elbow and leading her out the door.

Stopping by the front door, Lia sighed and glanced at Emily, who mouthed sorry to her before she put her shoes and coat back on. Edward looked at her slightly mud-caked boots with a look of disgust as he opened the front door and gestured for Lia to leave.

"See you tomorrow Emily." Lia called.

"Bye."

With a wave to Maureen before he shut the door, Edward punched a button on his car keys and opened the passenger seat door for Lia. Sliding into the seat, Lia placed her bag by her feet, ensuring that she still had a hold of the strap in case she needed to make a quick exit. Edward neatly slid into the driver's seat and tapped a couple of buttons so the engine and the radio came on. Lia relaxed slightly in the comfortable grey leather seats, as Edward flicked on the seat warmers but she kept one eye on Edward, knowing that the destiny conversation was not over.

"I will be in town until the 25th February, that should allow us time to have a couple of dates." Edward announced, as he pulled out of driveway.

"Edward, I really don't want to have to keep having the same conversation with you. As I've told you so many times before I am not interested." Lia told him.

"I really don't understand why this is so difficult for you to grasp. We are destined to be together, it is written all over our families' history."

"I understand that you see it that way Edward, but I'm sorry I don't. I don't want to date someone because somewhere, in a book written centuries ago, there may have been a promise of a marriage. That doesn't sound like a reason to begin a relationship." Lia explained.

"What would be a reason for you to enter into a relationship, Amelia?" Edward asked tensely.

Lia leant back in her seat as she pondered over Edward's question, she began to think about all of the happier times that she and Aidan had had during the few months that they were together. Smiling slightly, her head filled with memories of their dog walks where they would hold hands and talk about silly memories that they had of each other; at the Christmas party where Aidan had surprised her by arriving with mistletoe. Her smile got bigger as she thought about the snowball fight they had had at the beginning of December, when she realised she was in love with Aidan. They had battled with snowballs, hiding from each other in the trees before collapsing into the snow to form snow angels. As Lia had been waving her arms about in the snow, Aidan had leaned over and kissed her and she knew in that instant that she was in love with him.

"Amelia! I asked you a question!" Edward yelled, jolting Lia out of her thoughts.

"Sorry." Lia stated sarcastically, turning back to look at Edward who was glaring at her.

"So, why would you get into a relationship?" Edward repeated.

"I would get into a relationship if there was mutual respect and attraction. I want to know that the person I am with respects who I am and doesn't want to change me." Lia explained.

"All I'm trying to do is make you into the sort of person who would fit into my family. A quiet, respectful, non-argumentative, resourceful witch." Edward observed.

"But that's not me!" Lia exclaimed.

"Only because you continue to fight our destiny." Edward commented mildly.

"Edward. What you want is an old-fashioned house wife, I've not been raised to be like that. I like my independence." Lia told him, as they turned into her road.

"Independence is a wonderful quality to have but you also need to have someone in your life who you can depend on when decisions need making." Edward told her.

"Edward, this is never going to happen." Lia stated, as they pulled up at the bottom of her driveway. "But thank you for the lift home, I do appreciate it."

"It is destined to happen, Amelia. If you stopped skipping your lessons with your dad, our destiny would soon become apparent." Edward argued angrily.

As soon as the car stopped, Lia grabbed her bag from the floor by her feet and yanked on her scarf and gloves. Unclicking her seatbelt, Lia leapt out of the car as Edward leant across the seat towards her.

"This conversation isn't over." Edward warned.

Slamming the door shut in Edward's face, Lia stalked up the drive and around the corner, so that she was out of Edward's line of sight. Bending down slightly and leaning against the garage door, Lia rested her hands on her knees and focused on breathing slowly in and out, as she regained control of her temper, which had began to spike during her confrontation with Edward. Counting to ten, Lia eased herself back into a standing position and pushed away from the garage door. Brushing off any dirt and pushing her hair away from her face, Lia continued to walk towards the house. Just before she reached the path to the front door, she heard Aidan and Ben finishing a conversation at the front door.

Not wanting to have another confrontation, Lia glanced round for somewhere to hide. Realising that there was nowhere to hide, Lia walked as quickly as she could down to the bottom of the drive so that it would look like she was just getting in.

"Lia, it's nice to see you." Aidan said, when he spotted her slowly trailing up the driveway.

"Oh, hi Aidan." Lia said, trying to act surprised.

"How are you?" Aidan asked, pausing as Lia walked past him.

"I'm fine, how are you?" Lia asked, stopping and turning around, so she was facing him.

"Not too bad, just been playing Fifa with your brothers. Where were you?" Aidan asked.

"Oh, I was at Emily's studying and then Edward surprised us with a visit before driving me home." Lia told him, deliberately leaving out that she was not pleased to see Edward and that all they had done was argue.

"Oh. I thought you weren't interested in Mr London." Aidan commented, narrowing his eyes.

"Well, things change." Lia replied, starting to turn back to continue up the drive. "Not that it's really any of your business."

"I was simply commenting on the fact that when we were together you told me that you had no interest in him and yet, here you are just a couple of months down the line, spending loads of time with him." Aidan smirked.

"Well, it's none of your business so I suggest you just leave it alone." Lia told him, heading back up the driveway.

"All I was doing was trying to have a conversation, we never see each other anymore, so I just wanted to catch up." Aidan commented, with the smirk still on his face.

"No, what you want to do is pick a fight." Lia told him, as she whirled back round to face him.

"You're the one who started this one Lia." Aidan warned.

"How did I start this?" Lia asked.

"Telling me all about your new boyfriend and acting like it's no big deal." Aidan told her.

"You asked me where I had been!" Lia yelled back.

"Lia? Is that you?" Ben called.

"Yeah, I'm just coming in." Lia called back.

Aidan stared after Lia as she stomped towards the house and put his hands in his pockets. He knew Ben would probably appear in a minute or two once he had seen Lia's face. At the front door, Lia shoved past Ben and threw her bag on the floor before yanking off her scarf, gloves and coat.

"What's wrong with you?" Ben asked, watching his sister warily.

"I don't want to talk about it." Lia told him, before she ran up the stairs.

Sighing, Ben put his feet into one of the pairs of trainers by the front door and headed down the drive to see if he could catch up with Aidan. Meeting halfway down the driveway, Ben mirrored Aidan's position by shoving his hands into his pockets.

"I take it you bumped into Lia." Ben observed, staring up at the house, where Lia's bedroom light had just come on.

"Yeah." Aidan confirmed.

"What happened?" Ben asked.

"I want her back." Aidan told his friend, rather than offering an explanation as to what had gone on between him and Lia.

"Really?" Ben asked, turning so that he could look at his friend.

"Yeah, I've been missing her for ages and I thought it was just the fact we no longer spoke, but I realised tonight that it's not just that. I miss her laugh, I miss the way she would smile at me when I walked into a room, I miss our conversations and debates, the way she would lean against my shoulder when we were watching TV." Aidan explained.

"OK, what do you plan to do?" Ben asked.

"I'm going to win her back." Aidan told him.

"How?"

"Well, I was hoping that you could help me out a little with that."

"Why?"

"Because I made a mistake, one that I can't fix by myself." Aidan explained.

"Are you sorry about what you did?"

"I am beyond sorry about it. There are days when I actually try and convince myself that I didn't sleep with Sophie and ruin the best relationship of my life and hurt the person I care about most in the world. I would do anything to take it back."

"Will you ever do it again?" Ben asked evenly.

"Never, if Lia took me back, I would be the luckiest person in the world. I'm in love with her, I just need to show her that and prove to her that I would never intentionally hurt her again." Aidan stated firmly.

"How can I help?" Ben asked, accepting his friend's explanation.

"You know what she likes, her favourite things and what I need to do to prove that I want to be with her." Aidan explained.

"She loves romance. All of her favourite movies are those silly chick flicks. It's ridiculous, but she loves them, I suggest some sort of romantic gesture and telling her how you feel about her. I'll help you out with Sam and Charlie, getting them on board but you are on your own with Lia." Ben told him.

"How come you are so willing to help?" Aidan asked.

"If you hadn't been as honest with me just now I wouldn't help you, but you've told me how much you miss her and I believe you. Also, I know how much she misses you." Ben told him.

"Even though she is dating someone else." Aidan asked.

"Lia's dating someone else? Who is she dating?" Ben asked.

"Mr London, she was with him tonight." Aidan told him.

"Edward? She's not dating Edward. She was with Emily, they were working on some essay." Ben assured him.

"OK, well, that's good news. It would suck if she were dating someone new but I would still fight for her and I fight to win.

With that, Aidan turned and walked down the drive.

Chapter Twelve

15th February 2018

"Who is knocking on the door this early, the FIFA tournament doesn't start for another hour?" Sam groaned, at the knock on the door.
"It's Aidan." Ben told him, as he got up from the chair he was sprawled in.
"What is he doing here?" Sam snarled, angered at the thought of Aidan coming round and joining in his plans for the evening.
"I've been helping him with a plan to win Lia back and he needs our help." Ben explained.
"In what world would any of us help him after what he has done to Lia. How could you betray Lia by helping that pond scum?" Sam spat.
"Look, I've heard him out and you are going to do the same." Ben declared. "Go get Charlie."
Sam shoved himself out of his chair and stomped upstairs to fetch Charlie, while Ben pushed the dogs out of the way, so he could open the door to Aidan.
"So, you are in for quite a bit of resistance." Ben told Aidan, as he opened the door and let Aidan into the house.
"I guessed as much." Aidan admitted. "Does Lia know I'm here?"
"No and she just went back upstairs with another cup of tea to work on one of her essays, so she won't be down for a little while." Ben assured him.
"OK, let's get this first part over with." Aidan sighed.
"You can go straight to Lia if you want." Ben suggested.
"No, she relies too much on you guys. If I don't have your support, there is no way she will ever say yes to seeing me again." Aidan sighed.
With that, Ben nodded and headed through the house to the back-living room, where they both sank onto the sofa. Sam scowled at Aidan, as he and Charlie walked in. Aidan

met Sam's glare with a level look of his own.

"Why are you here, Aidan?" Charlie asked, as he sat down on one of the chairs.

"I wanted to talk to you all before I spoke with Lia. I want her back, she is the love of my life but she relies heavily on your opinions so I need you guys on side, if I am to have a chance of winning her back." Aidan explained.

"I'd leave now then." Sam announced, sinking back into his chair.

"I know you guys are pissed about the way I treated Lia and you have every right to be. The day you guys kicked me out of your house, I was so angry. Angry with Lia for just exploding about her feelings for me, I was angry with you guys for not hearing me out but worst of all I was angry at myself for hurting Lia and not being able to respond when she told me her feelings. I spent the afternoon thinking about what had happened and how I was going to sort things out with Lia. I tried calling her, only when she answered, I got scared of the enormity of what I was feeling towards her, so in a panic, I mentioned ending the relationship, which obviously upset her and then she hung up." Aidan explained.

"That doesn't cover the Sophie part." Sam observed.

"Sophie's dad lives a couple of doors down from me and when I went outside after the phone call with Lia, Sophie was just standing there. I had a one night stand with Sophie, as I was hoping it would stop what I was feeling towards Lia. Trust me, when I tell you guys it was the worst decision of my life." Aidan continued.

"Why were you together in town the next day?" Sam asked, not believing a word Aidan was saying.

"I was meeting Matt, Luke and Carl but Sophie and Marie just turned up. Sophie kissed me and although I was surprised initially, I did push her away."

"Is this what you plan to say to Lia?" Charlie asked.

"Yes, I'm going to tell her everything. Lay it all on the line and hope that she hasn't given up on me." Aidan announced, looking wistful.

"That should work." Ben declared thoughtfully. "On the phone, when we were working on a plan, I mentioned some of Lia's favourite things, are you going to use any of those to help you out?"

"You are letting him talk to Lia!!" Sam exploded.

"I'm going to give her the option of talking to him."

"Why?"

"Because Lia is miserable without him and I believe that Aidan really is sorry, so maybe they could work things out."

"Fine, what is the rest of your plan Aidan?" Sam asked finally.

"Well, I spoke with Ben yesterday and we discussed a number of Lia's favourite things to help me possibly win her back. Well, I'm going to completely open and honest with her and I have bought a bunch of pink tulips to give to her, then on the off chance that this does work out, I've booked a table at the little Italian place that Ben told me she loves."

"Will you ever cheat on her again?" Sam asked.

"No."

"Will you ever hurt her again?" Sam continued.

"Never."

"I suppose it would be OK if you spoke to Lia." Sam decided.

"Thank you."

Charlie half- odded his acceptance of Aidan's plan to win Lia back, although he hoped a tiny bit that Lia would refuse so he could keep talking to Emily. He knew that Lia would never date Edward but as long as she wasn't seeing anyone else, Edward would keep coming around and bringing Emily with him. Charlie was afraid that if Lia got back together with Aidan, Edward would prevent Emily from seeing them anymore. Feeling guilty about his thoughts, Charlie quickly left the room.

"I'll wait till everyone is here before I go and talk to Lia so that their arrival doesn't interrupt your conversation." Ben told his friend, as he settled down in his chair rather than heading upstairs to talk to Lia.

"Wanna have a practice game?" Sam asked, handing Aidan a controller.

"Sure. Just let me put these flowers on the shelf." Aidan said, standing up.

Lia settled herself at her desk, with her third cup of tea of the evening and wriggled her finger on the mouse of her laptop. Once her English essay had popped back up on the screen, she reread the paragraph that she had just written and deleted the second half as it didn't make sense. Picking up her copy of The Taming of the Shrew, she flicked through the play, searching for a couple of quotes she had highlighted. She knew that she had the rest of the evening to get as much of her essay done as possible because she had walked the dogs earlier and had her dinner.

Propping the book on her lap, she shifted so she could see the book and still type as best as possible. Her phone vibrated against the desk, stopping her just as she began to type.

Edward: Amelia, I was wondering if you wanted to have dinner tonight. Edward

Lia: Can't tonight got a massive essay to finish x

Edward: That's a shame I had a fun night planned.

Lia: Sorry x

Edward: How about tomorrow?

Lia: I can't tomorrow, got magic practice with Dad x

Edward: Ok I will try and visit at the weekend.

Lia sighed and threw her phone onto her bed, so she didn't have to text Edward back anymore, wincing when it landed against her wall with a loud thud, he was becoming more and more persistent about them dating, despite Lia's repeated protests. Turning back to her essay, Lia stared at the book on her lap trying to remember what she wanted to write before she was interrupted. Absently picking up the cup of tea that was resting on her chest of drawers next to her desk, she took a sip and started to type again.

After about an hour and a half, Lia paused to have a

further look through the play on her lap and flicked to one of the marked pages she had tabbed up earlier. She glanced up at the door when she heard someone coming upstairs, as her parents were away for a couple of days.

"Lia." Ben called, as he knocked on the door.

"I'm busy." Lia called back.

Ignoring Lia, Ben opened the door to her room.

"I said I'm busy." Lia told him, without looking away from the laptop on her desk.

"I'm only going to be a second." Ben told her, turning her chair, so she was facing him.

"What's up?" Lia sighed, putting her book down on her desk.

"Aidan is here." Ben told her.

"That's fine, I plan to be in my room all night as I need to get this essay finished." Lia said, gesturing to the laptop on her desk.

"He has asked if you would mind coming down and talking to him for a few minutes." Ben explained to her, crouching down in front her.

Lia ran her hands up and down her legs, as she thought about going down to talk to Aidan. Ben grabbed her hands and squeezed them in support.

"It's your choice if you go down and talk to him." Ben told her.

"How long has he been here?" Lia asked.

"About two hours, he came and spoke to us first but it is you, he is actually here to see. He really wanted us to understand what happened after we kicked him out of the house and his feelings towards you." Ben told her.

"What do you think I should do?" Lia asked.

"I can't make that decision for you." Ben commented, patting her knee before standing up and heading to the door. "He said he will hang out for a bit so you have a little while to think about what you want to do."

Once Ben had left the room, Lia stared at her door then she stood up and walked up to it but paused when she lifted her hand to open it. Frowning, she moved across her bedroom and checked her reflection in her mirror. As it was currently half term, she had been in the house for most of the day. Deciding that jeans and her pink striped jumper were completely fine, she ran her fingers through her hair and walked back to her door.

Forcing herself to open the door, Lia slowly began to walk downstairs. She paused when she reached the first floor and sank down to sit on the bottom of the stairs. Part of her was desperate to go down and talk to Aidan but she was scared that it was going to start a fight which she didn't want. They had only recently started to talk again but only if they were in a group of people. They had not been alone together since the fight on the driveway a month ago.

Shoving herself to her feet, Lia gathered her thoughts and made herself walk the rest of the way downstairs. Betty ran up to her, as soon as Lia reached the bottom of the stairs, Lia crouched down and hugged the dog.

"You make sneaking downstairs impossible." Lia told Betty, as she continued to pet her.

After a minute of petting Betty, Lia stood back up and walked to the doorway of the main living room where she could hear Sam, Ben, Aidan and a few others talking. Lia paused just out of sight and watched the boys, as they bantered with each other over the game that was underway. Smiling at the normality of the scene in front of her, Lia shifted so she could catch Ben's eye, as he had been half watching the doorway. Once Ben had spotted her, he tapped Aidan on the shoulder and inclined his head slightly in the direction of Lia. Aidan followed Ben's glance and spotted Lia, smiling he stood up.

"Hi." Aidan said, when he reached her.

Lia smiled in greeting and let Aidan lead the way into the second living room.

"So, how are you?" Aidan asked, as they entered the living room.

"I'm good, how are you?" Lia asked, glancing around the room feeling her own nerves and Aidan's taking over.

"I would like to tell you I'm great but the truth is I've

missed you." Aidan told her, walking to look out of the window.

Lia watched Aidan without responding, her heart starting to beat a million miles a minute. Aidan remained staring out of the window but met Lia's eyes, through her reflection in the window. Turning slowly, Aidan faced Lia. "I've missed you." Aidan repeated. "I know I've hurt you in more ways than I can imagine but I was hoping that you would hear me out."

Lia sat down on the edge of the sofa near the door and eyed Aidan warily, fiddling with her watch clasp, Lia nodded slowly.

Aidan remained standing and put his hands in his pockets, while he debated what he was going to say. Lia dropped her gaze and linked her hands on her lap, Betty and Veronica both walked into the room and settled themselves in front of Lia. Lia unlinked her hands and rested one hand on each of the dogs' heads.

"I suppose the first thing I need to say is that I'm sorry." Aidan started, walking back over to the window. "I'm so sorry Lia."

"I'm sorry too." Lia whispered.

"What are you sorry for, I'm the one who screwed this up." Aidan asked, turning back to Lia and walking over to her. "Wait! Don't answer that, just let me finish."

Lia stopped what she was about to say and settled back on the sofa, allowing Aidan to say whatever he needed to say. The air was charged with emotion and Lia was beginning to feel a tiny bit overwhelmed by what she could feel: frustration, guilt and something else she couldn't identify at present.

"First, let me apologise for the whole situation with Alice Foulds, I shouldn't have tried to keep what I had done with her a secret when I was asking you to be honest with me. The truth is that Alice and I went on a couple of dates, she wanted more but I wanted you. I thought she and her creepy brothers were trying to get me to change my mind by intimidation, I didn't want to worry you so I decided not to tell you." Aidan started, sitting down next to Lia.

"Why didn't you want me to worry?" Lia asked.

"I don't know. I guess, I just didn't want you to think badly of me or worry that I would choose her over you, I didn't treat Alice well, it was just a bit of fun but I knew whatever we had was going to be real and special." Aidan told her.

"Why did you think I would think badly of you?" Lia asked again.

"Because I haven't got a good track record with girls, I've cheated and I've lied and often I just go on a couple of dates and then forget to call on purpose." Aidan admitted.

"I knew all that Aidan." Lia told him. "It's not a secret. The girls you did those things to would talk about it and also you would occasionally brag to Ben and Sam, which I overheard."

"You still agreed to go out with me, even though you knew all that?" Aidan asked surprised.

Lia smiled slightly and nodded her head.

"Well, I feel stupid." Aidan admitted.

"I had a huge crush on you, I would have said yes, even if you were a mass murderer." Lia joked.

Aidan smiled and shook his head.

"That leads me to apology number two." Aidan told her and took her hands in his. "You told me that you had had a crush on me for years and that you loved me. I responded by not saying anything, running away and then having a one-night stand with Sophie. I have never felt worse than I did after I slept with her, except maybe, when Ben and Sam told me that you had seen me the next day."

Lia pulled her hands away from Aidan's and wrapped her arms around herself, trying to ward off what Aidan was saying to her.

"I will never ever be able to apologise enough for what I did." Aidan said, resting his hands on his lap.

"I'm sorry." Lia told him. "I shouldn't have sprung all my feelings on you, I was just angry and upset."

"You have no reason to be sorry, I asked you to be honest

with me and you were. I'm the one who screwed up. I'm so sorry." Aidan insisted.

"I forgive you." Lia told him.

"How?" Aidan asked surprised.

"Easy. As much as I don't want to, I still love you." Lia told him, placing her hands on top of his.

"I love you Lia." Aidan said, after a few seconds staring at their hands.

"Oh my God! What?" Lia gasped.

"I love you." Aidan repeated, gripping Lia's hands.

Lia tugged her hands free and half threw herself at Aidan. Surprised, Aidan fell back on the sofa but wrapped his free arm around Lia. Aidan laughed and hugged Lia close to him. After a few seconds, Aidan let go of Lia and eased her into a sitting position. Lia looked at him slightly suspiciously when he got up and left the room without saying anything. Aidan walked back into the living room holding a small bouquet of pink tulips and smiled when Lia's eyes went wide.

"Happy belated Valentine's Day." Aidan said, passing her the flowers.

"Oh my God! These are so pretty, they're my favourite." Lia told him, smiling and burying her face in the flowers. "How did you know?"

"I spoke to Ben and explained that I was going to beg for your forgiveness and I asked how to win you over. It took a bit of persuasion but eventually he agreed to help me. He told me how much you loved getting flowers and that pink tulips were your favourite." Aidan told her, sitting back down next to her.

Lia glanced over at Aidan, feeling the waves of tension coming from him. He was sat staring out of the window, despite only being able to see their reflections. After a few minutes, Aidan took Lia's hands and turned to face her.

"Lia? Please, could you give us another chance? Can you give me another chance?" Aidan asked, squeezing her hand.

Lia linked her fingers through Aidan's before she nodded.

"You'll give this another go?" Aidan asked her.

"Yes." Lia reassured him, before she rested her head on his shoulder.

Charlie came into the room a few minutes later and smiled when he saw the look on his sister's face but at the same time he got a sick feeling in his stomach when he thought about Edward and Emily. He knew how much Edward wanted to date Lia.

"I'm sorry to interrupt but your phone has been vibrating none stop for the last fifteen minutes Lia." Charlie announced, walking the full way into the room.

"Riverdale!" Lia cried, glancing at her watch.

"River... what?" Charlie asked, as Lia quickly stood up still holding Aidan's hand.

"Riverdale, we all watch and message about it." Lia explained.

"Who is we?" Aidan asked.

"Heather, Siobhan and now Emily." Lia explained, letting go of Aidan's hand.

"You all watch this show?" Charlie asked.

"Yes." Lia laughed. "I'll go and move my phone so that it stops bothering you."

Aidan sat back on the sofa and shook his head. Charlie started to leave the room but then he turned back and looked at Aidan.

"Everything OK, Charlie?" Aidan asked, when Charlie continued to look at him.

"I just don't know if you and Lia being together is such a good idea." Charlie admitted. "I love seeing her so happy but you made her cry."

"I know I did but trust me when I tell you that I will try my hardest not to hurt her again." Aidan told him. "When I spoke to you guys earlier I meant what I said, Lia is the most important person to me and I will do whatever I can to make her happy."

Charlie nodded and left the room. He still had the same sick feeling in his stomach, so he walked up the stairs two at a time, catching Lia just as she came back downstairs.

"Can I talk to you for a second?" Charlie asked, beckoning Lia into his room.

"Sure." Lia said, smiling at her brother.

Lia sat down on Charlie's bed and waited for him to say whatever was on his mind.

"Are you back with Aidan?" Charlie asked, sitting down on his desk chair.

"I guess so." Lia said. "I want to be, I love him."

"This is going to cause a huge problem." Charlie muttered.

"What is going to cause a problem?" Lia asked confused.

"Edward is going to go ape when he finds out. He absolutely believes that the two of you are destined to be together, the scene he will cause will be horrific and he'll probably ban Emily from ever speaking to us again."

"Oh, I didn't even think about that! Oh no!" Lia gasped.

"Oh yes." Charlie repeated.

"He knows I'm not interested in him that way." Lia insisted.

"He's interested in you though and he doesn't seem like a guy who will stop until he gets what he wants." Charlie told her.

"Oh God." Lia moaned. "I have to go tell Aidan otherwise this will be a disaster. I don't want him to think that there was ever anything between me and Edward. Edward can cause all the scenes he likes but I'm not letting him ruin things between me and Aidan. God his scenes are horrific though."

With that, Lia jumped off of Charlie's bed and ran down the stairs and skidded into the living room. Aidan glanced up at her entrance.

"Dramatic episode of Riverdale?" Aidan asked, when Lia all but fell into the room.

"Oh, they all are this season." Lia said smiling. "But that's not the problem."

"Talk to me, I can handle it." Aidan told her, when she stood in front of him.

"It's Edward." Lia told him, sitting down next to him. "I need you to believe me on this, I never dated him but he still wants to date me. I have explained to him that I have no interest in him so many times I have lost count but he refuses to accept that I'm not interested in him. You are the only person I want to be with."

"I believe you." Aidan told her, after her rushed explanation.

"You do?" Lia asked.

"Yes, I knew you weren't dating him. I was just jealous that you were spending time with him." Aidan assured her, taking her hands.

"I wanted to make you jealous." Lia admitted. "Whenever I see him, we just argue but I just skipped that part when I told you about being with him. I wanted you to feel some of the pain that I felt when I saw you with Sophie. Then, when we argued all I wanted to do was tell you he meant nothing and launch myself into your arms. I'm sorry."

"When Sophie kissed me I was in shock, but then I realised what had happened and I pushed her away. It was a one night stand, it meant nothing to me. All it did was make me realise how important you are to me." Aidan insisted, wrapping one arm around Lia's shoulder

Lia rested her head on Aidan's shoulder and felt better than she had done for the last couple of months.

"So, tell me about Riverdale." Aidan said suddenly.

"You want to know about Riverdale?" Lia asked, lifting her head from Aidan's shoulder.

"Yeah, Ben mentioned something about it being your current favourite show and I saw how you reacted when you realised your friends were messaging you about it."

Lia laughed, "How long did you and Ben spend talking about me?"

"Long enough for me to learn a few of your favourite things, like that your favourite flowers are pink tulips, that your favourite TV show is Riverdale, that you are a huge Taylor Swift fan and a large number of other things that I needed to know. Although, I knew about Taylor as you nearly always are playing her stuff when I am round"

"So, now you know everything about me." Lia teased.

"Not everything, just a few things I needed to know, I figure you will tell me the rest when you are ready." Aidan told her.

"Well, I will be as open as I can be." Lia promised.

"So will I." Aidan assured her.

"Everything OK in here?" Ben asked, popping his head round the door.

"Yeah, everything is good." Aidan said, nodding at his friend.

"Good." Ben commented, coming further into the room "It's after 9 on a Thursday, aren't you watching Riverdale?"

"Something came up." Lia retorted, with a grin.

"Is that so?" Ben teased.

"Ben." Lia warned teasingly.

"Dropping it." Ben laughed. "It's nice to see you two smiling again."

"Well, I believe you are partially responsible for this." Lia commented, looking at her brother.

"I may have passed on some helpful hints." Ben accepted. "But this is all Aidan's doing."

"Thank you." Lia mouthed.

"So what happens now?" Ben asked.

"Who knows?" Lia commented.

"We start working on this relationship and making sure that it works out." Aidan told both of them.

Lia turned to look at Aidan and saw that he meant what he had said. Ben nodded slowly, and got up from the chair he was sitting on.

"We are still playing FIFA, if you want to join?" Ben told Aidan, as he left the room.

Aidan looked at Lia, who laughed.

"Go, have fun! I have Riverdale to watch so I don't read spoilers from all my friends." Lia told him.

"Alright, I'll see you later." Aidan said, following Ben out of the room.

Lia smiled and relaxed back on the sofa. Betty and Veronica walked into the room and walked straight over to her.

"Hi girls. Can you believe what just happened?" she asked the dogs excitedly, as she bent down to pet them both.

Standing up, Lia followed the dogs out of the room to let them out and made herself another cup of tea, while she waited for them to come back inside. Lia laughed, when she heard the cheers and jeers from the living room, where Sam had just won what must have been the third game in a row.

When the dogs came back in, Lia went upstairs and fired up her laptop, which had gone to sleep while she was downstairs with Aidan. She minimised her essay and clicked onto the internet to open the Netflix tab she always had running in the background. Bringing up the latest episode of Riverdale, Lia curled up onto her bed and settled in to watch.

After about 30 minutes, Lia heard a knock on her door, so she paused the episode.

"Who is it?" She asked, uncurling herself from her blanket and heading to the door.

"Aidan."

"Hi." Lia said, opening the door.

"Hey, I just wanted to let you know I'm off." Aidan said, as he leant on the doorframe.

"Oh, OK."

"It's eleven at night." Aidan laughed.

"How did it get to be so late?" Lia asked, glancing at her watch.

"Anyway, I'm going to head home, but I was thinking maybe we could go for a dog walk tomorrow evening."

"That sounds like fun. I miss walking the dogs with you. My brothers aren't as nice when I stop to pet all the other dogs." Lia laughed.

"OK, I'll see you tomorrow." Aidan told her.

"Goodnight." Lia replied.

Aidan moved closer to Lia and placed one hand on Lia's waist, nudging her closer to him and leant down and kissed her gently.

"Goodnight Lia." Aidan said, letting go of her and heading off down the stairs.

Lia waited until Aidan had disappeared downstairs before she closed her door and she leant back against the door, smiling. Pushing away from the door, she headed back over to her bed and picked up her phone. She clicked on the Whatsapp icon and pulled up the group chat that included her, Heather and Siobhan. She thought about telling them that she was back with Aidan in the Whatsapp group that included Emily but decided it would be better to tell her in person, due to the whole Edward situation.

Lia: So me and Aidan are back together xx

Heather: What? xx

Siobhan: How? xx

Lia: He came over tonight

Lia: He apologised for everything

Lia: He brought me flowers and told me he loved me xx

Siobhan: Aww that's so sweet xx

Heather: So you have forgiven him?? Xx

Lia: I know... yes I have xx

Siobhan: What flowers did he buy? Xx

Lia: Pink tulips xx

Lia: He checked what my favourite flowers were with Ben so he could win me back xx

Heather: OK I would forgive him too xx

Siobhan: I'm so happy for you xx

Heather: Have you watched Riverdale yet? Xx

Lia: I was with Aidan when it was on... just catching up now xx

Heather: It's a good episode... message us when you've watched xx

With that, Lia put her phone down on her bedside table and drank a mouthful of the lukewarm tea which she had forgotten about. Pulling a face, she got up off the bed to go downstairs and make another one before she went to bed. Opening her door, she walked down stairs and bumped into Charlie as she reached the first-floor landing.

"You're up late." Lia commented, as Charlie was nearly

always in bed by eleven because he was always up by seven at the latest.

"I had something I wanted to finish." Charlie offered, distractedly by way of an explanation.

"You still working on your Physics presentation?" Lia asked, as she walked downstairs with him.

"Yeah, I just can't quite seem to work something out." Charlie commented grumpily.

"Take a break, there's no point stressing over it." Lia suggested.

"I can't, once I get this section done, I will be able to finish it." Charlie explained, twisting his fingers together.

"Charlie you need sleep, everything will be clearer in the morning." Lia said, resting her hand on his arm.

"Fine, fine." Charlie muttered, before turning to head back upstairs.

"Where are you going?" Lia asked.

"To bed, I was coming down to make coffee but you may be right, sleep would be better." Charlie told her, heading back upstairs.

Lia smiled and shook her head as she continued into the kitchen. She paused in the doorway to the living room where Ben and Sam were engaged in a further intense battle of FIFA. Lia went into the living room and settled on one of the chairs to watch her brothers.

"Everything OK?" Sam asked, spotting her.

"Yeah, everything's fine." Lia said smiling.

"You and Aidan sort everything out?" Sam asked. "OH, HE SHOOTS AND HE SCORES!!"

"You are cheating!" Ben declared.

"No, you just suck." Sam argued.

"You aren't even paying attention, you have to be cheating." Ben continued.

"I don't have to pay attention to beat you." Sam continued.

"It's a game." Lia told them both, before they started to fight.

Both of them turned to look at her, standing up, Lia quickly dodged Ben's playful swat at her legs.

"Oh no, I am so not playing tonight." Lia announced, laughing whilst fleeing into the kitchen.

She popped the kettle on, and busied herself refilling the dogs' water bowls. Then she grabbed a couple of dog biscuits out of the box, causing the dogs to come running into the room and start jumping up at her.

"Uh uh... No!" Lia disciplined the dogs. "No jumping!"

The dogs both sat down immediately and wagged their tails. Lia carried the dog biscuits through into the utility room to place one on each of the beds and they both settled down with their biscuits, as Lia turned off the light and closed the door.

"I've put the dogs to bed!" Lia called, as she went back to making her cup of tea.

There was no response from her brothers but Lia decided that it didn't matter, when she heard the sounds of FIFA coming from the TV. Once the kettle had reboiled, Lia made her drink and then headed back upstairs. She picked up her phone as she put her mug down and saw that Aidan had messaged her.

Aidan: I'm so glad you agreed to give us another go xx

Lia: I am too xx

Aidan: I missed you xx

Lia: I missed you too xx

Aidan: Can I ask you something? Xx

Lia: Go ahead xx

Aidan: How long have you had your crush on me? Lol Xx

Lia: I knew telling you would come back to haunt me. Lol xx

Aidan: Haha xx

Lia: See you tomorrow xx

Aidan: Goodnight xx

The next afternoon, Lia was once again sat in front of her English essay staring at the cursor as it blinked continuously. As she had written five words in an hour, she was feeling frustrated at her lack of progress. She fiddled with her music, changing from shuffle to Taylor Swift's, Reputation. She leant back on her chair in an effort to relax and think about the best way to proceed. Shakespeare was Lia's least favourite subject in English, she didn't like reading old English and found it hard to answer the questions and write essays. Lia closed her eyes for a few minutes, focusing on her breathing and continued to think about the essay in front of her. When she still couldn't come up with any words to write, she took her own advice and decided to take a break and text Emily.

Lia: You busy? Xx

Emily: No just watching TV x

Lia: Do you want to do something? Xx

Emily: What are you thinking? x

Lia: How about grabbing a coffee... I need a break from this stupid English essay xx

Emily: I'll meet you in 20 x

Smiling, Lia put her phone on one side while she changed from her pyjamas into her jeans and her blue Jack Wills cable knit sweater. She then pulled on her Ugg boots, then picked up her purse, shopping bag and phone to put into the small black bag and slung it over her shoulder. She shut down her laptop and headed downstairs. Grabbing her coat, she pulled it on over her clothes.

"I'm going to meet Emily for coffee." Lia said, popping her head round the living room door where Sam and Ben were sat playing yet another game.

"OK, bye." They both muttered absentmindly.

Lia stopped by the kitchen to check on the dogs and saw that they had plenty of water, she petted them both and then headed out.

Aidan: What are you up to? Xx

Lia: Meeting Emily for coffee xx

Aidan: We still on to walk the dogs later? Xx

Lia: Of course... can't wait xx

Aidan: See you later xx

Smiling Lia put her phone back in her bag and continued the walk into town. She paused as she passed the library and checked her purse to make sure that she had her library card. Once she saw that she did, she continued to walk past the last couple of shops to the coffee shop.

"Hi." Lia said, walking up to Emily who was waiting outside.

"Hi, how are you?" Emily smiled, opening the door.

"I'm good thanks. How are you? Enjoying half-term?" Lia asked, following Emily in.

"I'm good. It's nice to have a break but I'm starting to get a little bored of my house and endless lectures from Ed." Emily commented.

"You should have said something, I'm always free to hang out." Lia replied.

"Are you sure?" Emily asked.

"Of course. My house pretty much has an open door policy and I never mind going out." Lia explained.

"Thanks." Emily said sincerely.

The girls ordered their drinks and then found a table.

"So what's new with you?" Lia asked.

"Not much, Edward's still staying with us but I'm guessing you know that already." Emily observed.

"He's sent me a couple of texts, asking me to meet up." Lia commented.

"He's pretty intense about dating you." Emily commented.

"I know and no offence but I'm really not interested in him." Lia muttered warily.

"I know you're not interested in him." Emily reassured her.

"Good, because I have something to tell you and I really don't want to offend you." Lia said, looking up from her drink that she had been staring at.

"What?"

"Aidan came round last night. He apologised and he brought me flowers." Lia started.

"And…?" Emily asked.

"Well, he asked me to take him back and I said yes." Lia admitted.

"Wow!" Emily gasped.

"I couldn't say no, I love him." Lia whispered.

"Wow!" Emily repeated.

"Is this going to cause any problems between us?" Lia asked.

"Of course not." Emily reassured her.

"Good, I wouldn't want to lose you as a friend." Lia told her.

The girls fell into silence and sipped their drinks. After a few minutes, Lia looked up at Emily who had a weird look on her face. Lia grabbed her friend's hand and squeezed it, a few seconds later Emily blinked and refocused on Lia.

"Are you OK?" Lia asked.

"Yeah, I'm fine." Emily said, but she swayed a bit on her chair.

"Do you need water or fresh air?" Lia asked, squeezing Emily's hand.

"No, I'm fine." Emily assured her.

"What happened?" Lia asked.

"I had a premonition." Emily whispered.

"What sort of premonition?" Lia whispered back.

"I'll tell you once I understand what it means." Emily assured her.

With that, Emily lifted her coffee mug to her lips and sipped on her latte. Lia tried to relax and picked up her mocha. The girls sat in slightly awkward silence as they finished off their drinks. Once they had both finished, they stood up and left the coffee shop.

"I'm heading to the library before I head home, do you want to come?" Lia asked, once they were outside.

"No, I think I'm just going to head home, I'm a little tired." Emily commented.

"OK, message me if you need anything." Lia told her, as they headed off in their separate directions.

Lia walked into the library and headed up to the non-fiction area. Once there, Lia wandered around the History section and focused on the History of America, particularly the Civil War era, which was the next topic that they were studying in History. She picked up a couple of books and scanned through the contents page to see if they covered the particular areas that were highlighted in the syllabus. Choosing the best two books, in her opinion, she returned the others to the shelf. Moving over to the law area of the library, she pulled out a book on the legal system in the UK. Finally, after checking over her shoulders to ensure that no one was watching her, she walked over to the section on supernatural to look at books on Wicca. Selecting a couple of books about Wicca for beginners, she headed over to the self checkout. Once she had checked out all of the books, she placed them in her bag and headed back home.

"Lia!" Yelled a voice from behind her.

Lia turned round to see Luke and Carl jogging towards her. She waved before stopping and waiting for them to catch up.

"Hi." She said, when they fell into step with her.

"How are you?" Luke asked.

"I'm good, how are you two?" Lia asked.

"Not bad, thanks." Carl replied.

"Yeah, I'm good." Luke said. "Do you want a hand with that bag?"

"Oh no, it's fine." Lia said.

"Are you sure?" Luke asked. "It looks heavy."

"It's just a couple of books don't worry about it." Lia told him.

Ignoring her, Luke took the bag off her and hung it over his own shoulder. The three of them walked the rest of the way to Lia's house. Lia pulled her key out of her handbag and let the boys in. The dogs ran out to greet her and then jumped up at Carl and Luke.

"No!" Lia told the dogs firmly, grabbing at Veronica's collar before she could jump up again.

Betty quickly sat down at Lia's command and waited for Lia's next instruction. Once she was sure that the dogs weren't going to jump up anymore, she pointed into the house and the dogs ran in. Lia followed them in and closed the front door. She picked up her bag of books from the bottom of the stairs, where Luke had left it and headed up to her room. Once inside, she dumped the books on her desk chair, separating out the books on Wicca from the books that she had got for school. Lia checked her watch and saw that it was five in the evening. Knowing that Aidan would be round in about half an hour, she placed the books on Wicca on her bedside table and headed back downstairs to put water in the dogs' bowls and give them their tea. The dogs ran into the kitchen and greedily began eating. Lia made herself a cup of tea and grabbed a couple of biscuits from the biscuit tin before heading back upstairs. In her room, she began to look through the books on Wicca, starting on the origins of Wicca, Lia settled down on her bed and began to read. Lia's phone buzzed on the side and Lia glanced over to see that Edward was calling her.

"Hi." Lia said, answering the call.

"Good evening." Edward responded.

"Is everything OK?" Lia asked.

"Everything is fine, I was just wondering if you wanted to go for dinner tonight." Edward asked.

"I can't tonight." Lia told him.

"How about tomorrow?" Edward asked.

"Edward, I can't." Lia told him.

"Why not?" Edward demanded.

"I don't want to lead you on, I told you before I'm not interested in dating you." Lia explained.

"Our families are linked, we are destined to get married!" Edward yelled.

"Edward, I don't want to argue about this but I'm really not interested." Lia said, through clenched teeth.

Lia could hear Edward grinding his teeth and attempting to calm his breathing, so she knew that he was really annoyed.

"Edward, I'm going to hang up now." Lia said, after a few seconds.

When Edward didn't respond, Lia hung up the phone and placed it back on her bedside table. She glanced at the time and saw that it was getting towards half five. She put her bookmark in the book she was reading and then put both books in the drawer of her bedside table. She debated swapping her jeans from her slightly nicer ones to her dog walking ones but decided against it as it was the first time she and Aidan had been together, so she wanted to make the effort. To keep her feet warm while she was out, she pulled a pair of pink fluffy socks over the top of the Bambi socks she was wearing.

She then walked over to her chest of drawers and pulled out the hoody she had stolen from Sam, when he was having a clear out of his clothes last year. She pulled the jumper over her clothes and zipped it up. Checking her appearance in the mirror, she decided that she needed to brush her hair before she went out. Grabbing her hairbrush off her dressing table, she ran it quickly through her hair, then dropped it back on the dressing table. Checking the time, she saw that she still had about ten minutes before Aidan was due so she pulled her laptop out and reread the beginning of the essay that she had abandoned. Thinking that the essay did not make sense, she deleted it and decided that she would start again tomorrow. Picking up her copy of The Taming of the Shrew, she flicked to the first section that she had tabbed up and began reading, she rested a pad on her lap and made some notes, in the hope that they would help her write the essay tomorrow.

"Lia!" Sam yelled. "Aidan's here."

"Coming!" Lia yelled back.

Lia shoved her notes and the play on her desk, then jumped up, ran downstairs and skidded to a stop in the hall. She smiled at Aidan and then bent down to pet Buster.

"Hi Buster." She said, hugging the dog "I've missed you."

"You know, I'm sure you like my dog more than me." Aidan laughed.

"I like both of you equally, I just haven't seen Buster for a while." Lia offered, continuing to hug Buster, who was jumping up and licking her face.

Betty and Veronica hovered in the hallway and tried to nuzzle under Lia's arm.

"Sorry girls." Lia said, petting them both and standing up. "Let me get my shoes and coat then I'm ready to go."

While Lia was putting her shoes on, Aidan put the leads on both the dogs and then passed them to Lia, once she was ready.

"I'll see you later." Lia called, as she left the house.

Lia fell into step beside Aidan and shifted both leads into her left hand to let Aidan link his fingers with hers. Smiling, Lia walked alongside Aidan towards the woods. Once they arrived at the entrance, they let the dogs off their leads and they ran ahead. Aidan then pulled Lia close and tilted her head up, so he could kiss her. When they broke apart, Aidan hugged her close to him running his hands up and down her back.

"I missed you." he said into her hair.

Lia smiled and hugged him back tightly. Pulling away, Aidan laced his fingers through hers and began to walk into the woods.

"So, do you want to do something at the weekend?" Aidan asked, as they started to walk again.

"Yeah, what are you thinking?" Lia agreed.

"How about we go out to dinner?" Aidan suggested. "I was thinking we could go out for Italian."

"I love Italian food, pasta is my favourite." Lia commented "How much information did you get out of Ben?"

"Like I said yesterday, I got enough information to make this work and I will find out the rest." Aidan commented.

"OK but I'm not answering any questions about my crush on you." Lia told him laughing.

Aidan laughed and swung their hands.

"So, are we on for dinner?" Aidan checked.

"Yes." Lia agreed.

"Great, I'll come and get you at around seven." Aidan told her.

They walked hand in hand for a little bit enjoying each other's company in comfortable silence.

"I forgot how easy it was to spend time with you." Lia observed, after a few minutes.

"What do you mean?" Aidan asked, glancing at her.

"There is no ulterior motive to us being together, it's comfortable and most of all it's fun." Lia explained.

"And being comfortable is a good thing?" Aidan asked.

"It's the best thing, I hate second guessing everything I say and worrying about every little thing." Lia continued to explain. "I love being able to relax with you and know that you feel the same."

"That makes sense." Aidan agreed. "But don't you like the fun of getting to know someone?"

"I still get butterflies everytime you kiss me and sometimes have to check that it is me that you are smiling at, but I like that when I'm with you, I no longer ramble or forget how to speak like I used to." Lia told him.

"I never noticed." Aidan laughed.

Aidan pulled Lia towards him and bent his head so that he could kiss her, Lia leant into him, giving herself over to the sweetness of the embrace.

"Butterflies still there?" Aidan asked, resting his head on Lia's forehead.

"Always." Lia confirmed.

"Good."

With that Aidan released Lia but kept his arm round her shoulder, as they continued to walk round the woods. The dogs who were running around ahead of them but they kept checking on them. Slowly they walked round the woods and reaching the end, they clipped the leads back on the dogs to walk the rest of the way home.

"You coming in?" Lia asked, when they reached the bottom of her driveway.

"Sure." Aidan said, walking up the drive with her.

As they neared the house, Lia paused and stared at the black lexus parked outside her house.

"What's wrong?" Aidan asked, when Lia stopped.

"Edward's here." Lia whispered.

"OK, let's go inside and deal with him." Aidan said, tugging on Lia's hand. "Come on, there's no point in delaying this."

Lia trailed after Aidan as he walked into the utility room, unclipping the dogs' leads and letting them head into the house. Ben appeared in the doorway, shortly after the dogs had disappeared into the house. He was frowning hard when Lia looked up at him.

"What's wrong?" Lia asked, clinging to Aidan's hand.

"Edward is here and he's fuming." Ben told her.

Lia shifted slightly as she clutched at Aidan's hand for a few seconds. She took a few deep breaths and let go of Aidan's hand. Lia walked into the house after Aidan and nodded at Ben.

"Where is he?" Lia asked.

"He's in the front living room with Charlie and Sam." Ben told her.

"OK, I'll be back in a few minutes." Lia said to Aidan.

"Let her do this." Ben said to Aidan, when he started to protest. "She knows what she's doing."

Aidan nodded and let Lia go. Ben then gestured to Aidan to follow him. They met up with Sam and Charlie just outside the front living room as Lia closed the door. The four of them remained by the closed door, so that they could hear what was going in the living room.

Inside Lia moved away from the door and sat down on the sofa, as close to the door as she could get.

"How can I help you Edward?" Lia asked, when Edward glared at her.

"You hung up on me when I was trying to explain why we are meant to be together." Edward whispered harshly.

"I told you I wasn't interested in you that way." Lia repeated.

"We are destined to be together." Edward insisted.

"I don't believe that." Lia told him quietly.

"It doesn't matter what you believe, I am telling you that we are destined to be together!" Edward yelled.

"Well, that's not going to happen. Aidan came round yesterday and after a long discussion, we realised that we love each other and made the decision to get back together." Lia announced, suddenly feeling trapped.

"You stupid little girl!" Edward fumed heading towards her. "Do you think that matters? He can't understand you like I will."

"That's enough." Lia stated. "I want you to leave."

"I'm not leaving until you agree to date me."

"That's not going to happen. Now I want you to leave."

"I'm not leaving!" Edward growled, as he towered over Lia, who was still sat on the sofa.

"Edward, I want you to leave." Lia insisted, trying to shift away from him.

"You're a witch, Lia you can't date a mortal!" Edward yelled.

At that moment, Lia's brothers burst through the door. Sam and Ben moved so they were between Lia and Edward, Charlie stood holding the door open. Lia glanced through the door and saw Aidan staring at her.

"Lia asked you to leave." Ben said.

"I'm not done!" Edward snarled.

"Yes, you are." Sam told him, grabbing one of Edward's arms and towing him to the door.

Sam shoved Edward out the door and slammed it shut behind him. Once Edward was gone, Sam walked into the living room where Ben was sat next to Lia, Charlie had taken one of the chairs and Aidan was stood in the centre of the living room.

"What did Edward mean when he said that you were a witch?" Aidan asked Lia.

Lia glanced round at her brothers, who all nodded at her, giving their silent permission to tell Aidan their secret.

"He meant that I am witch." Lia whispered.

Chapter Thirteen

16th February 2018

Aidan laughed at Lia's announcement and looked round the room to confirm that Lia was joking but was shocked when none of them said it was a joke.

"What do you mean you're a witch?" Aidan asked, staring at Lia.

"Apparently, my dad's line of the family has some form of Wiccan heritage and on our 17th birthday we all inherited magical powers." Lia explained.

"You're kidding me right?" Aidan coughed.

"I can show you if you want." Lia stated, watching Aidan warily.

Aidan managed to nod, so Lia placed her hands out in front of her and moved Charlie's glass of water from where it was sitting on the coffee table, to have it float in front of her. Focusing her attention on the liquid inside the glass, Sam took over keeping the glass in the air, Lia lifted her right hand, pulling the liquid out of the glass. Concentrating hard on the water, Lia managed to manipulate its shape into a Poodle and then turn it into ice. Moving her focus onto Aidan, Lia moved the Poodle through the air and into Aidan's hands.

"What the hell." Aidan whispered, looking at the Poodle Lia had just placed into his hands. "You all have these powers?"

"We all have control over one of the four elements, Lia has control of water, Charlie has control of earth, Sam has control of fire and I have control of air." Ben explained.

"This is ridiculous." Aidan announced, standing up and placing the now melting Poodle back in the glass, which had now been returned to the coffee table. "This is just one of your Physics experiments, isn't it Charlie?"

"Trust me when I say that I wish it were all an experiment that I made up to help Ben play a prank on you but these powers are apparently real." Charlie admitted, in a somewhat resigned tone.

"I don't know what to say." Aidan announced, after a few minutes of silence.

"Do you have any questions?" Sam asked.

"You once said that you thought I was hiding something from you." Lia whispered, before Aidan could respond. "And you were right I was, I was hiding this part of my life from you but you know the truth now."

Aidan turned so that he could look at Lia, who was now perched on the edge of the corner sofa, watching him warily, with a mixture of fear and hope in her eyes. Breaking eye contact with Lia, he glanced at Ben who was sat down next to Lia, protecting her but without being obvious, his eyes clearly showing that he was concerned. Next, Aidan looked to Sam who was sprawled on one of the two armchairs, looking deceptively calm to anyone who didn't know him. Then across to Charlie who was watching him with his focused stare, as if trying to look inside his brain as to see how Aidan was going to react to the news. Finally, Aidan turned back to Lia, who had shifted her position slightly so it looked like she was hugging herself, a gesture Aidan knew was her way of protecting herself from something that had the potential to hurt her.

"This is a lot to process." Aidan managed evenly.

"I know and I'm really sorry that this has all just been sprung on you but please don't leave, I'll explain anything you want." Lia begged.

"I'll hear you out." Aidan assured her.

"What do you want to know?" Lia asked, unwrapping her arms from around herself.

"Do your powers have anything to do with all those library books flying off the shelves that day we had our fight at school?" Aidan asked, figuring that he would start by getting an explanation for some of the easy stuff.

"You sent a load of books flying?" Ben asked.

"Yes, Aidan came into the library after we had had an

argument and I was reading a book, trying to forget what happened. When Aidan tapped me on the shoulder, it startled me and I somehow sent a load of books flying off the shelves. But yes, my telekenisis sometimes gets the better of me when I get surprised, I have almost got it under control now but there are still occasions when I send stuff flying." Lia told him.

"I'm assuming that there were more of these accidents in the beginning." Aidan asked, with a small smile.

"I've had a lot when I first discovered my powers and you were around." Lia admitted, returning his smile.

"Oh yeah?"

"About a week after our birthday, I didn't realise that you were round and I bumped into you in the hallway. I was so startled I sent every coat on the pegs flying all across the hall." Lia told him, with a half-smile at the memory.

"I don't remember that." Aidan told her.

"The coats were all behind you and thankfully my mum saw what happened, she picked them up." Lia explained.

"Do your parents have any powers?" Aidan asked.

"Dad has the power to control air, like me but Mum's mortal." Ben told him.

"How did she handle finding out that you all had powers?" Aidan asked.

"She has known for a long time, Dad told her about his powers shortly before they got married, and when they started talking about having children, Dad told her that any children they had would likely inherit powers. I think they were both surprised when they found out that they were having quadruplets and that we are apparently destined to save the UK from the forces of black magic." Sam told him.

"Sam! That's far too much information!" Ben yelled.

"What do you mean you are meant to save the UK from the forces of black magic?" Aidan asked.

"Back in November, when we were having our magic lessons from our dad, he accidentally let slip some of our ancestry. It turns out that back in the day, there was this family who tried to start a war and gain the powers from one of our ancestors. He felt that he would not be able to fight them on his own, so he decided to split his powers down the generations and when the time was right, four would be born and they would work together to defeat the forces of dark magic." Sam explained gleefully.

"Is there something in the water in this house?" Aidan asked incredulously.

"God, I wish." Charlie groaned.

"Sam, we only needed to tell him about our powers." Ben told his brother.

"He asked Lia to be completely honest with him, I'm just helping her out." Sam argued.

"Ben, Sam, stop it! Now isn't the time." Lia sighed. "What are you thinking Aidan?"

Aidan reclined back on his seat and closed his eyes. He tried to process everything he had seen and been told over the last fifteen minutes. Ben patted Lia's leg as she started to stand up and go over to Aidan, effectively preventing her from getting up.

"Do you know who these supposed enemies are?" Aidan asked, as he reopened his eyes.

"We have found out." Lia admitted.

"Who is it?" Aidan asked.

"It's the Foulds family." Sam announced, when no one else answered for a few seconds.

"Are you sure?" Aidan asked.

"Unfortunately, we are." Ben admitted.

"How did you find out?" Aidan asked, looking at Ben.

"Do you remember the dog walk where you asked Lia out?" Ben asked

"Yeah, of course. How could I forget?" Aidan replied, with a half smile for Lia.

"Dean punched you in the face and you were knocked out for a minute or two. While you were unconscious, he tried to attack me using some sort of magic, I tried to dodge it but it sliced my arm open, which is why I had to have stitches. He also tried to attack me with a second one of those weird balls, which is when I used my powers to take him out with a branch from a tree." Lia explained.

"I remember Alice saying something about powers when we bumped into her in the woods and that was one of the main reasons that we started fighting." Aidan suddenly realised.

Lia didn't respond to Aidan's revelation, instead she shifted backwards, so she was leaning back on the sofa, partially hidden behind Ben, who had sat up when Aidan brought up their fight. With Ben's hand resting on her knee as a gesture of support, Lia moved her gaze from the floor up to Aidan's watchful stare.

"Do you mind if I had a few minutes just with Lia?" Aidan asked.

Lia nodded when all of her brothers turned to look at her. Accepting her decision, Sam and Charlie stood up and left the living room, Ben squeezed Lia's knee and gave Aidan a long look before he followed the others out of the room.

"When we had the fight the day after, I honestly thought I would never be more shocked than when you told me that you loved me." Aidan stated, after a minute or two of silence.

"And now?" Lia asked cautiously.

"I never imagined that your big secret would be this. I mean, I've come up with a number of truly insane theories over the last month or two but this is beyond anything I could imagine." Aidan admitted.

"What happens now?" Lia asked, staring at the floor.

"This is a lot to take on, I mean you are a witch and you have powers. I'm not sure if I can handle this." Aidan confessed.

"Oh." Lia breathed.

"Just give me a little bit of time." Aidan begged.

Lia nodded, feeling too emotional to speak. Looking ruefully at Lia, Aidan stood up and quickly left the room, before he said anything he would regret. As he was putting his shoes on, Ben came over to join him, while Sam went back into the living room to check on Lia.

"You off?" Ben asked.

"Yeah, I need to process this." Aidan admitted.

"Makes sense, we did dump a lot of information on you." Ben observed.

"Yeah. Secrets are safe with me." Aidan assured him.

"All of them?" Ben asked.

"All of them." Aidan confirmed.

With that Aidan opened the front door and headed out into the cold night. Closing the door Ben headed back into the living room where Sam was with Lia, who was sat staring straight ahead.

"Well, that was not the Friday evening I had in mind." Sam stated, as Ben collapsed down into one of the chairs.

"Yeah" Ben agreed.

As the Taylor family settled into a comfortable silence to process the events of the evening, Aidan was walking back to his house thinking about everything that he had heard and the ending the evening with Lia. Getting closer to his house, Aidan let Buster off his lead so he could run the last little bit of the way home, knowing that he would be able to get in through his dog flap. Once Buster had disappeared around the corner, Aidan paused to think more about Lia and her admission about her power. Realising that he had made a mistake telling Lia that he didn't think that he wanted to be with her now he knew about her powers, it didn't change anything about her, she was still the most caring and amazing person that he knew.

Turning around, Aidan began to head back towards the Taylor's house as quickly as he could. Out of nowhere he was struck by a bolt of electricity knocking him to floor. Groaning, Aidan rolled onto his back and scowled as Dean, Grant, Alice and Katie Foulds appeared above him. Before Aidan had a chance to get back on his feet, Alice grabbed his arm and teleported all of them to one of the local abandoned mines.

Back at the Taylor house, things were getting back to normal. Sam and Ben headed back into the main living room to continue battling each other, in whichever game they had been playing before Edward had disturbed them. Charlie headed into the office, so he could do some more research on one of his many engineering ideas. Lia had come out of her slight shock and was in the kitchen making herself a cup of tea before heading off to bed for an early night. Idly stirring the tea, Lia was staring out into the back garden where she saw an owl sitting, staring at her from on one of the fence posts. Remembering that she had once read that an owl could often be associated with approaching evil and darkness, Lia turned away from its mesmerising eyes, to quickly pick up her cup and leave the kitchen, switching the light off behind her.

Ignoring her senses telling her that something was wrong, Lia started to walk upstairs only to be interrupted by a knock on the door just before she reached the first landing. Placing her cup of tea, just behind the banister where no one could kick it over, Lia retraced her steps down the stairs, so she could grab the dogs' collars while Ben opened the front door.

"What the hell?" Sam asked, from just behind Lia, when he spotted Katie Foulds standing at the front door.

"What are you doing here?" Ben growled.

"I have something I need to say." Katie stuttered.

"We have an agreement." Ben growled back.

"This is nothing to do with that." Katie told him, before turning to look at Lia, who was clutching both dogs's collars as tight as she could. "My sister Alice, has a message for you."

Lia swallowed twice as she attempted to moisten her mouth, which had gone completely dry at Katie's statement.

"Alice wants to talk to you about you stealing her powers and her boyfriend. If you don't turn up, then she will ensure that something bad happens to Aidan. She's waiting for you in the old mine." Katie announced.

Before Lia even had a chance to respond, Katie turned away from the door and walked purposefully down the drive and vanished. Ben kept one arm across the door, while Sam put a supportive but restraining arm around Lia's shoulders as she tried to run after Katie.

Chapter Fourteen

Two minutes later

"We can't just chase after her." Ben told his sister, as he closed the front door and walked towards the back of the house.

"They've got Aidan!" Lia cried, fighting against Sam, who had put his arm across Lia's waist and was physically preventing her from getting to the front door.

"We are going to come up with a plan, we are going to get him back Lia." Ben assured her.

"Charlie!" Sam shouted.

"What?" Charlie called, from behind the closed office door.

"We need you!" Ben yelled.

"What's going on?" Charlie asked, opening the office door.

"The Foulds have somehow kidnapped Aidan and we need to get him back." Lia cried, following Ben and Sam into the garage.

The four of them entered the garage, Ben and Sam immediately began pulling down a number of books, which contained some spells that they may need.

"Do we even know anything about spells?" Charlie asked.

"Nope, probably don't need them." Sam agreed, tossing the books he was holding to one side.

Getting a map of the woods, Charlie set it out on the table so he could examine the area surrounding the old mine. Ben began flicking through some of the spell books, ignoring Sam and Charlie's conversation. Sam gathered up a few tools that he thought they might need. Lia watched her brothers as they began planning out how to rescue Aidan. Lia paced around the room, unable to focus on what her brothers were saying. Wringing her hands together, Lia realised that her brothers were no longer watching her, as they were too focused on what they thought they needed to do to rescue Aidan.

Quietly, Lia walked towards to the door, occasionally glancing over her shoulder to ensure that her brothers weren't paying any attention to her movements. Edging through the door, trying to avoid opening it too wide, Lia slipped out of the garage and back into the house.

"Sshh!" She whispered to the dogs, who whined slightly as she entered the kitchen.

Lia ran into the hallway and pulled on her coat as she shoved her feet into her trainers then sped out of the door. Before she had a chance to close the door, both dogs bolted out after her. Lia sighed, but made the decision that it would be better to take them with her, as they would alert her to any potential danger that she might run into, trying to rescue Aidan. Shutting the door quickly, Lia ran down the drive and into the woods, towards the abandoned mine.

While the boys planned and Lia ran on her way to find him, Aidan came to just beyond the main tunnel. Groaning, he rolled onto his back and reached around him, feeling the cold, uneven walls of the mine on his right side. He yelped when he reached out his left hand and was shocked by an electrical current. In an instant, he sat up to examine his surroundings. He could see clearly around the mine, as there was a lamp set up on one of the low lying rocks near him. Rubbing his head where he had taken the blow, he took stock of his surroundings. Glancing towards the main tunnel entrance, Aidan watched as someone began to come through the shadows towards him.

"Oh good, you are awake." Alice crowed, as she came into the light and stopped about a metre away from where Aidan was sat.

"What the hell, Alice?" Aidan asked, glaring at her.

"Is there something wrong?" Alice asked, feigning innocence.

"Why am I here?" Aidan asked.

"I feel that question is a little bit too philosophical for this time of day" Alice retorted, smirking.

"You know what I mean Alice. Why did you and your twat brothers knock me out and bring me here?" Aidan growled.

"Oh that's simple. You are bait to bring your goody two shoes girlfriend to me." Alice explained.

"Lia has no idea I'm here." Aidan countered.

"Don't be silly, Aidan." Alice laughed. "I sent Katie to tell her that I was holding you here. Dean and Grant are up by the entrance, waiting for her arrival."

"No." Aidan whispered.

"Well, of course she's going to come for you. I mean, she does claim to love you and she's going to act on those feelings." Alice told him.

"Why are you doing this?" Aidan asked.

"I want what she has." Alice answered, starting to pace.

"And what is it that she has?" Aidan continued.

Alice paused in her pacing of the mine's interior to turn back to face Aidan, who by now had managed to clamber to his feet and was leaning against the wall, watching Alice cautiously. Aidan pushed himself up and moved forward slightly.

"I wouldn't move too far if I were you." Alice warned. "Dean and Katie have set up an invisible force field to keep you in place. Get too close and it will knock you flat on your ass."

"Why?" Aidan growled, when Alice laughed at the end of her explanation.

"How much do you know about magic?" Alice asked.

"I only know what Lia and her brothers told me earlier today." Aidan responded carefully.

"And I bet they told you all about how their family is filled with good magic and my family is dark." Alice retorted. "But that's not the truth. The truth is that, Lia and her brothers' ancestors stole my family's powers and have been using them for their own gain since then."

"So, what's your plan Alice?" Aidan asked.

"That's easy, Aidan. I'm going to get little Miss Princess

goody two shoes to give up her powers by convincing her that the only way I'm going to release you is if she gives her powers to me." Alice crowed. "And then, using both her powers and those that our family has managed to hold onto, I'm going to make you love me, leaving her with nothing."

"Lia won't do that." Aidan told her. "I won't let her."

Alice laughed, before she sauntered out to the main entrance of the cave to see if there was any sign of Lia.

"OK, so we have a plan. Are you ready Lia?" Sam asked, rubbing his dusty hands on his jeans.

"Lia?" Charlie queried, when Lia didn't respond.

"She's gone." Ben declared, looking round the garage.

The boys all looked around, checking that Lia wasn't somewhere hidden somewhere. Leaving the garage, the boys headed into the house to continue looking for Lia.

"Lia!" Sam yelled.

"She's not here." Ben sighed.

"Are you sure? She could just have gone up to her room." Charlie commented.

"Her shoes and coat are missing and the dogs aren't here." Ben replied, gesturing around the empty hallway

"At least she took the dogs with her." Sam muttered, shoving his feet into his shoes.

As soon as they were ready, the boys left the house and hurried into the woods. Charlie took the lead for the journey, as he had worked out the quickest route through.

Further through the woods, Lia ran towards the mine. She got her foot stuck in an overgrown root and clattered into the ground, jarring her teeth as she landed. Pulling her foot out of the root, she gave her ankle a quick rub before pushing herself to her feet and whistling for the dogs to come back into her sight. Limping slightly, Lia continued as quickly as she could, pausing just before she got to the mine's entrance. Checking her surroundings, Lia crouched down so she was out of sight, in the bushes. Beside her, the dogs stood at attention waiting for Lia's command. She spotted Dean sitting at the entrance of the mine, while Grant was lying on the top of the grassy verge that kept the entrance to the mine slightly hidden. Lia motioned for the dogs to head round to the other side of the entrance as a form of distraction, so she could move closer.

Listening to the dogs rustle the bushes, and watching as Grant and Dean looked in the opposite direction. Lia started slowly edging towards the entrance but just before Lia could slip in, she stepped on a stick, which snapped loudly, causing Dean to notice her. Lia could see the menacing grin on his face as he advanced towards her. Faced with the choice of running back into the woods and leaving Aidan or standing her ground and hoping that she could somehow overpower the Foulds by herself, for the first time since she had left the house Lia began to regret coming out on her own. Swallowing, Lia met Dean's eyes as he generated one of his electrical balls in his palm. Advancing towards her, Dean grinned evilly as he cut off the entrance by shooting two electricity balls at her and diving in front of it.

Feigning left, Lia catapulted herself onto the floor to her right as the electrical ball barely missed her. Spotting a puddle on the floor, near where Dean was standing, Lia quickly turned it into ice and moved so that Dean would have to walk over it to get to her. Pushing herself to her feet, Lia winced as Dean came clattering down on the ice puddle that she had just created. Lia jumped, just in time to miss another electrical ball that Dean had created before he slipped. Recognising that Dean was just as dangerous on the floor, Lia used her full strength to pull moisture out of the ground and froze it so that Dean's hand and feet were encased in ice. With his hands completely covered by ice, he temporarily couldn't generate any more electric balls.

Running into the opening, Lia created an ice-covering for the entrance of the mine, hoping to cause a delay to anyone who was following her. She hadn't seen Grant, so she assumed he had followed the dogs into the woods, nor had she seen Alice or Katie. Stepping carefully over the slats of wood which used to form the tracks, Lia continued further in, ducking as she came across a few collapsed beams. Tripping slightly, as she was so focused on the collapsed beams, she winced as she caught her hand on something metal and sliced through the skin. Continuing on through the mine, Lia reached the point where the tracks broke off into several passages. Staring at all of the passages, Lia focused on the emotions that she could feel, once she had managed to untangle her own emotions from any others that were there. Sensing the hate that was flowing from the tunnel on her left. Lia headed that way. Once in the tunnel she could feel other emotions, fear and anger. Recognising the emotions as Aidan's, Lia picked up her pace until she could see a faint glow in the distance. Forgetting all sense of caution, Lia ran to Aidan.

"Lia stop!" Aidan called, just as Lia ran into the force field and was flung across the opening.

"Aidan!"

"Lia, go." Aidan told her.

"Aidan?" Lia questioned.

"Lia this is all part of Alice's plan. You need to go now." Aidan insisted.

"Now Aidan, you don't want to ruin all my fun, do you?" Alice cooed, appearing behind Lia.

Lia spun round so that she could face Alice, her fists clenched by her sides. Easing herself up, Lia stood cautiously, as she waited for Alice's next move. Without warning, Alice blinked and was then behind Lia, with her arm around her neck. Lia struggled to get out of the tightening hold on her. After a few moments, Lia managed to push Alice away from her, just long enough for her to spin around. Lia crouched down and charged into Alice, sending them both crashing into wall. In retaliation, Alice pushed Lia to the floor and kicked her in the stomach. Groaning in pain, Lia managed to trip Alice up, remembering some of the moves that she used as a kid when wrestling with her brothers. Telekinetically, Lia sent a couple of small rocks into Alice's falling body, ensuring that she landed on the floor. The girls grappled on the floor for leverage over the other; after a few minutes Alice's superior weight and height caused her to gain the advantage over Lia. Pinning her to the floor, Alice leaned over Lia with a wicked smile on her face. Lia struggled only to find that her legs were now pinned by some invisible weight. Looking over her captor's shoulder, Lia saw Katie standing just at the edge of the light and knew that she was not going to be able to overpower the Foulds alone. Winded after the fight with Alice and feeling the effects of using her powers on Dean, Lia didn't have the strength to move the rock she was trying to telepathically move, to try and distract Katie and hopefully free her legs from their stuck position. Deciding that she was trapped for the time being, Lia quit struggling so that she could conserve her energy for when she actually had a plan.

"Are you ready to have a grown-up discussion?" Alice asked, when she felt the fight go out of Lia.

"You've got me now Alice. You can let Aidan go." Lia said defeatedly.

"I'm in control here Princess, not you." Alice sneered, pushing herself off Lia, trusting her sister's powers.

"Don't give up Lia." Aidan begged, from his spot in the corner of the mine.

Lia glanced over, from her position sprawled uncomfortably on the mine's floor to meet Aidan's eyes, she managed a small smile for him, before forcing herself up into a sitting position.

"OK, Alice, what do you want?" Lia asked, reluctantly turning her attention away from Aidan back to their captor.

"Well, Princess, that's easy. I want your powers. I told you months ago that your powers were supposed to be mine and I intend to have them." Alice jeered, sitting down on one of the low-lying rocks, so she could watch and enjoy having Lia at her mercy.

"What do you mean?" Lia asked confused.

"I bet you have been led to believe that your ancestor, the scumbag, Isaac cast the power-splitting spell to stop my family from taking control of the elements. Well the truth is, Isaac stole the power of the elements from my ancestor but was injured before he could escape with them. The casting of the power splitting spell has been the bane of my family's mission to regain our powers. Each element only appears once every four generations until now, so I'm going to take back what is rightfully mine." Alice explained, leaning back against the cave wall.

"You're wrong." Lia told her.

"No, I'm not and then, as if to prove that your family is full of thieves, you came along and stole my boyfriend." Alice continued. "So, today I'm going to give you a choice. This is the only time that you will get this offer. You can choose to keep your powers but then you will never see Aidan again or you can choose Aidan and give me your powers."

"What do you mean I will never see Aidan again?" Lia asked.

"I have the power to blink myself to wherever I want to go and if you choose to keep your powers, then I will simply blink him all over the world with me, you'll never be able to keep up."

"She'll never let us be together, Lia!" Aidan cried.

"Quiet!" Alice snapped.

"If I give you my powers, will you leave Aidan and my family alone?" Lia asked.

"I, personally, will never bother you." Alice replied.

"I need your word that if I give up my powers, you and the rest of your family won't bother mine ever again." Lia told her, through clenched teeth.

"I'll see what I can do." Alice said, after a few moments of thought.

Lia looked towards Aidan, her eyes brimming with tears that she refused to shed. Aidan met her gaze and shook his head. Pulling her eyes away from Aidan's, Lia looked at the necklace she wore showing her affinity to water.

"I'm waiting Princess." Alice taunted.

"Stop calling me Princess." Lia snarled.

"Oh, is it upsetting you? I thought you liked to be called Princess. It's what Aidan calls you." Alice laughed.

Blinking the tears out of her eyes, Lia sighed and took one last glance at Aidan.

"I've made my decision." Lia announced slowly.

"Oh?" Alice asked.

"You can have my powers." Lia told her sadly.

"Lia, no!" Aidan cried.

"I love you Aidan, I don't want my powers, if they mean that I never see you again." Lia told him sadly.

"Lia, don't give up your powers for me. Alice can take me anywhere on the globe, I will find my way back to you. I love you." Aidan said, trying to prevent what Lia was going to do.

"I don't want to risk never seeing you again Aidan, it will destroy me." Lia admitted.

"If you give her your powers, she's going to cast some sort of spell so that I fall in love with her." Aidan told her.

"That is enough!" Alice snarled, blinking herself past the force-field to stand with Aidan.

Ensuring that Lia was watching her, Alice crushed her lips to Aidan's and wrapped her arms around him, plastering herself to him. At Lia's sound of pain, Alice pulled away from Aidan to grab a small rock from just behind her. She cracked it over Aidan's head, then blinked and appeared by Lia's side as Aidan crumpled to the floor.

"Now, this is the spell that you need to say in order to give me your powers." Alice told her, handing her a crumpled piece of paper.

Back at the entrance, Ben, Charlie and Sam, watched as Grant helped Dean out of the ice that Lia had encased him in. Silently the boys split up and headed to the positions they had agreed on en-route, while Grant and Dean were distracted.

While Grant was helping Dean to his feet, Ben sent a strong gust of wind into them, knocking them both over. Sam and Charlie then leapt out of their hiding places and ran towards the mine. Dean sent sparks of electricity into their path, as he and Grant struggled to their feet against Ben's wind. Dodging the sparks, Sam threw a couple of fire balls towards the Foulds brothers, ensuring they remained on the floor. Charlie then summoned up some willow branches and used them to tie Dean and Grant's hands behind their backs.

"Where are Aidan and Lia?" Sam demanded, once they were secure.

"In the mine… umph." Dean's laugh turned into a groan, as Sam punched him in the stomach.

"Tell us where they are." Sam repeated.

When neither of the brothers responded answered, Sam moved away, while Charlie opened the ground, causing Dean and Grant to fall into the hole he had just created. Ben, Charlie and Sam then gathered around the top and glared down at the Foulds brothers. After what felt like an eternity to the boys, Grant looked up at them.

"So, you want to know where your sister and her little boyfriend are?" Grant asked.

"Yes." Ben replied.

"I'm sure Alice will have sorted everything out by now." Grant stated. "If you let us out of here, we will take you to them.

Dean nodded begrudglingly and Charlie piled the ground back up, bringing the Fould's brothers back level with the rest of the world. Once everything was returned to its rightful place, Ben and Sam each grabbed one of the Foulds brothers and began walking them to the mine, with Charlie bringing up the rear.

Lia tried to focus on the piece of paper that she was reading but she kept glancing over to where Aidan lay, unmoving on the floor. Just as Lia was about to start reciting the spell, she heard some commotion at the entrance to the cave. Alice and Katie also glanced up at the noise and Alice headed towards the tunnel, leaving Katie to watch the prisoners. Using the distraction, Lia tore the crumpled bit of paper into pieces in an act of defiance and shifted her attention back to the rock she had been attempting to move earlier.

"Dean! Grant!" What the hell are you doing up there?" Alice yelled.

"We've encountered the rest of them but there's a problem." Dean called back.

A few moments later, Dean and Grant appeared, closely followed by Ben, Sam and Charlie, who were holding them hostage. The boys looked grimly round the cave and assessed the situation. Lia was sprawled on the floor struggling against an invisible force, trying to get towards Aidan, who was unconscious next to Alice, who had blinked herself back inside Aidan's force-field, while Katie stood semi-shocked at the back of the cave.

"So, the cavalry has arrived?" Alice enquired, appearing behind Ben, Charlie and Sam.

"Alice, I've made my decision, leave them alone." Lia cried, from her position on the floor.

"Shut up! We've been waiting for this." Alice snapped.

With that, Lia's legs somehow became free and she scrambled to her knees. Unfortunately, Alice spotted her and blinked herself back behind Lia to prevent her from getting up by putting her foot in the centre of Lia's back and shoving her down onto the floor. That caused Ben and Sam to forget about Dean and Grant for a few seconds, just long enough to allow them to escape from the willow branches. Within seconds, the two families were lined up against each other, staring each other down. Dean launched the first offensive, by flicking an electricity ball towards Sam. Sam ducked in time to send the ball crashing into the mine's wall. In retaliation, Lia swung out her hand, flinging all of the Foulds to the other side of the mine. Shocked by the strength of her powers, Lia and her brothers were momentarily stunned giving the Foulds enough time to recover.

Suddenly, Grant multiplied himself six times and formed a ring around the boys, separating them from Lia. As the boys shifted, so they were facing the Grants rather than each other, acorns began to pelt them from the ceiling, disappearing before they hit the ground.

"Acorns? Seriously?" Dean spat, as he hovered just beyond the Grants, electricity balls at the ready.

"Is that the best you can come up with?" Alice yelled at Katie.

"Sorry." Katie muttered, stopping the acorns and sliding away to stand at the back of the mine. "I haven't mastered creating anything else yet."

As soon as the acorns stopped falling, Ben nodded to his brothers and they charged at the three Grants in front of them. All three vanished into thin air, when the boys made contact with them, causing them to fall forward, stumbling over invisible rocks before colliding with the illusion of a wall.

Once again faced with Alice, Lia channelled the anger she could feel rolling off her. Focusing all of Alice's rage on the water she could see dripping down the walls of the mine, Lia created a wave of water, which she sent crashing into Alice, taking out her and the remaining fake Grants. Alice blinked herself so she landed at Lia's feet, rather than smashing into the wall, then kicked Lia's legs out from under her. Lia landed on top of Alice and froze the moisture in her clothes, making it difficult for Alice to move. Once Alice was temporarily incapacitated, Lia telekinetically moved a number of large rocks into a pile in front of where Katie was standing, blocking her from the rest of her family.

While Lia had been dealing with the girls, her brothers had managed to regain their balance and were dodging electric balls that Dean was throwing at them. Charlie was grazed by one and had fallen, Grant pounced on him, pinning him to the ground and punching him in the face. Seeing this Ben leapt to Charlie's aid and blew Grant off of Charlie, while Sam somersaulted into Dean, stopping him in his tracks. With the Foulds briefly stopped, Charlie made the ground tremble, bringing the rock barrier separating Katie from the rest down. Ben then created a small tornado, blowing all the Foulds together. Sam created a ring of fire to prevent any of the Foulds from moving, Dean then launched a giant electrical ball towards the four Taylor siblings, which sent them ducking in all different directions, while sparks flew all over the mine.

"Enough!" Alice shrieked, as Ben blew Sam's fire ring closer to them.

"This isn't over." Dean promised, as Alice blinked them all out of the mine.

Exhausted, the siblings all sank down onto the floor of the mine to regroup. Lia leant her head against Ben's shoulder and breathed deeply, as she dealt with the headache that she had gotten from channelling water so many times in quick succession. Dealing with a lot of emotions in such a short space of time hadn't been easy either. Ben reclined against the rock behind him and draped an arm over his sister's shoulder, while Sam lay sprawled on the floor and Charlie sat perched on a small rock, nursing his minor nosebleed from Grant's punch. For a few minutes the four of them remained in that position.

"What the hell were you thinking running into the mine, without a plan and without us?" Ben suddenly snapped.

Lia glanced round at him, having been startled out of her recovery.

"We were coming up with a plan." Charlie added.

"I couldn't wait." Lia told them.

"What do you mean you couldn't wait?" Ben snarled, pushing away from the rock and standing up.

"All I could think about was Aidan with Alice. I went a little crazy, I admit but I needed to rescue him." Lia said.

"What would you have done if we hadn't arrived when we did?" Sam asked, also getting to his feet.

Aidan groaned from where he was lying on the floor of the mine. Lia gasped and quickly crawled over to him, only to be repelled by the electrical force field, that was still trapping him against the wall of mine. Lia lay on the floor, momentarily stunned by the jolt she had just received. Ben strode the four steps to where Lia lay and hauled her to her feet.

"You OK?" Charlie asked, when Lia faltered a tiny bit as Ben let go of her arm.

"I'm fine." Lia insisted, resting her hands on her thighs getting over her minor dizzy spell.

"What the hell?" Aidan managed, as he stood up.

"Oh my God! Aidan are you OK?" Lia cried.

"What happened?" Aidan asked. "What are you guys doing here? Where's Alice? Lia please tell me you didn't give up your powers."

"Give up your what?" Sam exploded.

"I will explain later, just help me get to Aidan." Lia said, barely looking at her brothers as she stood as close to Aidan as she could get.

Nodding to each other, the boys all joined Lia standing about a metre from Aidan, respecting the invisible barrier that was keeping them apart. Sam lifted his arms and began feeling the air in front of them, looking mildly puzzled Charlie did the same thing, before nodding at Sam.

"I think that Dean and Katie have conjured some sort of invisible electrical force field to keep Aidan here." Charlie observed, putting his arms back down.

"What do we do?" Lia asked panicked.

"Lia calm down." Ben said mildly. "We are going to fix this."

"How? How are you going to fix this?" Lia cried, as she spun away from where Aidan was being held captive.

"Lia." Aidan called softly.

Lia turned around slowly and met Aidan's gaze.

"Trust your brothers." He said gently. "Just keep calm. Nothing else bad is going to happen."

Lia nodded her acceptance but moved away from the invisible force field, as her tears spilled over. Ignoring her brothers, who were huddled together whispering their plan, Lia swiped at her tears and then went back to stand in front of Aidan. Aidan lifted one of his hands up and held it as close to the edge of the force field as he could get, he nodded for Lia to do the same.

"OK, we have a plan." Sam announced.

"What is it?" Aidan asked, before Lia could jump down her brothers' throats.

"We are hoping that Lia can use her powers to short-circuit the electricity long enough for Ben and I to move the force field." Charlie explained. "Sam is then going to jump in and pull you to safety."

"How are we supposed to be able to see the force field?" Lia asked.

"I'm hoping to get it to glow by heating it up." Sam answered.

"This sounds dangerous." Lia commented.

Aidan chuckled, when Ben glared at his sister and Sam and Charlie sighed.

"Come on Lia, trust your brothers." Aidan told her.

"I trust them, I'm just not sure about short circuiting the force field. What if it goes wrong? What if I can't get you out?" Lia cried.

"You managed to knock the entire Foulds family flat on their asses ten minutes ago." Ben told his sister, coming round behind her and hugging her. "You are so strong."

"I don't know." Lia whispered.

"Lia? Do you love Aidan?" Ben asked, just loud enough for her to hear.

Lia nodded.

"OK, so use that and the strength that comes from it to get him out of this damn prison that the Foulds have created." Ben told her.

Lia turned in her brother's arms and squeezed him really tight before releasing him then nodded to her other brothers. With Lia's acceptance, the boys moved into position, Sam pulled Lia down to crouch with him, wedged into one of the corners as close they could get to the force-field. Sam clicked his fingers and managed to get a small flame to appear, resting the flame on his palm he let the flame get bigger until it was twice the size of his hand, satisfied he let the flame hover by the force field. Sure enough, the edges of the force field began to glow as it heated up. Watching as Aidan moved so he was pressed against the wall of the mine, Lia pulled a small amount of moisture from the ground and sent it flying into the glowing part of the force-field. The force-field hissed and sparks flew out in all directions. Sam shoved Lia out of the way, as he got ready to jump in and pull Aidan to safety. Feeling the ground vibrate and the rush of wind, Lia watched as the sparking wall began to move slowly away from the mine's wall. Once there was enough space, Sam dove towards Aidan and together they managed to jump out just before the cage door slammed back into place. The momentum of the force field slamming back into place sent sparks flying and all of the boys stumbled across the mine, while Lia remained sprawled on the floor. As soon as the sparks had stopped flying, they all got to their feet. The boys brushed the dirt from their clothes but Lia flung herself across the cave into Aidan's arms.

Holding Lia as tight as he could, Aidan closed his eyes and just as he began to relax, he noticed Lia trembling and crying in his arms. Keeping one arm wrapped tightly around Lia's body, he ran his hand over her hair to reassure her that he was OK.

"You saved me, gorgeous." He whispered into Lia's hair after a few seconds.

Lia lifted her head from where it was resting on Aidan's shoulder, to meet his eyes with her own tear-filled ones.

"You saved me." Aidan repeated.

Lia nodded before she wrapped herself back around Aidan, using his strength to comfort her. Aidan glanced over Lia's head and met Ben's assessing gaze with his own. Aidan nodded at Ben answering his friends unspoken question, Ben nodded back before clapping both his brothers on the shoulders.

"Right, shall we all head home." Sam suggested.

Everyone nodded their agreement and they began to gingerly walk out of the cave, using the light from the fire that Sam created to guide them through the darkness of the tunnels. Aidan laced his fingers through Lia's as they began to exit the mine, following her brothers. Lia went ahead of Aidan to scramble out and was almost immediately knocked to her feet when both dogs jumped on her.

The boys turned ready to fight again whn Lia shrieked as she hit the floor, but relaxed almost immediately when they realised that it was just the dogs.

"Hi girls." Lia cooed, wrapping one arm around each dogs' neck and hugging them close to her as she sat up. "You did so good."

"Come on Lia, let's go home." Sam called, after letting the dogs and Lia calm each other.

Lia stood up gingerly as all of the bruises she had gotten from the battle began to make themselves known now that she was relaxed. Once Lia was stood up, the five of them began the forty-minute walk back to the siblings' home.

"You staying over?" Ben asked, glancing over his shoulder to where Lia and Aidan were walking a couple of steps behind him with their arms wrapped around each other.

"What time is it?" Aidan asked.

"Little after two." Ben answered.

"Yeah I'll stay over, don't fancy explaining why I'm filthy and coming home in the middle of the night to my dad." Aidan   commented.

Chapter Fifteen

17th February 2018

The next morning, Lia woke up early due to some discomfort from the night before. Easing herself out of bed, Lia walked into her bathroom, where she wiped the dirt from her face, having gone straight to bed when they got in. She began running herself a hot bath to ease her sore muscles. After adding some scented bubble bath to the hot running water, Lia quietly walked down the stairs careful not to wake anyone who was still in bed. Noting that Ben's door was still closed, she smiled knowing that he and Aidan would still be asleep. Surprisingly Sam's door was also still shut but Charlie's was open. Continuing down the stairs, Lia stooped so that she could pet the dogs when they came running up to her.

"Good morning girls." Lia said, as she petted the dogs.

"Lia?" Charlie called.

"Morning Charlie" Lia called back, heading into the kitchen.

"You're up early." Charlie commented.

"Yeah, I was really uncomfortable with all the bruises. My ribs feel like I have gone ten rounds with Mike Tyson after yesterday, so I thought I would get up and have a hot bath. How are you this morning?" Lia asked.

"I'm fine." Charlie replied carefully.

"Are you sure?" Lia asked, turning to her brother, who was strategically avoiding her gaze, while she filled the kettle up.

"Yeah I'm just processing everything that happened yesterday. I didn't sleep very well once we all went to bed." Charlie commented absently.

"Yeah, it was a dramatic evening." Lia observed.

"I mean that scene with Edward was bad enough, but then having to rescue Aidan with all the magic and fighting." Charlie continued.

"Oh my God! I actually forgot that conversation with Edward happened last night, it feels like it happened ages ago." Lia remarked.

"Yeah." Charlie said awkwardly.

"Well, I would say, hopefully that's all over and done with but knowing Edward, I think there is probably more to come." Lia announced thoughtfully.

"Do you think there will be more battles?" Charlie asked suddenly, changing the topic slightly.

"What do you mean?" Lia questioned.

"I hate magic! I hate having these stupid powers! I don't want to have to give up my life to go out and fight everyday. If we keep having to go out and battle other people with powers, I'm not sure I can cope. And I mean what is next, we are battling witches this week, next week we could be out fighting dragons, ghost or mermaids, were does this bloody situation end?" Charlie cried.

Lia swallowed her laughter at her brother's over-exaggeration, before responding to his question.

"Charlie, I know last night was scary, I was really frightened right up until we got home but you have got to look on the bright-side, we all made it out pretty much unharmed." Lia soothed.

"So, you think there will be more battles?" Charlie enquired.

"I can't see the Foulds giving up that easily and like you mentioned, we don't know what else is out there." Lia admitted.

"What about Edward, he really wants to date you. Do you think he would start a fight to try and win you over?" Charlie queried.

"I don't think a battle is his style." Lia replied.

Charlie nodded and walked out of the kitchen. As the kettle boiled, Lia turned her attention back to making herself a cup of tea. Once the drink was made, Lia headed back upstairs, where she checked that the bath was still OK. Placing the tea on the side, Lia added a tiny bit of cold water so that she could get in as quickly as possible.

Leaving water running, Lia nipped into her bedroom, so that she could grab her book and dressing gown. Back in her bathroom, Lia shut and locked the door before sinking into the hot, scented water and opening her book, she relaxed back in the bath and let the water soothe her.

After she had been in for a while and was beginning to feel better, Lia put her book down on the lid of the toilet and quickly rinsed herself off, making sure that she removed all of the dirt that seemed to cover large parts of her body. Once she was clean, she turned on the in bath shower, so that she could wash her hair. Once she was convinced that she had every ounce of dirt out of her hair, she turned the shower off and lay back for a minute or two, allowing herself another couple of seconds of peace before she clambered out of the bath. Wrapping herself up in a big purple fluffy towel and pulling her dressing gown over the top, Lia left the bathroom to walk into her bedroom. She quickly pulled some of her more comfy clothes out of various drawers and dropped them on her bed. She then pulled her hair dryer out and plugged it in and began drying her hair.

Once she was dressed in simple grey leggings and a pale pink oversized stripy top, Lia pulled her hair into a loose ponytail before heading downstairs into the smaller living room to read for a little while. Placing her book on the coffee table, she headed into the kitchen, to make another drink.

"We need to talk about last night." Sam told her, when she walked into the kitchen.

"Good morning to you too." Lia retorted, switching the kettle back on.

"I'm serious, Lia." Sam told her.

"I know." Lia sighed. "I just think that it would be easier to do it all together, when Mum and Dad get back later."

Sam scowled at her.

"Have you spoken to Charlie?" Lia asked.

"No, why?"

"He seemed really bothered by everything that happened

yesterday." Lia explained.

"He was on form last night though. That plan to rescue Aidan was all his idea and it worked like a charm." Sam commented, frowning.

"Yeah, he just didn't seem like himself when I saw him about an hour ago." Lia observed.

"I'll go have a chat with him." Sam assured her. "Hold on a sec, did you just say that you were up an hour ago?"

"Yeah, I have a few bruises and sore muscles that made sleeping a little bit uncomfortable." Lia replied.

"Wow! There is something you won't sleep through." Sam quipped and laughed when Lia threw the tea towel at him.

Laughing, Lia turned back to the kettle, which was about to boil and made herself a small pot of tea then put some bread in the toaster. Grabbing the strawberry jam and milk from the fridge followed by a plate from one of the cupboards, Lia sorted out her breakfast while she waited for the tea to brew. Once she was satisfied it was brewed, she poured herself a mug of tea and headed into living room to read her book whilst eating her toast.

After about forty-five minutes, she heard movement above her head and realised that Aidan or Ben must be getting up. Checking herself for any crumbs and wiping around her mouth to make sure that she looked presentable, she pretended to read as she waited for whoever it was to come downstairs. However after a few seconds of pretending to read, Lia got sucked into the book and forgot about any movements from upstairs.

Upstairs in Ben's room, Aidan groped around in the dark, silently cursing Ben's blackout blinds, until he found the door handle to get out of Ben's room. He had the world's worst headache having been hit on the head twice yesterday. He blinked at the light in the hallway, when he left Ben's room. Getting a few painkillers out of the bathroom cupboard, he swallowed them with some water. Taking a quick couple of breaths, he headed back into Ben's room.

"Put some trousers on, my sister is around somewhere."
Ben growled, sitting up in his bed.

"Don't think she would mind, mate." Aidan quipped,
winking at his friend.

"Well, I'll mind for her." Ben retorted, tossing Aidan a
pair of his jeans as they were pretty much the same size.

Aidan laughed as he caught the jeans and pulled them on,
plus one of Ben's t-shirts which was precariously perched
on the top of Ben's laundry pile. Once he was dressed,
Aidan head back out of Ben's room and downstairs,
pausing to pet Veronica when she came out of the smaller
living room. He headed into the Taylor's kitchen and
poured some water into the kettle to make a cup of coffee
for himself and Ben. Veronica followed him into the
kitchen and whined slightly.

"What's the matter?" Aidan asked the dog.

In response, Veronica sat down cocked her head to one
side and watched Aidan. Smiling at the dog, he petted her
again. Once she was satisfied, Veronica stood up and left
the room. Aidan then found the container labelled coffee
and grabbed two mugs off the mug tree to quickly make
him and Ben some. No sooner had Aidan finished making
it, Ben strolled into the kitchen and grabbed one of the
steaming mugs off the side and took a huge mouthful.

"You mind if I talk to you for a sec?" Aidan asked, once
Ben had had a couple of mouthfuls of coffee.

"Sure."

"I want to talk about Lia." Aidan told him.

"I'm getting a strong sense of déjà vu." Ben commented.

"Funny." Aidan retorted.

"Well, we have had a couple of chats about her over the
last few months." Ben observed mildly.

"Do you want to have this conversation?" Aidan asked.

"Nah, I think this time, I'll let you talk to Lia first, Sam
says she reading in the front living room."

With that, Ben strolled out of the kitchen and into the back
living room without a backwards glance. Shaking his head,
Aidan smiled and headed out of the kitchen towards the

front living room. In the doorway, he paused and stared at Lia, who was curled up in one corner of sofa, oblivious to anything going on around her.

"Hey gorgeous." Aidan called, knocking on the living room door as he came into the room.

"Hey yourself." Lia smiled, sitting up.

"How are you this morning?" Aidan asked, sitting down next Lia on the sofa.

"Never better." Lia commented. "How are you?"

"All good, now that I've seen you." Aidan replied.

Lia glanced round at Aidan who relaxed back on the sofa with his arm draped over the cushions where Lia had been sat. Cautiously, Lia leaned back against the cushions and smiled when Aidan's arm shifted so it was wrapped around her shoulders, pulling her close to him and kissing the top of her head.

"So I've been thinking." Aidan said, after a few minutes of sitting in comfortable silence.

"Oh?" Lia replied, shifting so that she could face Aidan.

"I love you, that's the one thing that I'm absolutely certain of. With regards to everything else, it's part of you and as it's a part of you, I accept it. I was on my way back to see you yesterday, when Dean and Grant grabbed me." Aidan told her. "Don't interrupt I need to say this."

Lia shut her mouth immediately and settled back down, so that she could listen to what Aidan had to say.

"When I was sat in the mine with Alice, listening to her plan. All I could think about was how to ensure that you didn't get hurt and that no matter what, I wouldn't give up on us. Then you burst into the mine to save me. I would have done anything to stop everything that happened after that, you fighting with Alice and then having to make the decision between me and your powers. I certainly don't deserve to be the choice that you made, after all that I have done to you. But I love you and I'm here to stay as long as you want me."

"I'm always going to choose you Aidan." Lia whispered.

"Why?" Aidan asked.

"I love you, I'm pretty sure I've loved you as long as I have known you. You are one of the most important people in my life. You make me smile and laugh even when I'm sad. You make me feel like the most important person on the planet, even when I'm saying some of the silliest things that make no sense at all. You listen no matter what I have to say and you have so much faith in me. You said that you don't deserve me but that's wrong." Lia announced.

"So, I guess this means that you still want to stay together?" Aidan laughed.

"I'll think about it." Lia said laughing.

"Of course, I want to stay together." Lia laughed, when Aidan fake scowled at her.

With that, Lia curled up against Aidan with his arms around her, making her feel completely safe and invincible. After a few seconds, all of Lia's brothers burst into the living room and sprawled themselves on the various seats in the living room.

"I see that you two have sorted out everything." Ben commented, as he sat on the other end of the corner sofa to Lia and Aidan.

"Yeah, we have. Are you guys OK with this?" Aidan asked, looking at Ben in particular.

"Well, I'm certainly questioning Lia's taste in men but as long as she's happy then I am." Ben assured his friend.

"Yeah, what Ben said." Sam echoed, while Charlie nodded.

Once they were all in agreement, the five of them settled down in the living room. Sam flicked on the TV and began hunting for any sport that he could find. Once he had found something, all the boys settled down to watch, so Lia picked her book back up and resumed reading the romantic novel.

After twenty minutes of contentment, there was knock on the door. Lia untangled herself from Aidan's arms and went to grab the dogs, while Sam went to answer it. Holding both dogs' collars, Lia pulled them away, allowing Sam to open the door to the person who was intently knocking on the other side.

"What are you doing here?" Sam growled, once he had opened it.

"I'm here to warn Amelia that she could be in danger, there is trouble brewing." Edward announced, pushing past Sam and walking into the house.

"Edward, what are you doing here?" Lia asked, when he spotted her.

"Emily had a vision earlier in the week and she has finally figured out what it meant." Edward told her.

"Oh yeah, the vision that she had in the coffee shop. Oh, I'm so pleased that she figured it out." Lia beamed.

"Well you shouldn't be. That vision was a warning for you that there is a battle coming and that you are in danger." Edward told her.

"I think you might be a bit late on the warning, mate." Sam observed laughing, from his position leaning against the now closed front door.

His casual pose looked completely natural, unless you knew him. Lia knew that he was actually completely alert and ready for any action. Edward spared him a glance before turning his attention back to Lia, who was still holding the dogs' back.

"What does your brother mean that I'm a little late?" Edward demanded of Lia.

However, before she could answer, Edward interrupted. "Don't you think it's a bit rude to leave your guest standing out in the hallway?"

Shaking her head slightly at Sam, who had pushed himself off the door and balled his hands into fists, Lia led Edward into the living room where the others were all sat. Sitting down next to Aidan, Lia gestured for Edward to have a seat.

"What is he doing here?" Edward demanded, glaring at Aidan.

"He's my boyfriend, I told you yesterday that we are back together." Lia commented mildly.

"That is ridiculous Amelia, no-one with your powers should date a mortal." Edward told her.

"Edward, I really don't want to have this conversation again. Why don't you just tell us why you are here?" Lia sighed.

"Well, as you know my cousin Emily had a vision of you being involved in a fight, so I felt obligated to come round and tell you to avoid going to the old mine." Edward explained.

"Oh well, actually it has already happened." Lia told him, ignoring the sniggers from her brothers and Aidan.

"What do you mean that it has already happened?" Edward demanded, jumping to his feet.

"Well, it happened last night." Lia continued, watching Edward warily from her position next to Aidan.

"Just like Emily, always a day late and a dollar short. What's the point of being able to see the future if you don't tell anyone about it until it's too late." Edward muttered.

"Don't insult Emily." Sam said mildly.

"You don't get to tell me what to do." Edward said, dismissing Sam and turning back to Lia. "What happened last night?"

"So, the nefarious witches from all our ancestors' stories took Aidan captive last night and we rescued him." Lia told him.

"How did you rescue him?" Edward snarled.

"While Ben, Charlie and Sam were making a plan, I ran to the mine where I managed to temporarily disarm the two brothers and enter the mine. Once I got into the mine, I found Aidan who was being held in some sort electric force-field cage thing. Then I got into a fight with one of the two sisters but she was much stronger than I thought, so she was able to overpower me." Lia explained, standing up so she could move about the living room.

"What happened after she overpowered you?" Edward asked, watching Lia as she nervously moved round the living room.

"Well, she offered me an ultimatum of my powers or Aidan." Lia told him. "I chose Aidan but just as she was about to tell me how to give up my powers, my brothers came in and we had a battle. The battle was pretty evenly matched and sapped a lot of our strength however using all of our powers, we managed to temporarily defeat them. Then Charlie came up with a truly remarkable plan to rescue Aidan and well, here we are."

The room fell into complete silence, once Lia had finished telling Edward the summary of what had happened the night before. Lia was careful to keep her back to Edward so she couldn't see how his face had contorted in rage but all of the boys could see. Sam used some hand signals out of Edward's view to tell the others to be ready in case anything happened.

"What do you mean you chose Aidan?" Edward whispered menacingly.

"When I was offered a choice of my powers or Aidan, the choice was easy. Aidan is the love of my life and I don't want my powers if it means that I never see him again." Lia explained, turning back round slowly to face Edward.

Tilting her head up slightly, Lia met Edward's angry glare with her own defiant look. Not backing down, Lia remained standing and waited until Edward dropped his glare.

"Edward, have you heard of the soul-mate principle?" Charlie asked, diverting the attention away from Lia for a few seconds.

"Of course."

"What's the soul-mate principle?" Aidan asked.

"This is the guy you chose Amelia." Edward muttered disgusted.

"It's the principle whereby two people are intrinsically linked, like two halves making a whole. An unbreakable bond that two people share. I have been reading up on the subject for the last month in my spare time and I came to the conclusion last night that I'm certain that Lia and Aidan are soul-mates. There is no other reason why Lia would risk going into the mine alone to rescue Aidan and why she would be willing to give up her powers for him." Charlie explained. "And as that bond is unbreakable, no oath can break it no matter how old."

"Oh, Charlie that's lovely." Lia said tearing up a tiny bit.

"That's ridiculous, there is no way that Lia can have a soul-mate who isn't me. We have been destined to be together for centuries." Edward sneered.

"Makes complete sense to me." Ben observed, making his presence known for the first time since Edward had entered the room.

"Charles, I really thought you understood what was to happen between me and Amelia, I'm deeply disappointed."

"There is another way for our families' destinies to still be fulfilled." Ben commented.

"Oh?" Edward enquired.

"Well, Lia is not the only girl in our two families and you are not the only boy. All that needs to happen is for another girl and boy from our families to fall in love and the promise is still fulfilled." Charlie explained, realising what Ben was on about.

"Amelia, I must insist that you come with me now and leave this foolishness behind." Edward said grabbing at Lia's arm.

"I'm not going anywhere." Lia stated, carefully tugging her arm free.

"Come with me right now!" Edward bellowed, grabbing at Lia.

The force with which Edward lunged at Lia, resulted in her being knocked to the floor, as she tried to avoid him. Landing hard on the floor, Lia moaned as yesterday's bruises made themselves known. Momentarily stunned, Lia had no defence as Edward hauled her to her feet and began to drag her out of the living room. No sooner had Edward reached the doorway, his path was blocked by the growling dogs. He dropped Lia, who quickly ducked to the floor and began crawling away. Turning around, Edward found himself face to face with a furious Sam, who without warning, ploughed his fist straight into Edward's face. Howling in pain, Edward covered his face with his hands and blood began pouring from his nose.

"I would get that checked at a hospital." Sam told him smugly.

"You broke my nose!" Edward growled, through his hands.

"Yeah, I probably did but you manhandled my sister in my house." Sam acknowledged. "Ben, can you give me a hand taking this piece of trash out?"

"My pleasure." Ben grinned, taking one of Edward's arms as Sam grabbed the other.

Lia watched from her position on the floor as her three brothers left the living room. Charlie was slightly ahead, so that he could open the door with Ben and Sam half dragging and half marching Edward out of the room. Listening as the front door closed firmly, Lia took the hand that Aidan offered her and slowly got to her feet.

"You OK?" Aidan asked, running his hands over Lia's hair and arms.

"Bit fed up of being knocked to the ground endlessly but I'm fine." Lia assured him, taking his hands in hers.

"Did you hit your head?" Aidan asked, tilting Lia's face so that she was looking him in the eye.

"I caught it slightly on the coffee table but it doesn't hurt." Lia reassured him, when he let go of one of her hands to check for any bumps.

"Are you sure you are OK?" Aidan asked.

"I'm fine." Lia smiled, letting Aidan wrap his arms around her and relaxing into his natural strength.

Sitting down on the sofa, Aidan pulled Lia onto his lap and kept his arms tightly around her as she rested her head on his shoulder.

"You get a pass, if you don't want to deal with Edward always interfering in my life." Lia said, lifting her head off of Aidan's shoulder so she could look into his eyes.

"Never." Aidan told her.

"But he will never leave me alone." Lia warned.

"You heard what Charlie said, we're soul-mates, babe. You're stuck with me." Aidan laughed. "And like I told you earlier I'm all in. Edward is just a pest, he'll get the message. I'm pretty sure that he's got it already as Sam has almost definitely broken his nose. He should be glad that Sam was closer to him than I was because I would have done far more than broken his nose."

"Aww, would you have defended me?" Lia teased, batting her eyelids before she rested her head back on Aidan's shoulder.

"Any day of the week. No one puts their hands on my girl and gets away with it." Aidan told her.

"My hero. I love you." Lia whispered.

"I love you too."